A Cornish Christmas

Also by Lily Graham:
The Summer Escape

A Cornish Christmas

LILY GRAHAM

bookouture

Published by Bookouture

An imprint of StoryFire Ltd.
23 Sussex Road, Ickenham, UB10 8PN
United Kingdom

www.bookouture.com

ISBN: 978-1-78681-075-5
eBook ISBN: 978-1-78681-074-8

*For Mom and Dad, for making me believe
that anything was possible.*

And to Rui and Catherine, for their endless support.

CHAPTER ONE

The Writing Desk

Even now it seemed to wait.

Part of me, a small irrational part, needed it to stay exactly where it was, atop the faded Persian rug, bowing beneath the visceral pulse of her letters and the remembered whisper from the scratch of her pen. The rosewood chair, with its slim turned-out legs, suspended forevermore in hopeful expectation of her return. Like me, I wondered if it couldn't help but wish that somehow she still could.

I hadn't had the strength to clear it, nor the will. Neither had Dad and so it remained standing sentry, as it had throughout the years with Mum at the wheel, the heart, the hub of the living room.

If I closed my eyes, I could still hear her hum along to Tchaikovsky – her pre-Christmas music – as she wrapped up presents with strings, ribbons and clear cellophane, into which she'd scatter stardust and moonbeams, or at least so it seemed to my young eyes. Each gift, a gift within a gift.

One of my earliest memories is of me sitting before the fire, rolling a length of thick red yarn for Fat Arnold, our squashed-face Persian, who languished by the warmth, his fur pearly white in the glow. His one eye open while his paw twitched, as if to say he'd play, if only he could find the will. In the soft light Mum sat and laughed, the firelight casting lowlights in her long blonde hair. I shut my eyes and took a deep breath, away from the memory of her smile.

Dad wanted me to have it: her old writing desk. I couldn't bear to think of the living room without it, but he insisted. He'd looked at me, above his round horn-rimmed glasses, perpetual tufts of coarse grey hair poking out mad-hatter style on either side of his head, and said with his faraway philosopher's smile, 'Ivy, it would have made her happy, knowing that you had it. . .' And I knew I'd lost.

Still it had taken me two weeks to get up the nerve. Two weeks and Stuart's gentle yet insistent prodding. He'd offered to help, to at least clear it for me, and bring it through to our new home so that I wouldn't have to face it. Wouldn't have to reopen a scar that was trying its best to heal. He'd meant well. I knew that he would've treated her things reverently; he would've stacked all her letters, tied them up with string, his long fingers slowly rolling up the lengths of old ribbon and carefully putting them away into a someday box that I could open when I was ready. It was his way, his sweet, considerate Stuart way. But I knew I had to be the one who did it. Like a bittersweet rite of passage, some sad things only you can do yourself. So I gathered up my will, along with the box at my feet and began.

It was both harder and easier than I expected. Seeing her things as she left them should have made the lump in my throat unbearable, it should have been intolerable, but it wasn't somehow.

I began with the drawer, emptying it of its collection of creamy, loose-leafed paper; fine ribbons; and assorted string, working my way to the heart of the Victorian desk, with its warren of pigeon holes, packed with old letters, patterned envelopes, stamps, watercolour brushes, and tubes of half-finished paint.

But it was the half-finished tasks that made the breath catch in my throat. A hand-painted Christmas card, with Santa's sleigh and reindeer flying over the chimney tops, poor Rudolph eternally in wait for his little watercolour nose. Mum had always made her own, more magical and whimsical than any you could buy. My fingers shook as I held the card in my hand, my throat tight. Seeing this, it's little wonder I became a children's book illustrator. I put it on top of the pile, so that later I could paint in Santa's missing guiding light.

It was only when I made to close the desk that I saw it: a paper triangle peeking out from the metal hinge. It was tightly wedged but, after some wiggling, I pried it loose, only – in a way – to wish I hadn't.

It was a beautiful, vintage French postcard, like the ones we'd bought when we holidayed there, when I was fifteen and fell in love with everything *en français*. It had a faded sepia print of the Jardin des Tuileries on the cover, and in elegant Century print it read 'Carte Postale' on the back.

It was blank. Except for two words, two wretchedly perfect little words that caused the tears that had threatened all morning to finally erupt.

Darling Ivy

It was addressed to me. I didn't know which was worse: the unexpected blow of being called 'Darling Ivy' one last time, finding out she'd had this last unexpected gift waiting for me all along, or that she'd never finish it. I suppose it was a combination of all three.

Three velvet-tipped daggers that impaled my heart.

I placed it in the box together with the unfinished Christmas card and sobbed, as I hadn't allowed myself to for years.

Five years ago, when she passed, I believed that I'd never stop. A friend had told me that 'time heals all wounds' and it had taken every ounce of strength not to give her a wound that time would never heal, even though I knew she'd meant well. Time, I knew, couldn't heal this type of wound. Death is not something you get over. It's the rip that exposes life in a before and after chasm and all you can do is try to exist as best you can in the after. Time could only really offer a moment when the urge to scream would become a little less.

Another friend of mine, who'd lost his leg and his father in the same day, explained it better. He'd said that it was a loss that every day you manage and some days are better than others. That seemed fair. He'd said that death for him was like the loss of the limb, as even on those good days you were living in the shadow of what you had lost. It wasn't something you recovered from completely, no matter how many people, yourself included, pretended otherwise. Somehow that helped, and I'd gotten used to living with it, which I suppose was what he meant.

The desk wasn't heavy. Such a substantial part of my childhood, it felt like it should weigh more than it did, but it didn't and I managed it easily alone. I picked it up and crossed the living room, through the blue-carpeted passage, pausing only to shift it slightly as I exited the back door towards my car, a mint green Mini Cooper.

Setting the desk down on the cobbled path, I opened up my boot, releasing the back seats so they folded over before setting the desk on top, with a little bit of careful manoeuvring. It felt strange to see it there, smaller than I remembered. I shut the boot and went back inside for the chair and the box where I'd placed all her things; there was never any question of leaving it behind. On my way back, I locked up Dad's house, a small smile unfurling as I noticed the little wreath he'd placed on the door, like a green shoot through the snow after the longest winter. It hadn't been Christmas here for many years.

Back to my car, I squeezed the chair in next to the desk and placed the box on the passenger seat before I climbed in and started the engine. As the car warmed, I looked at my reflection in the side mirror and laughed, a sad groaning laugh.

My eyeliner had made tracks all down my face, leaving a thick trail into my ears, and black blobs on either side of my lobes so that I looked like I'd participated in some African ritual, or had survived the mosh pit at some death metal goth fest. With my long dark blonde curls, coral knitted cap and blue eyes, it made me look a little zombiefied.

I wiped my face and ears and grinned despite myself. 'God, Mum, thanks for that!' I put the car in gear and backed out of the winding drive, towards the coastal road.

Cornwall.

It was hard to believe I was back, after all these years.

London had been exciting, tiring, and trying. And grey, so very grey. Down here, it seemed, was where they keep the light; my senses felt as if they'd been turned up.

For a while, London had been good though, especially after Mum. For what it lacked in hued lustre, it made up for by being alive with people, ideas, and the hustling bustle. It was a different kind of pace. A constant rush. Yet, lately I'd craved the stillness and the quiet. So when *The Fudge Files*, a children's fiction series that I co-wrote and illustrated with my best friend Catherine Talty, about a talking English bulldog from Cornwall who solves crimes, became a bestseller, we were finally able to escape to the country.

In his own way, Stuart had wanted the move more than I did; he was one of those strange creatures who'd actually grown up in London, and said that this meant it was high time that he tried something else.

In typical Stuart fashion, he had these rather grand ideas about becoming a self-sustaining farmer – something akin to Hugh Fearnley-Whittingstall – and setting up a smallholding similar to Hugh's River Cottage. The simple fact of it being Cornwall, not Dorset, was considered inconsequential. Which perhaps it was. I had to smile. Our River Cottage was called

Sea Cottage (very original that), yet was every bit as exquisite as its namesake, with a rambling half acre of countryside,
alongside rugged cliffs that overlooked the aquamarine waters
of the Atlantic Ocean in the gorgeous village of Cloudsea with
its mile-long meandering ribbon of whitewashed cottages with
window frames and doors in every shade of blue imaginable,
perched amid the wild, untamed landscape, seemingly amongst
the clouds, tumbling down to the sea. It was the place I always
dreamt about when someone asked me where I would choose
to live if I could magically supplant myself with a snap of my
fingers or be granted a single genie's wish. Cloudsea. And now. .
. now we lived here. It was still hard to believe.

So far our 'livestock' consisted of four laying hens, two grey
cats named Pepper and Pots, and an English bulldog named
Muppet – the living, slobbering and singular inspiration behind
Detective Sergeant Fudge (Terrier Division) of *The Fudge Files*,
as created by Catherine, Muppet's official godmother.

Despite Stuart's noble intentions, he was finding it difficult
to come to terms with the idea of keeping animals as anything
besides pets. Personally, I was a little grateful for that. We as-
suaged our consciences though by ensuring that we supported
local organic farms, where we were sure that all the animals were
humanely treated.

But what we lacked in livestock, Stuart made up for in vegetation. His potager was his pride and joy and even now, in the
heart of winter, he kept a polytunnel greenhouse that kept us
in fresh vegetables throughout the year. Or at least that was the
plan; we'd only been here since late summer. I couldn't imagine
his excitement come spring.

For me Cornwall was both a fresh start and a homecoming.
For the first time ever I had my own art studio up in the attic,
with dove grey walls, white wooden floors, and a wall full of
shelves brimming with all my art supplies; from fine waterco-

lour paper to piles of brushes and paint in every texture and medium that my art-shop-loving heart could afford. The studio, dominated by the mammoth table, with its slim Queen Anne legs, alongside the twin windows, made it a haven, with its view of the rugged countryside and sea. One where I planned to finish writing and illustrating my first solo children's book.

Now, with our new home and the news that we'd been waiting seven years to hear, it would all be a new start for us.

I was finally, finally pregnant.

Seven rounds of in vitro fertilisation, which had included 2,553 days, 152 pointless fights, five serious, two mortgages, countless stolen tears in the dead of the night in the downstairs bathroom in our old London flat, my fist wedged in my mouth to stem the sound, and infinite days spent wavering between hope and despair, wondering if we should just give up and stop trying. That day, thankfully, hadn't come.

And now I was twelve weeks pregnant. I still couldn't believe it. We hadn't told Dad yet; I didn't want to get his hopes up, or tempt fate; we'd played that black card before.

Our hopes. . . well, they'd already soared above the stars.

It was why I so desperately wished Mum were here now. It would have made all of this more bearable. She had a way of making sense of the insensible, of offering hope at the darkest times, when all I wanted to do was run away. I missed how we used to sit up late at night by the fire in the living room, a pot of tea on the floor, while Fat Arnold dozed at our feet and she soothed my troubled fears and worries – the most patient of listeners, the staunchest of friends. Now, with so many failed pregnancies, including two miscarriages, the memory of which was like shrapnel embedded in our hearts, so that our lives had been laced with an expectant tinge of despair, primed for the nightmare to unfold, never daring to hope for the alternative; we were encouraged to hope. It was different, everyone said so, and I needed to trust that this time it would finally happen, that we'd finally have a baby, like the doctors seemed to think we would. Stuart had been wonderful, as had Catherine, but I needed Mum really, and her unshakeable, unbreakable faith.

There are a few times in a woman's life when she needs her mother. For me, my wedding was one and I was lucky to have her there, if luck was what it was, because it seemed to be sheer and utter determination on her part. It had been so important to her to be there, even though all her doctors had told us to say our goodbyes. I will never know what it cost her to hold on the way she did, but she did and she stayed a further two years after that. In the end, it was perhaps the cruellest part, because when she did go, I'd convinced myself that somehow she'd be able to stay.

But this, this was different. I needed her now, more than ever. As I drove, the unstoppable flow of tears pooling in the hollow of my throat, I wished that we could have banked those two years, those two precious years that she had fought so hard and hung on for, so that she could be here with me now when I needed her the most.

CHAPTER TWO

Missing Paint

The desk fitted under the alcove in my attic-turned-studio, as if that was where it was always meant to be. With its view spanning the ocean and the evergreen countryside, the little writing desk seemed a familiar, yet unfamiliar object. In a way, I was grateful for its unobtrusiveness. In the weeks before I summoned the courage to fetch it, I'd wondered if I would ever be able to actually use it. But having it here, removed from my childhood home, felt different, not quite as embedded in the salt-sting memory of her, so perhaps I could. I'd brought it upstairs as soon as I arrived home. Thankfully, Stuart had gone to the country market.

I needed a quiet moment alone with the desk to get reacquainted and to sift through my emotions. He'd left a hurried note in blue ink, held in place on the fridge with a porcelain magnet that read:

Gone to see a man about turnips. Jam a possibility. . .

Good lord, I thought. Let's hope not. I was still recovering from the pak choi jelly.

I had to laugh at how different our lives had become. Just a few months ago in London, a message from Stuart would ping on my mobile telling me to have dinner without him, or that I should go along to friends alone, because he was stuck in some or other long-winded executive meeting. As a senior marketing director for a large pharmaceutical company, Stuart had run on the fumes of lack of sleep, filter coffee, and the unmistakable and unrelenting feeling that he was living a life against his values. As much as he'd tried to convince himself that their practices were ethical, that they were helping save millions of lives, he couldn't help but notice how some products were rushed into the market barely out of trials, when a few more months of analysis and study could have halved the side effects, or how expensive and inaccessible their medications were for those who really needed them and how fat and wealthy the top administrative flotsam had become.

He would come home to find me seated at the large dining room table (the one I'd painted French white and vowed we'd dine on every night after a holiday in Provence and that we'd yet to eat a meal on, as it housed all my various and sundry art supplies). He'd pull up a chair next to me, look at one of my latest illustrations of Muppet, aka 'Detective Sergeant Fudge', or my pet project, the one I dabbled with in that twilight hour after midnight, when the world was asleep and I created my own magical forest realm, capturing the adventures of a most adventurous mouse named Mr Tibbles, who made his home amongst the enchanted toadstools in the Lake District. Stuart's tired espresso-coloured eyes would light up and he'd stare at the images and exclaim, 'Mr Tibbles went to Devon?' picking up from where I'd left the story the night before.

I would smile, showing him Mr Tibbles's most recent expedition, which on that occasion included cream tea with his cousin Molly and a trip to the seaside.

'Tonight they are going to a night market in the forest.'

Stuart's face lit up, his dark eyes hopeful. 'With fairy lights?'

'With fairy lights,' I agreed.

'That's good, I like fairy lights. . .' he mumbled, resting his weary face on his arms, and closing his eyes. I smoothed Stuart's dark, silky black hair off his forehead, worried at how stressed he'd become.

So this year, when he'd suggested a different pace, I readily agreed. We were fortunate enough to have some savings and, with the royalties from *The Fudge Files*, the most we'd ever achieved, we were able to buy the house. But to keep the inflow of cash ticking over and I suspect, more importantly to keep Stuart busy, he'd begun a series of successful and some not so successful (see pak choi incident) home industry creations under his Sea Cottage label, which I'd helped design.

I placed Mum's box of things on an empty spot on one of the heaving shelves that lined the wall at the back of my studio. Only to pause, open it, remove the unfinished postcard and Christmas card and place them in the writing desk, along with a display of my fine watercolour brushes in a glass jar, a haphazard pile of watercolour paper, a large dusk-pink paper peony, blotting pads and a photo of Mum and me – both with identical grins and teary eyes – taken on my wedding day.

Stuart found me sitting there not long after, staring at the little Christmas card, deep in thought. 'Pretty,' he said, giving me a kiss, his head nodding towards the card. 'Getting in the spirit?' He smiled at me with those dark, gentle eyes that crinkled at the corners.

'It was Mum's – I found it in her desk. She hadn't finished it.'

He studied it, and then shook his head. 'She was very talented; it's gorgeous. Are you going to finish off his little nose?'

I tilted my head, considering. 'I've been trying to decide.'

He pulled up a chair from the old dining table that was now my official studio table (the long-ingrained paint marks had helped this decision along), his impossibly long legs stretched out in front of him, and stared at me, his hand in his palm, dark eyes thoughtful. 'What's to decide?'

'Well. It's a bit mad, I know. My first thought was that I would. . . but now. . .'

'But now?'

'But now, I'm not sure I should.'

He nodded slowly, eyes solemn. 'Well, you'll figure it out.'

I smiled at him and shook my head. 'You know, that's one of the things I love about you. You always get it.'

'Just one of the things that you love about me?' he said in mock affront, eyes wide, sitting up straight.

I raised a brow. 'Well, it certainly won't be turnip jam,' I replied, unable to hide my grin.

He frowned. 'Am I due a talk?'

I nodded. 'Mr Everton, we need to talk,' I said seriously.

He sighed, dramatically, flinging his forearm across his head in mock horror. 'Is it about the jam?'

I nodded. 'It is about the jam.'

He hung his head.

I patted his knee. 'My love, the truth is. . . not everything is meant to be jam. I think that some vegetation is destined for other possibilities, wondrous and transformative, definitely. . . but not in the jam family really. Maybe they'd be better off as pickles, or curd possibly, not that I am entirely sure what curd is, but possibly that, or even chutney.'

'Chutney?' he said, his eyes lighting up at the possibility.

'Chutney,' I concurred.

He got that look in his eye, so I hastened to add firmly, 'But not for turnips.'

'Ah.' His shoulders drooped. 'Tomas said much the same thing,' he said, with a small sad sigh, referring to his eighty-five-year-old French vegetable guru, who lived at the far end of the village and who was giving Stuart a very practical education on vegetable preservation, to Stuart's rather creative chagrin.

'Good man,' I said with a wink, silently thanking the heavens for Tomas's wise counsel.

He nodded, eyes amused, laughter lines crinkling at the corners. 'He's trying.

'And what's this?' asked Stuart, picking up the empty post-card. 'My God,' he said, looking at the old card in awe and not-ing Mum's fine script. 'It's addressed to you,' he breathed.

I nodded.

'Level?' he asked, eyes grave.

'*Eight* on the *Everton Scale*.'

Stuart and I had developed our own emotional pain scale based on our surname, during the Mum passing and our failed conceiving years. *Eight* was code for: *Mild heart attack.*

'I can imagine,' he said, leaning over and giving me a hug. 'Though the weird black tracks leading to your ears are a bit of a clue,' he teased.

I smacked his arm.

'It's just so strange. I mean, why would she start writing me a postcard from a place we'd gone to together?' I asked. 'And then. . . stop?'

He shook his head and leant the card back against the pink paper peony. 'Very strange,' he agreed. 'But it's nice that she was thinking of you.'

I nodded. Still, I couldn't help but wonder. . . what had she left unsaid?

Stuart didn't offer much in the way of speculation. He was comfortable with it just being a mystery.

Men. Honestly.

He gave the card a last frown and said, 'I'm thinking rocket pesto and prosciutto linguine,' and I answered with, 'I'm think-ing: yes. Starving,' and grinned.

He left with a salute, clicking his brown wellington-clad heels together. I shook my head and laughed.

I am one of those lucky marvels whose husband has banned them from the kitchen; the last and now permanent ban was dur-ing an *Everton Three: Door slamming on hand* when he'd lamented, in a crazed manner, to no one in particular, after my failed tomato soup experiment, 'She'd burn air, so she would,' accompanied by wild pacing around the tomato-splattered linoleum.

I took the time, while he was occupied, to call my best friend, Catherine Talty, from our first day of primary school, when Ted Gramble lifted her long red plait and asked if he'd get gingivitis from touching it, and she replied, 'No. . . but I'll give you something, anyway,' and she punched him point blank. I was thoroughly impressed and offered to match his other eye for her. Now we write children's books together that I illustrate.

She answered on the second ring. 'Was it brutal?' she asked, in lieu of a hello, well apprised of the writing desk expedition. Muppet seemed to sense her presence and began whining for her favourite unlawful feeder, while gently scraping off the skin of my shin with her paw.

'You've no idea,' I said, filling her in on the day and how difficult it was packing up Mum's desk, while I redistributed my shins to safety.

When I told her about the postcard though, the creator of Detective Sergeant Fudge offered a few ideas. The last – and the worst – unfortunately seemed to offer the most sense and I had to conclude that it seemed the most likely.

Catherine suggested, 'Maybe it was just a mistake – like she was talking to you and meant to write a card to someone else and put your name instead? I mean, it happens to me rather a lot, I'm afraid. Just the other day Ben was trying to get my attention, shouting at me that he wanted to watch the bloody Minion movie again, and I wrote "Minion" four *bloody* times. . .'

Since she was a writer, I took her word for it. But the prospect that it was simply a mistake was rather awful. I'd hoped, despite the pain that it would no doubt cause me, that maybe Mum had had some final thing left to say; perhaps one last 'I love you' or a bit of her typically idiosyncratic, but usually sage wisdom. Anything besides this.

At my silence, Catherine hastened to add, 'Ivy, I could be wrong. I mean, who knows? You know your mum. She wasn't the kind of woman to leave things unfinished. If she'd done that – made a mistake with your name – chances are you would have gotten it anyway. She'd have told you the funny story and that it was probably because she was meant to tell you that she loved you, or something, and mailed it to you. She was like that. . .'

I smiled at the recollection, my throat a little tight. She was right too. It still amazed me how well Catherine knew Mum. Though, then again, we'd grown up together. Catherine hadn't had a mum – hers had died when she was born – and she loved Mum rather fiercely. It was a very mutual affection. Mum had loved absentminded Cat, who spent most of our childhood with her head in a book, dearly too. So perhaps her intuitive knowledge of Mum wasn't surprising at all.

She had a point though; Mum wasn't the type to leave things undone. She was thrifty and imaginative and could be counted on to turn a *faux pas* into something special. It was one of her best qualities that I hoped to emulate some day. My eye fell onto the little Christmas card and Rudolph's missing nose.

Why would she have left these unfinished?

Perhaps the simplest answer was that, in the end, faced with such pain, it was hardly surprising that a few things would have come undone.

After Catherine rang off to 'feed the horde', which consisted of her husband Richard and three sons Tim, Jason, and Ben, all under the age of seven (I didn't mention that Stuart was cooking dinner as it seemed far too cruel), I decided I'd give Rudolph his nose. I crossed the wooden floor to the shelves behind, in search of the perfect shade of crimson gouache, only to shake my head in puzzlement as my search left me empty-handed. I scratched around and behind all the boxes, paints, and paper, to no avail. I walked the length of my studio, searching the long table and even the open writing desk, though I knew I hadn't placed it there. Nothing. And I knew I'd had it. I'd bought the crimson just days before, in an art shop in Penzance; it was the colour I'd used for Mr Tibbles's special raincoat.

The more I looked, I noticed something stranger still: it wasn't just the crimson that was gone, but every last shade of red in every medium I owned was missing as well. From my water-colours, acrylic, ink, pen, gouache. . . all the burgundies, clarets, scarlets and all the shades in between. . . it was all simply gone.

It was desperately odd. I have my scatter-brained moments, sure, but nothing like this. Especially not as a professional artist. We're often, despite the label of 'creative messiness', neat and tidy out of sheer necessity, as damaged £100 paintbrushes can attest. So where were they?

I set Rudolph down next to the empty postcard, wonder-ing if perhaps Stuart had decided to take up homemade signage with my supplies. Though I really would have thought he valued his life more than that.

I found him in the kitchen, his face bathed in steam from the simmering contents in the pan, which he was scenting with blissful intensity. He caught me staring and beckoned me over with a dreamy smile and inclination of his head. I breathed in the aromatic bouquet of garlic and cream, forgetting instantly why I had come down to confront him in the first place.

'You should bottle that,' I said.

'Eau de Sea Cottage?' he asked, with a grin.

'Oh yes.'

He laughed. 'Well, it's ready if you are.'

I quickly fetched two plates from the Welsh dresser I'd re-stored from a charity shop in the village, and painted a deep Provençal blue, piling the thick ceramic plates high with the creamy pasta, while Stuart carried the cutlery to our little con-servatory in the front of the house, where another charity find had become our dining room table, the repaired legs and old, scarred wood painted a soft dove grey.

The conservatory had become a favoured winter retreat, catching the last of the sun and the sunset while we dined.

I had plans for a velvety, blue chaise longue and a fireplace and perhaps some flowers and plants. I'm sure I could keep one alive. Stuart would probably help.

'Red?' he asked.

'Yes! I've been looking everywhere!' I exclaimed over my shoulder, almost cricking my neck as he passed me on his way back into the kitchen. Suddenly reminded of why I'd come down, before I was distracted by Stuart's kitchen wizardry.

He pivoted on his heel, two wine glasses in his hand. 'Sorry?' he said, dark eyes puzzled.

I shifted the plates in my hand. 'Oh, you meant wine. . . though you know I can't. I thought you were referring to my missing red paint.'

He frowned. 'Missing paint? I was going to offer you apple or cranberry juice so you don't feel left out.'

'Thanks, the cranberry please. Never could abide white wine; not about to start now,' I joked, and then raised a brow, undiverted. 'You didn't by any chance take all my red paint? Like every last shade in every single bloody medium I own, by any chance?'

His eyes popped. 'You're joking. I value my neck a little more than that. . . I still remember the brush incident of '06, *Everton Four: Broken toe* at least.'

I laughed. 'Damn straight. . . that was a pure, Kolinsky sable red, a legend amongst watercolour brushes, at an eye-watering seventy pounds a pop and you used it. . .' I took a steadying breath; the memory, even now, caused mild panic.

'To paint glue on the loose skirting board,' he said, head down, foot doing a half circle on the wooden floor in mock shame. 'Muppet and I took shelter for weeks afterwards,' he said dramatically, a theatrical shudder at the memory.

I raised a brow. Muppet, who had been eyeballing our exchange and the plates in my hands hopefully, cocked her head, almost in doubt.

'I'd hardly say weeks. . . and Muppet was on my side,' I pointed out.

Muppet didn't argue; she just stood in a puddle of her own drool.

'Days surely? And, no, she wasn't; she hid with me in my shed,' he insisted, in mock horror.

'More like an hour or two and if by "shed" you mean your man cave outside with your Xbox, well. . . Muppet knows where you keep the crisps,' I laughed.

Muppet gave me a rather scornful look, followed by a bulldog huff. All she saw, apparently, was that we were ignoring food, food that could be coming to her.

I took the food outside while he went to fetch the bottle of red and my cranberry juice. Later, after we had finished dinner and cleared up the kitchen and were relaxing and watching the last remnants of the sunset with its wash of pink and gold, Muppet snoring loudly, I remembered the missing paint, and considered the possibility that I had in the emotional residue of the day just overlooked it in some way. Though I didn't see how that was possible.

Just before bed, my mobile rang. It was 12.30 p.m. Turning to look at the screen, I stifled a groan.

Genevieve. Stuart's mother.

Let's just say that taking her only son to live far away from London was causing her some distress – no matter how much Stuart pointed out that the move was his idea, she remained, resolutely, unconvinced, and since he refused to answer her calls in general, she phoned me instead. Because there was the faint, *very* faint possibility it could be important, I invariably answered. I blame my own mother for this; I find it hard to be rude due to years of her coaching against bad telephone manners and so I habitually find myself on the receiving end of countless marketing calls. . . and endless tirades from his mother. I never learn.

In the months since we'd moved, Genevieve had found several, admittedly creative, ways to try to get us to change our minds. As if selling our old house, working out the notices on both our jobs, buying a home over five hours away, and packing up all our belongings hadn't been decisive enough.

The trouble was that Stuart turning sustainable farmer was not how the Everton men were meant to go, apparently. As far as she was concerned, she'd indulged him long enough. Yes, that's what she termed it, an *indulgence*. Which was laughable really, as Stuart didn't and wouldn't ever ask for her indulgence in the first place.

Thankfully, John, Stuart's father, didn't seem to share her opinion. In fact, every time he visited he seemed to stay just that little longer, with a look in his eyes of unmistakable longing. When he'd suggested that they consider retiring down here, she'd snapped, 'Don't be ridiculous, why would I ever retire?'

He never pointed out that maybe he would like the opportunity. Which, to me, was the saddest part. When I'd opened my mouth to tell her, Stuart had said, 'Just leave it.'

John would either stand up for himself or he wouldn't. Though why we should stay out of things that weren't our place when she never gave us the same consideration was at times beyond me.

'Hi Genevieve,' I said, attempting and failing to stifle a sigh. 'Everything all right?'

'Yes, of course,' she replied in her customary clipped tones, completely oblivious to the hour. I could picture her sitting in their London manor house in Knightsbridge (one of several homes here and abroad), in her velvet-lined Queen Anne chair, twisting her Cartier watch around her wrist, legs crossed at the ankle (naturally) in their silk trousers. Her bobbed hair neat in its no-nonsense style – the same one she'd been sporting in every company brochure since the 1990s. A CFO for a large global firm she co-founded called 'Women in Finance', Genevieve was so well-used to issuing orders and subsisting on her customary five hours of sleep a night – a source of baffling pride to me – that it would never occur to her that other people would feel differently. And as I suspected most of her employees were a little afraid of her, I sometimes felt a kind of contrary-like sense of duty to introduce her to the real world, or at least the part of it that didn't fall under her reign.

'Oh. . . well, it's a bit *late*, Stuart and I were just about to turn off the light.'

Stuart gave me a sympathy eye roll, and held his hand out for the receiver, his shoulders slumping ever so slightly. I held up my own to say *don't worry* – it usually took him much longer to calm down following one of her calls than it did me.

Genevieve didn't miss a beat. 'Oh, well, good that I caught you then.'

I sighed again, and she continued, oblivious, impervious, or both. 'I've come across a rather interesting article about a fertility specialist, Dr Marcus Labuscagne in Chelsea. It says that he's developed a new technique that has shown real promise for women in the last years of their fertility cycle, like you. He has a sixty-eight percent success rate.'

My eyes closed. Mentally, I counted to three. I was barely in my mid thirties. As far as Genevieve was concerned that meant I was premenopausal. Despite me pointing out to her time and again that women were able to have children much later in life and that the fertility cycle only started slowing down at around the age of thirty-eight, a woman who was responsible for the financial success of entire organisations, whose mission it was to enhance the lives of women in business, just failed to grasp it.

The truth was, unless it was on a spreadsheet in black and white, it was a grey area for her; one that needed to be resolved, now.

'Anyway,' she continued, 'I've made you an appointment for this Friday. Shall I send James along with the car, or will Stuart be driving you?'

James was her assistant. Her rather abused assistant. She took pleasure in having a male secretary. James did not. Though he had on more than one occasion corrected her with the term 'executive assistant', she pish-poshed it every single time – even though I had once heard her go to war with her husband, John, for daring to call the flight attendant an air hostess. Somehow, to her, sexism didn't occur the other way. If it did, she referred to it as 'sexism in reverse', which was both confusing, and well, frankly insulting as far as I could see.

I took a breath. 'Actually, Genevieve,' I began. 'The truth is, we've decided to take a break. . . just for a little while. You understand.'

There was a pause.

'A break?' she repeated.

'Yes,' I lied.

Stuart gave me a look. It was almost a *Should we just tell her and get it over with?* sort of look. I shook my head vigorously: no. I was not prepared for that, not yet. The last time we'd told Genevieve, she'd quite simply taken over.

My house, my health, and the absolute edge of my patience.

Without word or warning, I'd come home after a long day at my full-time post as an illustrator at a busy publishing house to find a nurse with the figure of an army tank and the personality to match ensconced in my spare room, who'd followed me around only to bark orders at me to my complete and utter bewilderment. Looking back, I'm not entirely sure why I didn't send her packing straight away. Perhaps it was simply shock. She'd strapped a heart rate monitor onto my arm, dismissing all my protestations, and within the first hour she'd hollered at me, 'Your heart rate is up!'

'That's because I was laughing!' I'd told her, looking away from Muppet, whose antics had caused the wire monitors to start beeping.

The same thing happened two hours later when I was working on a particularly sad scene when Mr Tibbles had to say goodbye to his Aunt Flossy, the wise mouse of the forest, who died to save the Red Fairy and keep her promise to fairyland.

'Keep calm!' she barked. In what I imagined the tone Miss Trunchbull would have used while catapulting children out of the window, in Roald Dahl's *Matilda*.

The irony of having her shout the instruction at me seemed lost on her though, so early the next morning, I decided to follow her 'orders' by sneaking out, so that I *could* actually keep calm.

When I'd come home that evening though, I found Genevieve sitting in my living room, white-knuckled with fury, her jaw clenched as she hissed, 'Odessa is one of the city's most experienced nursing sisters, I *cannot believe* that you just left her here without telling her where you were going.'

Odessa? Somehow in all her barking she'd never imparted her name.

'Oh! You're a nurse?' I'd said, in mock surprise, my own annoyance clearly displayed. Who did she think she was to employ someone in our home without consulting us, and then come here to reprimand me as if I were a child? I cursed Stuart for being away on a business trip to Berlin. Though, in retrospect, that was no doubt the very reason she had acted when she did, by employing the nurse and installing her in our home, with the spare key we had given her for emergencies. I made a mental note to have the locks changed as my own emergency action that night.

'Odessa said you hadn't even had breakfast when you left.'

I was fairly certain that what I had for breakfast was my concern but in the interest of not appearing defensive I'd said wearily, 'I did.'

'Toast is not breakfast,' contradicted Odessa, who resembled a female SS officer.

'And you never said when you'd be back,' Genevieve continued. 'Odessa has been worried sick,' she accused, folding her thin, silk-clad arms.

'Right,' I'd said, setting down my bag. That was quite enough of that. 'I'm afraid, Odessa, no one consulted me on your appointment. . . because if they had, they would have known that it was entirely out of the question. I do not want, nor require the need of a. . . nurse, as you term yourself, so we will not be needing your services any longer. Please see yourself out.'

When she failed to leave, my voice lowered. 'Now.'

While Odessa had mumbled incoherently, and Genevieve had stood up to lecture me, I'd escorted Odessa out, and suggested that Genevieve, likewise, follow suit.

To her credit, she did actually leave. Her parting shot had been cutting though, a curse disguised as a warning. 'Well, don't blame me if this pregnancy goes as well as your last.'

I'd slammed the door so hard that the glass cracked in two, like our lives two weeks later when things did, in fact, go as badly as the last.

She never did say 'I told you so' when she heard about the miscarriage, but her words haunted me for months afterwards, despite my obstetrician, Dr Josef Tam, assuring me that I had done nothing wrong, that my blood pressure, diet, and health were all fine, that it was simply a cruel act of fate.

Genevieve's words had coloured an already strained relationship, and it had taken me months to speak to her again. Now I only do it for Stuart, though if it were up to him I wouldn't need to bother – sometimes I was sorely tempted not to.

'That's really interesting,' I said now, remarking on her news about the fertility specialist in London with his novel approach and encouraging results.

And it *was* interesting, and a few weeks ago there was no doubt I would have been pushing her for more information. But now that we were finally pregnant and my new obstetrician, Dr Gia Harris – a referral of Dr Tam's based in Falmouth – assured us that we were likely to stay that way, provided I stayed away from any undue stress, I wasn't as interested as I would ordinarily have been.

It didn't feel like the right time to bring up the baby either. To be honest, I didn't know when it would be the right time. The trouble was that even though she meant well, and I didn't doubt *that*, she had a way of making a stressful situation worse. She had a tendency of not trusting us to make our own decisions, to insist that I visit a battery of professionals that she had sanctioned, as if only via her own investigations they could be degreed to the right level, despite what I, or science may have to say on the subject.

Three years ago when I'd refused to change my gynaecologist and see her experts instead, she had implied that because we hadn't seen 'the best' professionals, who would have advised against my fondness for long walks (which she believed weren't good for the baby), there was a chance we wouldn't have miscarried. Three guesses why we've decided to keep the third pregnancy – the one all our doctors were calling the lucky one – secret.

'But Ivy, is that a good idea? These are the last good years, you don't want to throw them away!'

Last good years? I gritted my teeth. 'We're not throwing them away!' I gasped. Couldn't she just understand that we'd been through hell and needed a minute to recover from it all? Even if, yes, right now I was lying and probably going to hell. . . it was a *good* lie, for all our good really, even hers, a lie that would reduce the stress all round rather considerably.

Genevieve pressed on, 'You've got to push through – I know it's hard, but this could work. It takes around six months to get the body ready apparently, with twice-weekly appointments. You could both come stay here, I could arrange for James to fetch you, and take you back, you wouldn't have to worry about a thing. Or. . . you know, I could set up an area for you to live in the manor house, just to make things a little easier. . . John said the other day that they could install a whole kitchen in the east wing in a week. . . It'll be no trouble, I'll call the builders tomorrow.'

Come live with her? *What?* The woman went from zero to a hundred faster than I could blink, and after the day I'd had all I really wanted to do was go to sleep. I was regretting not handing the phone to Stuart when he offered.

I took a deep breath. I didn't need to explain myself to her. Something that I kept forgetting, and something she needed a reminder of as well. 'I appreciate your help, Genevieve, I do, but please respect our decision.'

A long silence followed, where I suspected Genevieve, too, was attempting to find her own inner calm. 'Well, all right, that's your choice. I'll respect it. Give my love to Stuart,' she said, then hung up.

I closed my eyes.

'Scale?'

I opened an eye and gave a dry, humourless laugh. 'About a *Five: Third degree burn.*'

'Ah, well that's good then. . . shows she's grown,' he said with a wink.

I couldn't summon a laugh; all I wanted to do was sleep.

He looked so worried that I said, 'She means well. . . in her own twisted sort of way.'

Stuart patted me on the knee. 'I'm sure I'm the one who is meant to tell you that.'

I snorted. 'Maybe we can tell her. . . when it's about nine.'

'Nine?'

'Nine years old.'

He gave me a look. 'Just say the word.'

Stuart was sorely tempted, but I couldn't do that. I might not have wished her to know about the pregnancy just yet. . . but I couldn't do that. She might drive me mad, but you couldn't fault the fact that she cared. Finally, we put out the light, where I tried, and failed, to put aside all the anxiety speaking to her had caused, dredging up more than one old ghost.

CHAPTER THREE

Rudolph Has a Shiny Nose

I dreamt of Mum that night. Perhaps, it wasn't surprising. After bringing the desk home, a part of me knew I was bringing something else along with it too. Something I'd been trying to bury, along with everything else. A piece of her, I suppose.

I hated it when I dreamt of her.

Hated how easy it was to forget. How easy it was to slip back to before.

I hated it, because I loved it so much. Because when I dreamt of her, it was as if she was still there. My traitorous mind was always so quick to peel away the years, to erase all the pain and heartache, and put me once again back in my childhood home, without a moment's hesitation.

Except that night, I wasn't a child. It was now, just after the phone call with Genevieve, except now I was calm. What had I to fear? There she was, just when I needed her. Soon she'd tell me not to worry. . .

In my dream, she sat at her writing desk, penning a letter. I smiled, at how often I'd found her sitting there, doing that. Her hair was once again long and dark blonde, a loose tangle of curls that flickered in the soft firelight. When I entered the room, she smiled, patted the seat next to her, making Fat Arnold, our squashed-face Persian, glare as he was made to relocate. She laughed, and then took a sip of tea, out of that old pink and gold teacup that she loved so much, and in the pause, I glanced over and saw that she wasn't writing a letter at all.

It was a postcard. A familiar one, with a pretty French cover. As I peered I saw her wink, as she picked up her pen, and addressed the card to *Darling Ivy.*

I smiled in return, and watched as she began to write.

I opened my mouth to ask her why she was writing me a postcard but found that no words came out. I tried again. But my voice was gone. My heart started to beat faster. What was happening? I tried to touch her arm, get her attention, but my hand felt like it was coming from very far away. No matter how hard I tried, I couldn't touch her. I couldn't reach her.

'Mum?' I cried, until I was hoarse. My throat sore. The words ricocheting in my head like a machine gun. But no sound came out of my mouth at all.

I stood up fast, and all at once I was peering at her from the end of a long tunnel. A tunnel that was getting fainter and fainter, as I called her name over and over again, till I could taste the blood in my mouth. But she never looked up. She never heard my cries. She just sat there, with that soft smile on her face as she wrote and wrote the words I would never, ever read.

I awoke to painful, gasping tears. The kind where your lungs forget to breathe. Somehow in my fog-covered gaze, I saw Stuart's gentle eyes, and felt his arms hold me tight. 'It's okay, love,' he said while stroking my hair. 'Just a dream, just a dream,' he added, trying to soothe me.

But I could find no solace. She'd been there. Her face so vivid. The room so real. . . and that bloody postcard. That postcard with its cruel emptiness filled with nothing but silence, a silence that seemed to both haunt and taunt me. All I could do was sob for it. For the sheer waste and cruelty of it.

'What is it?' asked Stuart, his eyes tired, worried.

I tried to squeeze the words out past my grief, past everything that had been left unsaid, but I couldn't. Somehow, though he must have guessed.

He held me closer. Finally when the words came, they were a jagged rock-heap of things, from missing Mum, to the ever-present fear that when our dream of finally having a baby was so close to being realised it would be taken away. Like it had so many times before.

'We've just got to trust, my love. That's all we've got to do. I'm sorry that I kept encouraging you to get your mum's desk. I thought it would be good for you, I should have known. . .' he said, his brow furrowed.

I shook my head. 'Don't, it was. . . it is good. It's so hard to explain. . . but as hard as it is, and it's well, brutal in a way, it's the closest I've felt to her in years.' I took a shuddering breath. 'It's just. . . no one tells you about this, that it can come back and hit you again when you least expect it to. When finally everything seems to be going all right.'

Stuart sighed, then said wisely, 'But that's the way of it, isn't it? We're so wired to expect the worst that when something good happens, it's like our subconscious minds need to find something to torture us with, because if we dared to trust, well then there's a chance we'd be disappointed.'

I nodded. 'Though in my dream. . . it was only realising she was gone again that was the torturous bit.'

Stuart gave me a sympathetic squeeze.

I always appreciated that about him, he didn't tell me I was silly, or try to sweep away my emotions. Or worse, try to cover them up. He just let me feel them.

Finally, I drifted off again, this time into a dreamless sleep.

* * *

It was the first thing I noticed as I entered my studio in the early chill of the morning, despite my tired, swollen eyes. I pulled my cardigan close and stood just inside the doorway and swallowed in sudden trepidation. Like a sentinel guiding me in, burning so brightly, it appeared to have an almost otherworldly glow, the little card with my mother's reindeer and his missing guiding light: Rudolph had a very shiny nose.

A perfect little nose in a shade I'd never seen; like crimson mixed with stardust, seemingly lit from within. I blinked, unable to move; it took a while before my legs obeyed my command.

It was all some mad joke of Stuart's, surely? A strange pre-Christmas trick? I rushed forward to the desk and picked up the card. Up close, the little nose seemed even more delicate, like red spun fairy dust. If he had done it, I couldn't even be upset. It was exquisite. Except, when could he have done it?

Perhaps last night as I slept, maybe he had tiptoed out. . . Maybe that would explain the missing paint, even though he said he hadn't taken it.

I frowned, remembering Stuart hadn't even been home when I'd brought the desk, he hadn't seen the card until later. . . and wouldn't have had the incentive to steal the paint. . . unless he found some and thought it would be a way of making me feel better, after last night?

I set the card down, a sudden thought occurring to me as I crossed the room to look again through the boxes, only to pause in bewilderment. They were all still missing.

Perhaps Stuart had found a bit of paint somewhere and had done it as a surprise, though I wondered why. It was sweet, a beautiful gesture in a way, but still unlike him; he would have usually left well alone; left me to sort out how I felt about it; or so I had thought.

I placed it next to the postcard, noting how, in the early morning, the postcard seemed to glow. Then I turned away from it, last night's dream still fresh in my mind. A part of me wanted to simply shut it in the drawer and out of sight. A bigger part knew I never would.

I rubbed my eyes, thinking 'coffee', and retreated downstairs to put on a pot. Muppet heard the sound of my footfall and roused herself to follow. I stepped over Pepper and Pots, lounging by the Aga in the kitchen, and gave them both a morning rub. 'Hello boys, where've you been?'

They circled me, while Muppet looked on disdainfully. They had a mutual understanding, which I understood as follows: when the curly-haired human, 'The One Who Feeds', is in the holy place with the most saintliest of deities, whom the humans call 'Fridge', which opens with a great holy light to reveal 'Food', we are all on our best behaviour.

When my back was turned, of course, all bets were off.

I fed the livestock, popped some homemade bread (Stuart's) in the toaster and made some filter coffee, sighing as I examined our impressive collection of preserves, which included squash, cucumber, and even beetroot. Wishing that, just once, Stuart would think 'strawberry'. . .

'Beetroot it is,' I said to Muppet and Pots, who'd lingered by the Aga, while Pepper slouched off in search of a vacant bed.

I unhooked my navy parka from behind the back door and slipped on my wellies, fetching a tray that I filled with two cups, toast, jam and the coffee pot. If the mountain won't come to Muhammad, Muppet and I would meet him in his polytunnel.

'Slugs,' he moaned in despair, a bucket at his feet into which he dropped the soft molluscs, favouring each one with a pointed glare and a disgruntled shake of his head, as if each little shell-less slug owed him a personal debt.

'Coffee?' I asked, interrupting his morning tirade against the slugs.

'Bless you,' he said, crossing the cabbage patch, looking rather fetching in an emerald green jersey that brought out his dark eyes. He gave his runner beans a fondle as he took a cup and joined me, perching on one of the raised cement beds.

'Back to the 2 a.m. patrol?' I asked.

'Looks like it. Little buggers!' He glared at the bucket. 'You will not get my prize lettuces,' he declared, like a general announcing war.

'Lettuces,' I mused, 'is that the plural? Sounds odd.'

He frowned. 'Lettuci?'

'That sounds vaguely diseased. Mrs Sprout, I'm afraid you've got a nasty case of lettuci. . .'

He laughed and took a sip from his cup. 'I'll ask Tomas.'

'I'll Google,' I said, having more faith in the search engine than an eighty-five-year-old Frenchman who insisted on calling me Eve, despite numerous corrections. Stuart's vegetable guru lived alone in a small rundown cottage at the end of Cloudsea, where he had placed a collection of handmade 'Keep Out' notices in a violent shade of red paint all along a rather grim-looking path of stinging nettles, to his neighbour Gertrude Burrows's long-suffering despair. The small front garden looked like something out of *The Addams Family*. Ironic, considering the back resembled something that could be entered in the veggie division of the Chelsea Flower Show. There had been a petition to declare that bit of Cloudsea – the bit belonging to Tomas – as a no man's land for the last, oh, twenty years. All of which had only encouraged Stuart to get to know the odd gardening recluse who lived there more, because, well, Stuart is Stuart.

The geriatric Tomas had long grey hair that swept his shoulders, wore a green beret at all times, even inside, had purpled, arthritic fingers that perpetually smelt of kale, and bright blue eyes that got a distinct twinkle whenever he saw Stuart's long-legged approach up the hill, and a distinctive glint whenever he saw Gertrude Burrows's more laborious shuffle.

No one really knew what the old Frenchie was doing here, but the rumours were pretty intense. Some said he escaped the French Foreign Legion, others that he was a Nazi spy, a very small sect maintained that he'd followed his heart and the village baker, Robyn Glass, here, after she holidayed in Marseille – he certainly seemed to blush a ripe prize-winning radish shade every time she handed him one of his favourite iced buns. But I suspected that the truth was stranger than fiction: the old goat was a closet Anglophile.

For instance, an offering of coffee whenever he came around to inspect the state of Stuart's polytunnel was met with a distinct shake of his head, as were any other teas *except* English breakfast, which was greeted with a faint, yet affirmative nod. Once I even caught him grin (when he thought no one was looking) as he dunked a digestive into his 'Building Tees', without getting any of it into the mug en route to his gummy maw. . .

Stuart snorted, the laughter lines around his eyes creasing.

'So. . .' I began.

'So?'

I gave him a look, waiting for him to say something about the Christmas card.

'Yes?' he said, pointing his ear towards me, his expression for 'I'm all ears', so I threw a bit of toast at him.

He ducked. 'It sounded like you wanted to ask me something?'

I rolled my eyes and smiled. 'Fine, have it your way.'

He frowned. 'Okay, what way?'

'Stuart.'

'Ivy.'

'Stuart. . .'

I sighed. Fine. 'I love his nose.'

Stuart blinked. '*Whose* nose?'

I glared. 'Stuart, stop teasing. I'm serious. Rudolph's nose, it's beautiful. I have no idea what you used, but frankly it's incredible.'

But Stuart looked at me as if I'd gone crazy. 'What are you talking about? Who is Rudolph?'

I stared at him, feeling a bit off-kilter. 'Rudolph. . . the little reindeer from my mother's card. You. . . you painted in his little missing nose. . . didn't you?'

Stuart's eyes went wide. 'Ivy, I would never do that.'

'But. . .' I said, feeling suddenly like the ground beneath my feet was shifting.

He came over, touched my arm, his face concerned.

'But someone did,' I insisted, feeling my blood turn cold.

He shook his head. 'Can't be, love.'

'It is, I saw it. . . his nose is there now,' I exclaimed. 'Come, I'll show you.'

Stuart looked at me, but didn't move.

'Come,' I insisted.

'Ivy, love, it was probably you. You know how you get caught up in your work. Maybe you did it without realising?'

I blinked. 'Are you serious? I just popped Rudolph's nose on my dead mum's old Christmas card and. . . forgot?'

'Love. . .' he began, but I shook my head.

'It's okay. Next, you'll tell me that I'm tired, I'm stressed. . . It's the pregnancy hormones. . . But I know what I saw. I didn't do it. For one, it was . . . well, luminescent really.'

'Luminescent,' he repeated in some surprise.

'Yes. . . It was like, like a really beautiful technique that I don't know how to do, or special paint because it shimmers. . . I couldn't do that.'

He laughed. 'Darling, you are one of the best illustrators in the business. Of course you could. . . and if you thought you couldn't, why on earth would you think that I could?'

I stared at him, mouth slightly ajar, hoping that he'd just jump out and say, 'Gotcha'. . . Though I'd probably punch him out at this point if he did. 'I don't know. . . I just thought maybe, maybe you had some really great paint,' I said, somewhat faintly.

He turned towards me. 'Some great paint that *you* didn't know about? That would be a little like telling Einstein you've found a neat way to work out the seven times table. I think the best explanation is that you probably did it without realising. I mean, remember Mr Tibbles's Moroccan slippers? You drew that one and even you were surprised.'

'That they ended up Moroccan, yes, but I always knew I was drawing a pair of slippers,' I pointed out.

Stuart shrugged. 'A little nose. . . I mean, it could have happened.'

I sighed. 'Maybe.' Though I knew that wasn't the case. How could it have been? I was in no state to have done that yesterday.

'You okay?'

'I'm fine. . . it was just a bit weird.'

He nodded. 'I can imagine.'

I didn't think he could though because I knew that it wasn't me who had done it. I would never have just done something like that. . . something so intricate and unique on autopilot. For one, someone had made sure that I couldn't, considering that there was no paint for me to do it with.

Which left, what exactly?

I didn't know.

I was confused and a little anxious. The shimmering nose haunted my thoughts, hanging around like an unwanted guest.

I cleared up the cups and breakfast things and gave Stuart a kiss goodbye. He was off to sell his wares at a market in North Cornwall and to see a man about Christmas ham.

So with Muppet in tow, I set off on our regular morning walk on the beach, determined to shake it off.

Even now, edging nearer to the clutches of winter, I couldn't believe that we lived here, how fortunate we were. That I could stroll on the beach every day if I wanted. That I could live surrounded by such beauty. My childhood home was further inland, just outside the village of Cloudsea in Tremenara, so the beach, though close, was always a delight.

As Muppet and I walked along the rocky outcrop that bordered Sea Cottage, breathing in the fresh seaside air, my nose and cheeks turned pink with cold. Muppet ran ahead and came trotting back every few metres or so until we reached the golden sand. Today the sea was a rich sapphire, the waves thundering at high tide. The wind had picked up and there was no one about except for a few egrets that circled above, their strange caws piercing overhead.

Muppet ran off to bark in doggy delight though even she wouldn't dare step her paws in the icy waters.

Shells dotted the beach, as if the ocean had gently pulled back its skirt to reveal a frothy garter studded with jewels, each one glistening in the spray. I bent to pick up a particularly pretty one. It was purple and lacy black. The fine detail reminded me of an evening dress. I popped it in my pocket. Often I drew inspiration from nature, especially when I captured the fey folk of my imagination.

Muppet barked at a length of calk and I laughed. The metre-long seaweed was large and full of sinewy tendrils – alien. It looked almost alive.

Here, now, I was able to shake off the disconcerting events of the morning for a while; the long walk had helped clear my head.

Afterwards, Muppet and I headed out towards the village. There was a little café, not too far from the beachfront, that we often frequented, called Salt. The owner had a soft spot for Muppet and could always be counted on to offer a tasty treat for her and a cup of tea or hot chocolate for me, while we thawed before the fire and considered the day's itinerary.

In truth, it had been a little bit of an escape for my sanity when faced with the likes of pak choi jelly, or the perils of beetroot jam. I couldn't bring myself to take generic, store-bought food home, but every now and then a little scone with strawberry jam and clotted cream did the illicit trick.

Today I lounged in the comfy blue and white checked wingback, cradling a tall mug of hot chocolate in my hands while I warmed myself by the fire.

'So, it looks like Detective Sergeant Fudge will be solving *The Case of the Missing Brolly* and later Mr Tibbles will be throwing a party for his friends in the Fairy's Forest,' I informed Muppet.

Muppet cocked her bulldog head to the side, tongue lolloping about as if she were considering her role in the activities. Which would no doubt involve lying beneath the desk, a rather faithful artist's assistant, if not a very productive one.

'Can I tempt you with a slice of cake before you solve the case?' asked Terry, the café owner, in his soft Scottish burr that was at odds with his powerful, over six foot size.

Just into his sixties, and still fit and trim from his years in the Navy, his hair reflected a vivid shade of burnt auburn in the firelight, sky blue eyes above ruddy cheeks aglow, beefy arms on his red and white striped apron-tied hips.

I winked. 'Go on then.'

'We've a particularly good chocolate orange, or triple chocolate fudge?' He raised his faded blond brows, temptingly.

'Good lord, how would one choose?' I dithered. 'Long day, so I'm thinking the triple chocolate fudge.'

'Good choice,' he said, with a slightly crooked smile. 'Cappuccino?'

I nodded. 'You're bad for me, Terry. . . one day my husband will find out about us.'

'Not from me. How do you eat what you do and stay so slim?' he asked, eyes amused.

I laughed, shaking my head at such blatant flattery. 'Must be the miraculous powers of pak choi jelly. . .'

He grinned. 'To be fair, it tastes great.'

I laughed. 'Well, perhaps. . . but even though he calls it jelly instead of jam, I still can't get over the fact that it is in fact jam and that "pak choi" is really just Chinese for cabbage. But if you could get over that, it would be quite good really.'

Terry sniggered, 'Jelly is just the American for jam.'

'Don't tell Stuart, you'll break his heart.'

His smile widened. 'Well, I ordered twenty bottles.'

I laughed aloud.

Terry had rather a soft spot for Stuart's culinary creations, declaring him a man after his own heart. Still, he kept my clandestine cake visits a secret, knowing that woman can't live on pak choi, or indeed, beetroot jam alone.

Back at the cottage, I found the most welcome of sights I've had in weeks sitting amongst the raised vegetable beds, a look of contentment on her face as she stared out at the sea beyond.

Victoria. Stuart's sister. Younger by eighteen months. Curly black hair in a constant tumble to her waist, large brown eyes, and a perpetually lopsided smile that made her look naughty even when she was trying to be serious, which was also oftentimes at odds with her rather posh accent. That and her penchant for Converse trainers in every shade imaginable, which she wore with everything, even suits – *especially suits* – was a sort of finger to her mother, who was the kind of woman who would know just when to wear white and who still believed women shouldn't wear jewellery in the morning.

'Smudge?' I said, not daring to believe my eyes.

Victoria turned to look at me, then started jumping up wildly, as if it was me who had startled her and not the other way around. 'Ivy?' she exclaimed in glee, and we went racing into each other's outstretched arms at a very slow, movie pace, laughing like idiots as we do.

'What are you doing here?' I asked, between giggles. After the emotional residue from the last two days, her presence was exactly what I needed, a tonic.

Stuart's sister was a rather famous biographer whose work had taken her all around the globe, trawling through the forgotten libraries of ancient civilisations and the secret tombs of history's most interesting personalities.

'Manderley. . .' she said enigmatically, with a quirk of her lips.

'Du Maurier?' I breathed. 'Really? You got approval for the biography!'

She nodded. 'It seems an old family friend has recently come forward with some never-before-been-seen letters and, well, I've got first pick.'

'What? How?'

'I'd tell you, sister dearest, but then I'd have to kill you, and, well, I'm used to you being in the family now.'

'Oh shut up!' I said with a giggle, knowing that Victoria's network of sources spanned many continents. She had a way of charming anyone, anywhere, and getting information out of the most reticent of people.

I was delighted for her. Victoria had long wanted to write a biography of Cornwall's most famous author's life, but our publishers had been hesitant as, without a new angle, it would simply be yet another tome vying with all the others about the mysterious author who had made Cornwall her home.

Victoria and I had met at the Christmas party of the publishers we shared, Rain River Books. Though at the time I never did think we would ever meet, as her reputation was so established.

While I loved what I did, in a room full of Booker-Prize-winning novelists, at events like that, as a children's book illustrator and co-author you couldn't help but feel a little like you'd entered through the back door. So when my editor, Jeff Marsons, steered me towards Victoria Langley, the world-renowned biographer, who'd recently scooped up several international awards for her latest biography of a South African anti-apartheid activist, and she had expressed a desire to meet me, I'd somewhat reluctantly agreed.

He had tapped a tall woman with a mad tumble of curls down her back, who turned to look at us from behind a pair of large, square frames. When she saw me, her eyes widened and she began jumping up and down.

'Detective Sergeant Fudge?' she said, as if I had morphed into Catherine's and my creation. 'Look!' she commanded, holding up a toy version of Detective Sergeant Fudge that hung off a key chain. 'I ordered it online. I love The Fudge!'

My mouth fell open. It was still a surprise that anyone even knew about our books; we had a few promotional type items that you could order off the publisher's site but nothing extravagant. *The Fudge Files* was just something that my best friend and me dreamt up one afternoon and started to create, when Catherine said, 'Imagine if there was a terrier division in Scotland Yard and Muppet was in charge?' I didn't know if it was the incongruity of this illustrious author with our imaginary detective on her key chain, the 'Supergirl' T-shirt she was wearing underneath her stylish black blazer, or the bemused looks on everyone else's faces who had come over to have an intellectual conversation with this renowned biographer, but after that we were firm friends.

It was Victoria who had introduced me to Stuart. She still accused him of stealing me. Which, as he pointed out, was payback for coming along, the second child, and smudging the 'perfect' family that had existed before she arrived. Where, as the only child, he had been quite literally the little lord of the manor – he'd grown up in a rather stately manor home in London until she came along and 'smudged' it all, not only by wrecking the 'happy trio' but by being a certifiable genius to boot. Whereby afterwards and forevermore she was doomed to be known to one and all as 'Smudge'.

It was true too, she was technically a genius. She had been tested, and had one of those IQs that meant she should be building spaceships or 3D printing our moon colony. While that would probably appeal, she resisted the traditional route of maths and science as she found it 'too easy' – somehow I still liked her after this statement. But mostly I liked her because she was also a bit of rebel, as if the cute trainers and superhero outfits weren't enough of a clue. Though as Victoria maintained, 'A rebel with a nerd herd.' Apparently, nerds were her people.

As someone who hadn't been cool a day in her life, I suppose I was definitely part of that club. My collection of knitted hats with ears definitely qualified.

And despite its rather acerbic nature, Stuart's nickname for her was one of endearment – for few siblings were closer. There were times, like right now, she just knew when she was needed. 'So I believe you do not negotiate with terrorists?' she said with a smirk.

I laughed. The Terrorist. That was their name for Genevieve. Yes, this too was a term of endearment – though actually, sometimes, not.

'Ah. . . no, no, I don't,' I said with a chuckle. 'So you heard?'

She nodded. 'Oh yes! But look, I agree, you have to lie just now in the beginning before she causes World War Three. . . It's for her own good, and ultimately, the baby's,' she winked.

Victoria was one of the few people who knew about the baby.

I don't know how she knew, mostly she guessed. . . She was not a genius for nothing, and years of studying people had made

her something of an expert, I suppose. Though she did say that
the irony was that she was oftentimes blinded by her own husband Mark, who was also a well-known biographer. She, like
Catherine, were the two people in this world that Stuart and I
both felt like we could tell about the baby, either way. As much
as I wanted – and needed – to tell Dad, having him look as helpless as he did the last time meant that I just couldn't face that yet.

'So we'll be seeing more of you?' I said hopefully.

'Oh yes,' she said, giving me a big hug.

'How long are you in town?' I asked.

'Just a flash visit right now, I'm afraid. I have some transcrip-
tion work to do around the corner. . . I'm not allowed to remove
the letters from the home, so I thought I'd stop by here for a
coffee if that's all right? Took a chance that you'd be home as I
pass this way – only realised while I was driving, else I would
have called, but I'll come this way again in a week, if that's good
for you, spend a night or two?'

'That's perfect!' I said, delighted at the surprise, making a
mental note to get some new things for the spare room, something Christmassy definitely. . . would be good to put it in use
for the first time.

'How's Mark?' I asked.

A cloud seemed to settle over her face for a second, but
passed just as quickly. 'Oh, great, great, working on a biography
of Marcus Aurelius. He's in Rome till the end of the month,' she
said with a bright smile that didn't quite reach her eyes. I didn't
push it, though it did make me worry. Victoria and her husband
Mark hadn't had the easiest of relationships – they both had
careers that took them to opposite ends of the earth, but somehow they'd made it work. Everyone has their ups and downs.
They didn't want children just yet as it wouldn't quite fit with
their careers, though of course, Genevieve persisted in trying to
persuade them anyway. At least Stuart's mother shared 'the love'.

'How's the great jam experiment coming along?' she asked, changing the subject.

I snorted. 'Splendidly. You very narrowly missed out on turnips. . .' I said with a chuckle.

We heard footsteps approach, then, 'Ah, I thought I heard your dulcet tones! Hullo Smudge,' came Stuart's voice from behind.

She rolled her eyes. Smudge's voice was a bit high-pitched, not overly so, but it could get extremely high-pitched when we had had a few glasses, which was when Stuart said she was able to break the sound barrier with her giggles. Sibling love. . .

She quirked her brows. 'Turnip jam?'

His shoulders started to shake in laughter. 'Touché! It seemed like a good idea at the time, a bit like you, Smudge,' he said, face deadpan.

She glared at him, and elbowed him in the ribs. Then they linked arms and he took her on a tour of the polytunnel, while I brewed us a pot of tea, glad that Victoria was here. I knew that Genevieve's latest call had been weighing on Stuart's mind, and Victoria was one of the few people who would be able to ease his worries. It was hard for him not to tell his mother about the baby, and I knew that he felt bad about our decision to keep it to ourselves, even if it was for a good reason.

Victoria had about an hour before she had to get to her appointment, so I made us a quick lunch – simple cheese sandwiches with Stuart's homemade bread. (Stuart made her try each and every one of his condiments, while I rolled my eyes, especially when she said that the pak choi was her favourite, then laughed like a lunatic at my expression.)

Victoria entertained us all by telling us what she had so far learned about Daphne du Maurier, and her amazing life.

I was sorry that she wouldn't be staying longer, but glad that she was at least in the county, and we agreed to meet later on in the week, for an exclusive tour of the country surrounding the author's old stomping grounds. It would be incredible to see this part of Cornwall from the eye of a biographer, and I was already looking forward to it.

After she left, I got started on *Detective Sergeant Fudge and the Case of the Missing Brolly*, doing my best to ignore Rudolph's shiny new nose. The day moved swiftly and I managed several illustrations for *The Fudge Files*. Catherine would be pleased. At this rate, we'd be early with the publishers. . . a first.

Later, Tomas came over to consult on a case of septic-looking greens that Stuart had been examining with a magnifying glass. As Tomas passed me en route to the garden, he lifted the edge of his green beret with a gnarled finger, and drawled out a greeting, ''Ello, Eve. . .'

His lips twitched, as I corrected, 'Ivy,' automatically.

He shrugged his thin shoulders, in a manner that promised that he'd do it again, held up a bottle of sloe gin to Stuart with a twinkle in his clear blue eyes, and the two disappeared to discuss 'business' in the polytunnel.

I scoffed – not looking forward to dealing with the after-effects of *that* in the morning, and headed back to the studio to work on *Mr Tibbles and the Fairy's Forest*, where Mr Tibbles was about to receive a rather strange gift, from the Red Fairy. Only, she wouldn't have any red hair if I didn't find the missing paint.

Somehow in the events of the day I'd forgotten about it. I had another search and sighed in frustration. Then I moved over to the writing desk and looked there again. Still nothing. Absently, I opened the bottom drawer which I hadn't touched since I'd unpacked it the day before, only to stare at it in absolute, fearful shock. I jumped back, my heart pounding, the colour draining from my face.

There they were.

Every last tube. Every last pot. Every last bottle of red paint that I owned was there in the drawer. Not in a fan or in a row, or just scattered about.

No.

They were all grouped together to commit a single felony, to form one simple, damnable word, and it belonged to me: Ivy.

CHAPTER FOUR

The Scarlet Ribbon

There were two explanations really. The first, obvious, and least inspiring was that I was indeed going mad. Surprising really that it would happen now, after we seemed finally to be over the worst of our troubles.

The second was that someone was playing a rather befuddling joke on me. Someone who thought I had a better handle on my sanity, because I'm quite sure it would backfire when the men in little white coats appeared to take me away. I couldn't quite believe that Stuart would do that to me; it just wasn't his style. He was far too aware of how it would hurt me.

There was a third option too, of course, which was absurd.

If I considered it I'd have to believe in fairy tales or magic, or ghosts. . . really.

And I didn't know if I was quite ready to believe that.

So I did what any sane person would do. . . I went to the kitchen, opened a bottle of red wine and sat with my eyes closed while I sniffed it, breathing deeply of the luscious berry scent.

'And now?' asked Stuart, coming in from the back door and looking at me quizzically, while I sat at the pale cream island with the bottle of wine held reverentially in my hands.

'I'm hoping that it will impart its magic. . . via osmosis.'

He raised a brow, an amused smile playing on his lips.

'I think you'll find,' he said, placing an enormous ham on the countertop and giving it a firm, yet tender pat, 'that you actually need to drink it for it to have any effect.'

I gave him a look. 'Yes, well. . . That's off the cards for at least what. . . seven months?'

He grinned. I did too – couldn't help myself. 'Small sacrifice,' we both said together.

'Still. . . you could probably have half a glass of some champagne or something if you're really desperate. . .'

I made a face. 'I'm rather desperate. But still. . . I don't want to risk it.'

He nodded. 'Bad day?'

'Not exactly. . .' I looked at him and cleared my throat. 'I found my paint,' I said, and searched his face for telling signs.

'Your paint?' he asked, confused, staring at the ham, no doubt deciding where its Christmas future lay. Considering it was only November, the plan was obviously rather grand.

'My missing red paint?'

He frowned. 'Oh yes. . . was it all there when you looked again? Told you,' he said, crossing the kitchen towards his cookery book collection. 'You were overwrought when you came home with your mum's desk, maybe you just didn't see it.'

My eyebrows shot up. Stuart was many things, a dear generally, with the most expressive eyes this side of Cornwall and a talented creative cook, who had the fabulous ability to look good in anything he wore. But he wasn't an actor. Unless he took his cues from the Christmas ham, there was no way he would have been able to maintain that air of nonchalance.

I sighed deeply and went back to sniffing the wine bottle. Dammit. I had really hoped that I wasn't getting an all-express ride on the lunacy train.

'Chocolate,' said Stuart suddenly.

I paused from my sniffing. 'With the ham?'

'No, bit too rich, I think. More of a steak accompaniment in the culinary stakes. I'm considering a classic honey glaze.'

'Glad to hear it,' I said.

'With some wasabi, perhaps. . .'

I sighed.

'I was thinking that perhaps some chocolate would make you feel a bit better. . . if you need a glass of wine?'

I looked at him in surprise. . . See, he's a dear. 'I'm okay, thanks. The sniffing helps.'

'Okay, well, I'm fully prepared, just so you know. For the cravings. . .'

I laughed. 'You are?'

'Oh yes,' he said mischievously. 'I've thought of all the possibilities. The boot, pantry, fridge and freezer are fully cognisant of any eventuality. . . I did my research.'

'You spoke to Tomas?'

'I spoke to Tomas,' he agreed.

'And what did Tomas have to impart?'

'Well, always have *pains au chocolat* on hand, condensed milk in the fridge and a *tarte tatin* in the larder. . . if you want to avoid having a cranky wife.'

'A cranky *French* wife,' I corrected. 'My tastes don't run to condensed milk.'

'Well, to be fair, probably neither do the French wives. Tomas said he kept it for himself, to keep his energy up. He had two wives, you know.'

'*What*! At the same time?'

'No, one after the other. Sisters, apparently.'

'Oh. . . that's. . . a bit, well, gross really.'

'Depends on the sister,' said Stuart, with a lascivious wink.

I laughed. 'One of the few reasons I'm rather glad that I didn't have a sister.'

'Pity!'

I smacked him.

He grinned. 'No, I just meant it would have been nice.'

I smacked him again.

He laughed and backed out of my reach to safety. 'For you. . . I meant for you.'

'Uh-huh. I believe you, but thousands might not,' I said.

He laughed, but said somewhat seriously, 'Not sure how I would have handled The Terrorist without Smudge.'

I nodded. This was very true. 'Though Smudge is my sister too now, and Catherine. . . she's always been like one.'

'Oh yes, always did like red-heads. . .' he said, before running to hide in the pantry.

'Very amusing. I will have you say that in front of Richard next.'

'Mercy!' he called from behind the pantry door.

Richard, Catherine's husband, played professional rugby for a well-known London team. He was six foot three and when you thought of him, the terms 'brick and 'house' sprang to mind.

'Can I come out?' called Stuart, in mock fear.

'Can I have that chocolate?' I asked, setting the bottle aside.

I heard a rustle. 'Hazelnut or orange?' he called from behind the door.

'Orange, please.'

He came forward and handed me the chocolate with arms outstretched, careful to keep his body out of my reach.

I laughed. 'It's fine, you're safe. So what else is in my emergency stash?' I asked him, curious.

'Ah. . . well, you know, I'm not going to tell.'

I looked at him in surprise. 'You're not?'

'I'm not.'

'Stuart Stanley Everton. . .'

'Ah! Do not Stanley me. . . my bloody parents,' he muttered, shaking his head disappointingly at his second name. 'I'm hold-

ing firm, Ivy Rose Everton. Incidentally, you will never understand the scars that are caused by awful second names. Rose. . .
I mean, honestly. No moral fibre learnt with a name like Rose.'

I laughed. 'Stanley is hardly a terrible name. Moral fibre indeed. Were the boys at Eton brutish over Stanley? How could
they be when faced with the likes of Basil and Eugene?'

Basil and Eugene were two of Stuart's friends from school.

'Eugene isn't too bad. Then I would have shortened it to
Gene; that's rather nice.'

I nodded, conceding. 'Not bad. Anyway. . . I can just check
the fridge and the pantry.'

'You could, but you won't,' he said assuredly, eyes amused.

'I won't?'

'Course not. What's in the fridge now?'

'Pak choi jelly?'

'Besides that.'

'Cheese?' I ventured.

He shook his head. 'Hopeless! Apart from toast, you would
starve.'

'That's not true. . . before we met, I, er . . . you know, cooked
a bit.'

He looked nonplussed. 'You cooked? What did you cook?'

'Er. . . there was the chicken Parmesan.'

'No, that was me, you just grated the cheese.'

'Oh, really?' I said, surprised. 'Okay. Well, there were the
cinnamon pancakes. . .'

'Oh God, I forgot about those. The batter never set. How did
you do that? I will never forget it just refused to solidify.'

I laughed. 'Well, I forgot to put in the egg, didn't I?'

He threw his head back and laughed. 'A ten-year mystery solved!'

I looked at him, a little worried. 'Stuart. . .' I bit my lip. Was
I that hopeless? 'I can do it. . . I'll learn some new recipes before
the baby comes – I want to be able to cook for him or her.'

He hugged me. 'I'm just teasing. You're going to be fine. You've made us lots of meals in the past. They were. . . you know, not exactly tasty, but edible, mostly. . . Children seem to like things like fish fingers,' he said with a shudder.

I smacked him but felt better. I'd never be a great cook, but in fairness babies don't eat very exciting food and that I could manage. 'So what you're saying is that our child will have to come to you the second we're off the bottle?'

'Just if it values its taste buds.'

I narrowed my eyes and shot him a look that said 'pak choi jelly', but we both knew. I could live with that.

In light of the events of the day, I was grateful for Stuart's calm presence, his banter. And the chocolate – the chocolate was definitely helping.

I slept fitfully that night. My dreams vivid, haunting. Mum was there, just at the edge of a blink, and every time I turned she was gone. I dreamt of paint, brilliant stardust paint that flecked into little moons all over the studio, creating luminaries that glowed in the dark and turned the room moonbeam bright. When I awoke, I was tired, my mood subdued. I crept off downstairs in search of coffee, but two cups later, I felt more tired still.

At barely dawn I set off for the beach, leaving Muppet and Stuart to sleep as I trekked alone in the bracing cold, a scarf looped around my face, mitten-clad-hands wedged into my parka and feet frozen, despite being ensconced in a pair of rose-print wellingtons. Without Muppet, it was a solitary walk, with only the sounds of the barren sea for company.

When I got back, I took a cup of tea up to my studio. I found Pots dozing on the window seat, wedged in a pile of cushions. Pepper, no doubt, had gone on his dawn patrol.

The two cats had come with the house. We'd found them sleeping beneath the stairs that led to the front door after we arrived that first afternoon. No one knew to whom they belonged.

The previous owners hadn't lived here for years as they'd decided in their retirement to finally give up their family home, emigrating to Australia to be closer to their children who'd moved there. Our nearest neighbour couldn't recall seeing the cats before. But after we moved in, they stayed too. They kept to themselves mostly, two solitary shadows, but they could be counted on for meaningful visits, often later in the night.

Eyeing me by my desk, Pots stretched and opted for the comfort of my lap. I looked down at him, only to frown – as tied around his neck was a silken ribbon in vivid scarlet.

Stuart must have found his Christmas spirit. Pots looked sweet with his handsome adornment. I took a sip of tea and touched the glossy fabric, lifting the edge in my fingers, only to frown in sudden disquiet when I noted two faint black marks near the edge. As I craned my neck for a closer look, my body froze, and I felt suddenly faint. For there, on the fabric, were two faded letters, written in large childish script: *F.A.*

My heart pummelled my chest.

F.A. Short for Fat Albert. Letters I'd etched onto the silken cloth myself, stolen and trimmed from Mum's desk on his last Christmas with us.

It couldn't be. Could it?

I picked up Pots, placed him back on the window seat, and crossed the room towards the shelf where I'd stored Mum's box of things.

My fingers shook as I lifted the lid, only to gasp aloud. There was nothing there. Nothing at all.

This time though, I didn't question. . . I crossed the room, my throat tight, to open the latch to the desk, my eyes closing for a beat, then opening in real, sudden fear, for there, neatly folded back where they belonged, was every last letter, every last line of thread, and every last silken ribbon, save one.

I shut it quickly and fled.

CHAPTER FIVE

Moonshine and Gossamer Things

'Shovel?'

'Thanks.'

'Fork?'

'So kind.'

I spent the rest of the morning helping Stuart in his poly-tunnel, avoiding the studio. Here, at least, in the warm glassy bubble, I could almost forget the mysterious ribbon and the paint, and what any of it might mean.

'Not that I'm not grateful for your help, but may I ask why you're here when *The Case of the Missing Brolly* is yet to be solved?' enquired Stuart, after a much-needed tea break. He handed me a kale, radish, and fennel sandwich with watercress pesto that I accepted dubiously, and a cup of strawberry tea, that met with more approval.

I paused mid-bite and scrunched my face, trying to think of a way to not sound like I was going, well, crazy. 'It's. . . I just needed a little change of pace, feeling tired, not the best for work.'

He raised an eyebrow. 'So you opted for manual labour instead?' His dark eyes looked amused. He was wearing his emerald green jersey again, his dark hair shining to high gloss, every bit the gentleman farmer.

'You know, it's rather unfair, how do you look so good in that? I mean, it's got about seven holes, yet on you, it's beautiful.'

He grinned. 'You only love me for my looks. I'll have you know that I'm more than a pretty face. See these. . .' He lifted up a rather incredible runner bean, longer than a ruler. 'These are a thing of beauty and magic. No one else has runner beans *in winter*,' he stage-whispered, while looking to Pots and Muppet for support, who were both lounging on one of the raised beds, warm in the polytunnel. 'But does she care?'

'Of course, it must be so hard being a trophy husband.'

He sighed heavily. 'You have no idea. . . but I persevere.'

I shook my head, laughing, and took a sip of my strawberry tea, sighing with pleasure. If I closed my eyes I could imagine it was a lovely summer's day. . .

'So, what's the real reason you're hiding away?' he asked, inspecting a head of a cabbage with a worried frown.

I spluttered a little tea in shock, opening my eyes. He may be a smallholder now, but it wasn't wise to forget that Stuart had been one of the most sought-after marketing executives in the city. His eye for detail was razor sharp.

'No reason. . . just tired, like I said.'

He gave a long slow nod. 'Uh-huh. . . this from the girl who spent all day illustrating at her day job at a publishers and who then came home to work on Mr Tibbles until well after midnight, only to get up and do it all again? Since when has being tired ever stopped you?'

I sighed. It's always harder to fool the people who know you best. I wanted to tell him about everything that had happened, to have him offer support or help provide some sane explanation, but I didn't know where to begin. So I just shrugged and said, 'It's more like I needed a break. Not from my work, but from the space. . . just for a bit.'

This was true at least.

Stuart topped up my teacup and shrugged. 'It's good to break a habit every once in a while. Besides. . .' he said, pointing at the dog and the cat, 'you're not the only one who wanted a change of scene.'

I nodded, grinned at the two unlikely allies, drained my cup and helped him trellis the rest of his miraculous runner beans.

I couldn't avoid my studio forever, but I could join Stuart for a sneaky glimpse into the day in the life of a smallholder, which was just the escape I needed. So I helped him pack boxes of his assorted jams, jellies, and condiments into the delivery van that I had helped paint; Stuart had gone for a bright cherry red, with his Sea Cottage label in white.

Subtle, it was not.

Together with Muppet in tow, we set off to deliver the orders that had come through over the last few days from his online shop. Today he had over twenty – a new record. It seemed news of his unusual culinary skills was spreading, at least in Cloudsea and the neighbouring town where I'd grown up, Tremenara. Fortunately most of the villagers were the sort who liked to support local businesses, and were, I suspect, a little curious about the tall, odd Londoner and his weird concoctions.

It helped that Stuart was part of the Cloudsea Facebook Group – *yes*, there really was such a thing and, no, I did not belong to it for purposes of sanity preservation. (Mostly, as far as I could tell, it was a forum to endlessly discuss the lack of parking on the high street, mad drivers around the sea front, and why no one had as yet committed Mrs Aheary, the batty old postmistress, to an asylum. Or Gertrude Burrows, for that matter. Or Tomas, but maybe that was just me.)

Also, every so often someone threw in a mention about the foiled plans for the mass supermarket that had finally been denied planning permission and all hell broke loose, as it was still a very sore point. Some wanted it (morons who should just go live somewhere else, really). Stuart slotted in with record time when he showed his outrage at one of the pro-supermarketers at the idea of blighting the countryside with a ginormous new Payless Hypermarket. As a result, most of the village, or the bit that liked the village to remain a village, were now pro-Stuart. This, of course, didn't mean he was now One of Them, this was Cornwall after all – I mean, Leuon Davington had lived in Cloudsea for thirty-seven years and they still called him 'The Welsh Bloke'.

Still, it meant that Cloudsea showed their support. Or you know, maybe they really *did* like beetroot jam and pak choi jelly.
. .

As we travelled into the village, the mild winter sunshine warm on my face, my eyes fell upon the throng of whitewashed cottages that meandered up from the coastal path towards the hill, where swirling clouds vied with the tumbling sea, the view that centuries ago was said to have inspired the village's name, though there is some contention over the matter.

The old vicar, Jeffrey Morris, claimed that his great-grandfather had given it the name when they'd opened the vicarage in the 1800s and brought the word of God and other essentials to the town.

Like the first outbreak of German measles, according to the Willises, who have lived in Cloudsea for longer than memory.

Bess Willis, who ran the local launderette and comes from a long line of Cornish fishermen, told me one night over a glass of ale at The Cloud Arms that the village was called Cloudsea long before the vicar's relations rolled their diseased carriages into the town. 'Hogwash, what would 'e know about it? From upcountry, the whole lot of 'em. I heard was an artist who came up with the name. . . Some poncy impressionist painter, I believe.'

Ah well, it could have been worse, I'd said.

Gertrude Burrows, who had the honour of being the oldest Cornishwoman in the village at the ripe old age of ninety-seven, blamed the English for the name. She lamented once when I popped into Cloud Nine, the village shop where she worked part-time, that no one in Cornwall could speak Cornish any more.

'Even this place. . .' she said with a shudder, as if it was So-dom and Gomorrah, 'Cloudsea,' she spat. 'It was called Kelym Treth originally, that was its *real* name. . . Then the English came and it got lost in translation. . .' she added darkly. 'Means Sea Holly, not sure how they got Cloudsea from that. . . the daft blighters, 'tis shameful having an English name, shameful. . .' she repeated, while shoving my things into a five-pence carrier bag I hadn't asked for.

Of course, I never dared tell her that I was rather partial to the name Cloudsea. . . You really didn't want to get on the wrong end of Gertrude Burrows. Though, as her warring neigh-bour, Tomas, was likely to point out, 'Is zere a right one, I ask you, Eve? Is zere?'

Our first delivery was for April Blume, who ran the local pub, The Cloud Arms. We met her flowery print bottom in-side, while she was giving the place a vacuum. She paused the whirring monster, which looked like a yellow version of R2-D3, straightened up and gave us a sweaty palmed shake.

'Wonderful, wonderful,' she murmured, wiping a brow, and tucking in a few stray wisps of bright magenta hair behind her ears, before Stuart handed over five bottles of his beetroot jam.

She gave an amused-looking grin at my befuddled stare. 'The punters like it, had to order *two* bottles for them,' she explained, jerking her head upstairs to one of the two en-suite rooms that she ran as a holiday let, sounding quite pleased at the prospect of offering a taste of the exotic to her clientele. 'From *London*,' she stage-whispered, though there was no need because next thing she said, 'Been waiting half the morning just to give the place a bit of a spit and polish, they've finally gone for an explore now. . . They'll be back in around half a minute, I don't doubt. The missus was wearing something she'll be regretting soon enough when she feels that icy wind coming. Not a decent fleece or a proper parka amongst them, just thin fashion jackets. . . They didn't even have *wellies*, had to point them towards Ol' Grumpy's hardware store, bless 'em,' she added with a grin that we couldn't help match. In the village the local hardware store, run by the rather dour-faced John Usett, who found speaking about as painful as passing a kidney stone, sold everything that you'd have to go to the bigger market towns to get, such as clothing and speciality pet food. Thank you, Muppet. . . Hence, some people wanting the big supermarket. . . and the resulting cold, civil war.

'They thought it would be milder here,' she told us with a throaty chuckle, referring to the London visitors. 'Poor devils,' she added.

While Cornwall was known to have one of the mildest climates in England, when it got cold, it got really cold, and it could stay that way for some time, especially in the countryside. Out here, having feet that were well shod had little to do with fashion – you were either slipping on mud, slipping on slush, or slipping on wet grass.

We passed the visitors en route to our next delivery, looking rather cold, yet determined in their new green wellies, holding each other close for warmth.

'Hard to believe that was us a few months ago, right?' whispered Stuart, as we headed towards Frank's Butchery.

I scoffed, 'Speak for yourself. . . I knew how to dress for this weather. . . I am a Cornishwoman,' I reminded him.

He stopped point blank. 'Really? That's why you bought out half of Usett Hardware's winter line when we moved?

I scoffed. 'Winter line? I'd hardly call Ol' Grumpy's stock a "winter line".'

His eyes narrowed. 'You bought four bloody parkas, even that daft one with the bulldogs all over it that makes you look

like the village weirdo, fifteen fleece-lined jumpers with matching tracksuit bottoms, and *seven* sets of wellingtons, all in various shades of passion killer.'

I rolled my eyes. It was hardly *that* much. . . more like two
pairs of wellies, a parka, and five tracksuit bottoms. Bloody
men! I shot him a look of disbelief. 'Me? The village weirdo?
Pots and kettles, darling. . . you're the one who sells cabbage jam
for a living.'

He shook his head. 'I can't help it if you've got the refined
palate of a three-year-old,' he quipped, opening up the butcher's
shop door just as I attempted to throttle him. At the sound of a
tinkly bell, a heavy-set man named Frank, with a crime-scene-
looking apron tied around his barrel chest, popped out from the
back and beckoned us to come through. I quickly removed my
hands from around my husband's neck and gave him a smile.

'All right there, love?' he asked, while I laughed. 'Good man!'
he added with a grin, eyeing the eight bottles of pak choi jelly that
Stuart popped on a nearby steel slab. 'Thought I'd use it in the next
batch of sausage I'm making now. . . quite the Christmas treat!'

I sighed as Stuart gave me a look that said, 'You see?' Next
thing he rather enthusiastically rolled up his sleeves and asked if
he could help, eager to learn. I couldn't help my nose wrinkling
at the sight of the sausage skin. Ugh! I felt a sudden queasy feeling in my belly. Nope, I couldn't handle the smell of raw meat in
normal circumstances – but pregnant? Forget about it.

'I'll. . . er, carry on and take these to Bess, shall I?' I said, a
little pointedly to Stuart, who didn't spot my pointed look at the
remaining stock in the box – six bottles of turnip chutney – nor
did he receive my extremely loud but silent plea of 'LET'S GET
THE HELL OUT!'

'Sure, sure,' said Stuart dismissively, with a wave of his hand.

I swallowed a growl. Bloody men! And set off with the box
down the path to the launderette, taking deep breaths of the

fresh clean air, trying my best to get the sight *and* smell of sausage casings out of my mind.

'Ivy, you're looking a bit peaky, my lovely. All okay?' asked Bess, who had long grey hair, thick glasses like the ends of jam jars, and a ready smile.

The smell of detergent, it seemed, was okay. A surprise, as the other day the aroma of my hand soap almost made me lose my dinner. Why did they call it morning sickness, when you could feel sick all the live-long day?

'Fine, fine,' I said, handing over her order.

'Shall I make us a cuppa?' asked Bess, above the hum of the washing machines.

'That'll be great,' I said, following her into her little office, where things were slightly quieter.

Her office was painted a greyish blue and looked out towards the high street, filled with shelves that gave a nod to her family's long seafaring heritage. From toy fishing boats to vintage photographs of men sporting old-fashioned sailing garb and pulling in the catch of the day to old log books, a key chain that looked like a codfish, and rope knots in all sizes and shapes. On her desk, though, sat a very scrummy-looking lemon drizzle, which despite my earlier nausea resulted in a sudden, urgent craving. Bess said to my delight, 'Just got it in from Salt café. Love that place. That old fox, Terry, sure knows how to bake. . . You'll have a piece, won't you?'

I grinned. Old fox indeed! But Terry's cakes were indeed legendary, thinking fondly of the triple chocolate fudge I'd had the other day.

While we waited for the kettle to boil, Bess shared the latest village news. Apparently, Gertrude Burrows had given up on trying to have Tomas's house removed from the village boundary and had moved on to trying to get Tomas deported instead.

'Don't understand it meself – they got on for years, then they had a big fight in the nineties, which was when he put up all those godawful notices in his front garden, all to stop her poking her nose in his business.'

At this I burst out laughing – I hadn't known that!

'Maybe she's got the hots for him?' I suggested with a giggle. 'Spurned lover?'

Bess sniggered, then added, 'Perhaps 'e didn't want to be her toy boy?', making us both howl.

Just as she cut us a slice of lemon drizzle, which made my mouth water in anticipation, Stuart suddenly appeared.

'Hi Bess, sorry to barge in. . .' He looked at me pointedly, and said, 'Love, got to head back home, the web designer just phoned to say he's on his way to test the Sea Cottage site – apparently there's a few things it'd be better to go through in person, so I must go. It's raining now, so I think I should take you back as well.'

I picked up my slice, but Stuart shook his head. 'We're already running late. . .'

I looked from the window where the rain was indeed coming down in buckets, and then back at my slice of lemon drizzle sadly, and with a sigh stood up to say goodbye to Bess.

Bloody men!

It was during the still hum of the night, with only the mournful sound of the waves crashing softly outside, echoing through the bedroom, that I understood.

I'd been tossing and turning, and in my dreams it felt like I was on the edge of remembering something.

Three a.m.

I crept out of bed and up to the studio, leaving Stuart asleep, Muppet in his arms. Now, under cover of night, I realised this was meant solely for me.

Three a.m., the witching hour, when ghosts roam free. At any other time of the day you could convince yourself otherwise, but when the night made that shushing sound and the world held its breath and the hairs on the back of your neck stood on end. . . anything, anything at all, seemed possible.

It was then in the early hours of the morning that I began to remember something that I'd long thought forgotten, or perhaps I blanked it from my memory, because remembering it would only serve to cause me pain.

It was long ago, before she fell ill.

One of those comments that had just made Mum, well, Mum. We'd gone to visit Haworth, the home of the Brontës, just the two of us. It was an obsession we shared, a mutual love of the dark, gothic sisters growing up on the Yorkshire moors. I was only thirteen at the time, but still the trip was one of those special moments that live on in your memory. The house, with its accompanying graveyard and lingering memory of a family who had known such deep suffering, was incredibly affecting. We couldn't help but wonder if, like Emily's Heathcliff and Cathy, the sisters still roamed the moors to whisper their secrets after dark.

I remember saying that I hoped that they did, so that they could see the effects they had had, long after they were gone. And Mum had said if it were her, she'd find a way to come back to let me know that she was fine, that death wasn't the end.

She meant it, I knew she did, and at the time I believed her with childish conviction, comforted that she would.

Years later, when she fell ill with Stage IV ovarian cancer, I thought of that day and of her words – of her promise – and thought perhaps she had told me what she wished would be true.

Yet now, I had to consider what I'd spent years trying to deny. The rational side of my brain said no, it wasn't possible. It was a manifestation of years of childish hope and grief. Yet despite knowing it was absurd, hope had found me, nonetheless.

As I stood in the still air of the studio, the moonlight entering the window and falling upon the desk, I knew somehow there was something waiting for me.

I crossed the room slowly, reverentially. . . barely able to breathe, only to pause, my throat swelling with emotion. On the desk, made by air and gossamer wisps of moonlight, lay a single perfect baby bootie, glowing in the dusky starlight. My hands shook as I picked it up and cradled it in my palm, the size of a whisper, the weight of a kiss.

I closed my eyes and let the tears fall. She'd found a way, after all.

CHAPTER SIX

The Letters Appear

I stared at the little bootie for hours.

Knowing, without knowing how, that it could only be Mum. Three letters that I haven't been able to think about, let alone feel, without the accompanying swell of my throat. Staring, wide-eyed, wondering, hoping, selfishly wishing for more.

At some point though, I must have fallen asleep, which even now seems mad because there was this part of me that felt like I may never dare sleep again.

When I awoke, I knew. I sat up quickly and opened my palm. A wild search confirmed.

Gone.

I felt an indefinable sense of loss.

Had it just been a dream? My eyes fell on the little Christmas card, relieved to see Rudolph's nose still shimmering, gold and red.

I don't know how, but I managed to get through my day, finishing up four more illustrations for *The Fudge Files*, Detective Sergeant Fudge hot on the case of the missing brolly, despite risk to life and paw from a rather bristly porcupine named Solstice Spike.

At teatime, Catherine surprised me.

'What's this I hear about you sniffing wine bottles?'

I looked up to see her leaning against the door jamb, olive green eyes amused, her long sleek red hair striking against her cashmere shawl, behind which Stuart was attempting to hide his six-foot self, but he was unable to hide his sniggers.

I narrowed my eyes in a mock glare at him for his betrayal, '*Et tu*, Everton? You had to call in for some reinforcement?'

Stuart backed away, like a man leaving a firing squad, arms above his head. 'I'll put the kettle on. Shall I uncork you a bottle?' he asked.

'Very funny,' I answered.

Catherine shook her head as she watched him leave, her even smile showing her dimples. 'I've brought dessert. I wouldn't want you to sniff on an empty stomach.'

I laughed. 'Good thinking! How did you get in – did you drive?' I asked. Catherine still lived in London, with her husband and three children. I hated to think that she had spent hours driving to get here, just to look after me.

'No, don't worry, we're down here for an extended Christmas/New Year's holiday. The children are at my dad's place – the school's closed so we're making the most of it.'

'Ah, brilliant!' I said, thrilled to think that she'd be in the area for some time. It was Catherine's fondest wish to also return to Cornwall, but with Richard playing rugby in London, it wasn't possible just yet.

'Oh, are these the latest?' she asked, peering over my shoulder at the finished illustrations of Detective Sergeant Fudge, paw pinned onto Solstice Spike, the red brolly in his claws.

'Hot off the press,' I concurred.

Just then the inspiration behind Britain's beloved, slobbering detective came caterwauling around the corner, running with her trademark sideways sprint, treading air for half a beat, eyes slightly crossed. In total, mad glee.

'Muppet!' exclaimed Catherine, giving her god-fur-child a hug.

'Oh wow' she added, as she straightened, holding Muppet in all her fifty-five-pound glory in her arms, her eyes falling on my mother's desk. 'It seems so strange to see it here. It's smaller than I remember, but it looks good. . . right?'

I nodded. 'I know, it's strange, I thought so too. I thought it would look out of place, but it fits.'

Catherine smiled sadly and shook her head. 'You know, often when I think of her, it's from behind that desk. Even when I would visit your dad, it was hard to see it. . . without her. I can't imagine what you must feel, having it here,' she said, touching the fine rosewood.

I sighed. 'It's been. . . strange. Really strange,' I said truthfully. 'But good too – I feel more connected with her in a way.'

Catherine nodded. She cocked her head to one side in contemplation, her soft green eyes considering. 'You know, seeing it there I almost feel like she's here. . . like the desk is waiting or something.'

I blinked in shock.

Her face coloured slightly. 'Sorry, just being silly. . . that sounded mad even for me. Just had a weird feeling – ignore me. Come, cake. . .' she said, swiftly changing the subject and nodding towards the door for me to follow, while Muppet grinned at me happily over her shoulder, encased in her cream, cashmere-covered arms.

Gobsmacked, I stared at her retreating back, momentarily rooted to the floor, heart pounding. I compelled my feet to follow, giving the desk a final glance. She was right, it did appear to be waiting – she wasn't being silly at all.

After tea and cake, Catherine and I took Muppet for a walk, while Stuart retreated to the safety of his polytunnel, giving us both a hug and Catherine a meaningful look that conveyed their shared concern.

'It's not the baby, is it?' she asked, as soon as we'd left the house, wind whipping her hair across her face. Catherine had a rip-the-stitches approach that I'd always appreciated. I realised, out of respect for Stuart, she'd kept this fear to herself while we all sat together eating and laughing this afternoon. It must have been killing her.

I shook my head. 'No, thank goodness. The doctor is very positive this time,' I said, though hating to say those flimsy words aloud, even now, tempting fate. I'd been burnt before.

She sighed in relief. I'd told Catherine about the baby the same day I found out. Not telling her would have been unthinkable and impossible. She'd have figured it out – she's like a bloody bloodhound.

'Still haven't told Dad yet,' I added, my lips tightening at the thought. 'Just wanted to be sure first.'

Catherine gave me a sideways hug, eyes full. 'He's going to be so happy.'

I nodded, closing my eyes for a second, knowing that when we told him it would feel more real.

Muppet raced ahead to bark at the waves and we shared a laugh at the crazy dog who was yet to solve this particular mystery.

'So. . .' she said with a raised eyebrow, green eyes serious. 'It's the desk, isn't it? That's what's driven you to sniff bottles,' she guessed.

I sighed. It was very hard to keep secrets from Catherine.

'Yes. . . I don't know how to explain it. . . I'm not sure I understand it myself, but I just have this feeling like. . .' I swallowed, wondering just how much to tell her. Part of me wanted to bare all, tell her everything in exchange for her opinion. Have her tell me I wasn't going insane.

'Like?' she asked, puzzled.

I took a steadying breath. 'Like. . . she's trying to tell me something.'

Her pale brows shot up in surprise. 'Really?'

I nodded. 'It's mad. . . when you say it out loud.'

She shook her head. 'No, I don't think so. It's your mum. . . I mean, God, it would be just like her, you know.'

I did know. Mum was one of those people who believed in the inexplicable, in magic. It's why she loved this time of year so much. She'd always say that anything could happen. And when she was around, the funny thing was, strange things often did.

Catherine stared at the beach. 'Remember that time after dinner, that day when she suddenly looked at me like the world was ending, her face went awfully pale, and she told me to run home immediately and look behind the dresser in my dad's room?'

'Of course.' I wasn't likely to forget. It had been really strange. One minute Mum was fine and the next all the blood had drained from her face; she'd looked terrified, like she'd seen a ghost.

'That's when you went home and found your mum's wedding ring?' I prompted, remembering.

She nodded. 'Dad was so shocked. He came in and found me there holding the ring, and, I never told you this, but he just started crying. Sobbing. He was broken. I'd never seen him like that before. It was only years later that he told me that I saved his life.'

I looked at her in shock. 'What – why? What happened?'

'Well, he'd just lost his business. That idiot Dave, remember him, his old partner at the factory? He'd been siphoning off the cash for years, while Dad tried to raise us alone, not realising his partner was robbing him blind, and that day, he'd found out just how bad it was. We were going to have to hand over the keys to everything. Essentially we were penniless. I never knew Dad with my mum, but everyone said that after she passed it was like the light went out of him. And this was. . . like the final straw really. None of us were home, so that's when he decided to do it.'

I gasped. 'He was going to kill himself?'

She shrugged. 'I don't know. . . He was in such a depression. He hadn't made any definite plans, but he says that just before I came home he'd started the car in the garage. When he heard the front door bang open and me rushing upstairs, he realised he wasn't alone. . . and with Mum's ring he realised that he wasn't alone in more ways than one.'

'What do you mean?'

'Well, after that, he took it as a sign from Mum, you know, like she chose that moment to make me find the ring. If it hadn't been for your mum telling me to go home right then. . . I mean, who knows what would have happened?'

I couldn't believe this. I remembered her finding the ring and afterwards her dad seemed to come back to life. They moved house, closer to ours, which was great, and Catherine's dad started writing his first novel. This was before he became one of Britain's top thriller authors. Brian Talty was the reason Cath and I started writing our own stories.

'My God, I had no idea. . .' I breathed. 'I mean, I think I always did believe a little in her ability to see things that others didn't, but nothing like this. . . well, until now.'

'Now?'

'Now, I just feel like she's here. I mean, things have gone missing. . . only to reappear in her desk and. . .'

'And?'

At this I stopped myself. I would tell Catherine, but just not yet. Not until I had a better handle on it myself. What was happening was so delicate. . . holding my hopes edged on the weight of a breath. I was afraid to disturb it too soon, expose it to the light, so I just said, truthfully, 'And I think it's her.'

She nodded, eyebrows raised. 'That's incredible and it would be so like her. . . I mean, she could have chosen any time to tell me about my mother's lost wedding ring, but somehow she knew. . . knew to tell me about it then. It's so like her to reach out now. . .'

I swallowed. 'When I need her the most,' I said, echoing my own thoughts and wishes of only a few days ago. I blinked. Was it possible?

She nodded, answering my unspoken question. 'It would be.'

We walked the rest of the way, arms linked. Catherine wondered just which of her sons my baby would marry, certain in their pre-destined love.

'I could have a boy, you know,' I said.

'Don't be mean and put that out there. . . it listens,' she whispered theatrically. 'We need a girl.'

I laughed. 'What listens?' I asked, smiling.

She gave me a pointed look. 'It. . . the universe. . . Murphy, whoever runs this mad, bloody show,' she said, green eyes narrowing as she looked up at the sky. Catherine lived with three robust, rowdy boys under the age of five, her husband, and her male dog, Trouble (a Jack Russell terrier who lived up to his name). When it all got a bit too much, when she'd tripped over yet another piece of Star Wars Lego and Trouble had run the carpet bare fetching his ball, Catherine would get that look in her eye, the one that said 'One word of complaint and someone is going to lose an eye' and she would hand over the boy reins to Richard, who despite his sheer mammoth size and Christmas-ham thighs, would stand there meekly, watching her go with a forlorn expression in his hazel eyes, while Catherine sought some female company with Muppet and me.

'Anyway. . .' I teased. 'Even if I had a boy, they may still marry. I mean, look at Ben.'

She laughed. Ben, one of my three godsons, had taken to wearing pink. A lot.

'True!' she laughed. 'It's hard work getting Tim and Jase not to tease him too much. Brothers, you know. . .' she sighed. 'Though it's a nice change. . . the pink.'

'The Guilt?' I asked

'The Guilt,' she concurred.

Catherine and I had spoken about The Guilt at length. Where you just never knew if you were doing the right thing. Everyone had an opinion and being a mum in today's age was not easy: far too many people with a platform and an axe to grind. You could only try your best and do what you thought was right. For now, that was letting the little bugger wear his tutu if he wanted to.

'Claire Thomas,' she sighed.

'Ah,' I said, nodding, though I had no reason to.

'She had a little speech at the school gate the other day.'

'I hate Claire Thomas,' I said, with narrowed eyes.

She laughed. 'You don't even know who Claire Thomas *is*.'

'Even so. . . I hate her on principle. . . people who give speeches at school gates. . . Besides, I've never known a nice Claire before.'

Catherine giggled. 'That's not true! Claire Braithwaite was very nice.'

I raised a brow in mock shock. 'No, she wasn't. . . Don't you remember what she called me?'

'Er. . . was this before or after you stole Derek Jones from her?'

My mouth twisted wryly. 'Okay, well. . . after, but I hardly stole him. . . I was seven.'

She grinned. 'Your first kiss. Anyway she was seven too when she called you. . . what was it again?'

I laughed. 'A mutton chop – she said something about me being a mutton dressed as sheep's lamb. Not sure she really got the metaphor. Either way, it did the job; I was Muttons after that. . . the only seven-year-old on the playground worrying about wrinkles.'

Catherine laughed uproariously. 'Muttons! Yes. . . that went on for a while.'

I nodded, gravely. 'All through primary school, bloody Claire Braithwaite!'

Catherine laughed. 'Well, anyway, the new Claire isn't much better. Claire Thomas told me that I was creating a precedent.'

I curled my lip in contempt. 'A precedent? I hate people who use the word precedent.'

She laughed. 'Quite! Apparently I was confusing a gender norm, making life harder for Ben. Sadly she seemed to think things had come to a head when he asked for a pony for Christmas.'

'What's wrong with that?' I exclaimed. Though it was expensive and out of the question in their pretty London home in Chelsea.

Catherine sighed. 'A My Little Pony. . .'

I laughed. 'Well, still, I always thought it was a crying shame that girls get all the sparkles. . . Personally, I think it's great when I see a little girl with a bit of Star Wars Lego too.'

She sighed. 'Me too. I gave her what for. . . but afterwards, you know. . . I just wanted to smack her on her velour tracksuit bottom.'

'Velour? Good lord! Are people still wearing that?' I patted her shoulder. 'Well, you can always make her the baddie in your next book and put that in velour.'

She laughed. 'Oh yes, and in honour of Claire Braithwaite perhaps an ewe will do? What do you say?'

'Ewe know revenge is sweet,' I quipped, while she laughed and rolled her eyes. We were total nerds when we got like this; if Stuart and Richard were around, they would have shaken their heads in exasperation and slunk off to miss the worst of our giggling.

After we worked out the case of the silly ewe, Detective Sergeant Fudge's latest escapade, which Catherine said she'd work on and send me the pages for in the next fortnight, I bade her goodbye and promised to bring Muppet round for a visit in the week, while they were on holiday.

When I got back, Stuart was busy decanting jam into jars in the kitchen, the cream island filled with dozens of little bottles. 'A fifty-bottle order for my pak choi jelly. Can you believe it?' His dark eyes were alight with happiness.

'Wonders never cease. Well done, my love,' I laughed, giving him a kiss.

'Good chat with Catherine?'

'Mmm,' I said, leaning over to breathe in the tantalising scents of a simmering pot on the Aga. 'Good lord, it's heaven sent. Or heaven scent. . . I suppose,' I said, tapping my nose. 'What is it?'

'It's Christmas.'

'In a pot?' I said in surprise, my eyes wide. 'How did you manage that. . . is it like a Mary Poppins pot?' I added with a wide grin.

Stuart laughed. 'Very funny. . . I meant it's for Christmas, for the mince pies.'

'You're making homemade mince pies?' I breathed in wonder.

He nodded.

'Trying out my new pastry kit.'

'You have a pastry kit?' I asked in surprise, wondering what a pastry kit consisted of.

'Yes.'

'Have I told you lately how much I love you?' I asked.

He shook his head, his face a picture of long-suffering. 'No. I mean, I cook, I clean and nothing. . .' He wielded a spoon, pointing it at Muppet, who sat staring at it hopefully. 'She just keeps me around to feed her.'

I crossed the counter and fetched a biscuit for Muppet, which she inhaled, giving us a hopeful stare afterwards that I was unable to resist.

'Clean?' I asked. 'Since when do you clean?'

He shook his head, looking at Muppet for support. 'Typical. . .'

I giggled, pressing my face into his soft navy jumper, to breathe in the smell of cinnamon and Stuart. 'It's not just about the food,' I said.

He hugged me back, raising a brow. 'But it helps?'

'Yes. And you look nice too.'

'You're not so bad yourself. Though the hat?' he said, playing with the flaps.

'What's wrong with my hat?' I said in mock affront. I had a rather sizeable collection of knitted hats, chosen more for their amusement value than their style.

'It has ears, for a start,' he pointed out.

'All the better to hear you with. . .' I quipped, taking it off and shaking out my hair. 'Better?'

'Better.'

I rolled my eyes. Men!

Later, I glanced at my phone and sighed – there were three missed calls from Genevieve, Stuart's mother. I listened to one, and then tried to take a deep, calming breath. It seemed she was not about to go down without a fight about getting me to visit that fertility specialist she mentioned. I swallowed a feeling of mild guilt that we still hadn't told her about the baby. The idea of telling her just made me feel. . . tired. *So* tired. At this time of the day, I was finding that I could cheerfully just go to sleep for a week – a not-so-great side effect of the pregnancy as oddly enough in the wee hours of the morning I was often wide awake. So I decided to put it off.

After Christmas, maybe? When I had more energy?

Perhaps in the New Year? Thinking about how impossible she was likely to be no matter the date, I mentally shook my head. When the sun decided to rise in the bloody west, *that's* when we could tell her without having her hijack my sanity. I'd think about that later. . . possibly.

I went upstairs with a cup of strawberry tea to soak in the claw-foot tub. Apart from the studio and the conservatory, the bathroom was my favourite room in the house. Painted duck-egg blue, with pale wooden floors, it had a breath-stealing view of the sea. The bath was in the centre of the room and on cold nights its silver toes sparkled in the glow from the open fireplace opposite.

We'd made the offer for the house shortly after we saw the bathroom. I hadn't even seen the bedroom yet or the rest of the grounds, but I knew that this was what I needed, a place to soak any troubles away. I had a lot of fun becoming a lady who bathed. Buying scented aromatherapy candles and bath milks. I'd even installed a small bookshelf, where I kept a collection of my waterlogged favourites, so that I could lie back and read in the scented steam to Stuart's book-preserving dismay.

He had his own bathroom down the hall and subscribed to the get-up-and-go, power-shower ablution, though he did enjoy visiting my steamy sanctuary on wintry nights.

As I lounged in the bubbles, thinking about Catherine's startling revelation earlier, the image of the closed garage door and the running car haunted me. What if she hadn't got there in time? I wondered how Mum knew and why she never told us about it.

'Place for two?' Stuart asked, coming in from downstairs and leaning against the open door.

'Always,' I said with a smile, soaping my arms.

He smiled, espresso eyes reflecting the firelight, and undressed. I admired my husband from the tub and, as the flickering light played over his silken hair and across his lean muscles, all thoughts of Mum and Catherine's dad evaporated.

'You're looking rather fit, Mr Everton,' I remarked, eyeing his taut stomach appreciatively.

He smiled, teeth startlingly white and even. 'And you thought gardening was for the elderly.'

I laughed as he slid in behind me and leaned against him. 'Did I?'

He wrapped his arms around me, moving aside my long, wet hair. 'No, not really.' I turned and kissed him. 'See now, that's the trouble with us having a bath together. . . we never actually bathe. . .'

He grinned. 'And that's a problem?'

It wasn't, not really.

I woke at quarter to three, a feeling of excitement expanding in my chest. With a hammering heart, I tiptoed out of bed to the studio.

I had a theory.

Born in the seconds before sleep opened its arms to claim me, but I wouldn't know until tonight if it were true. I crept along the passage and opened the door, hugging my dressing gown to me. The room was still and quiet, the crash of the waves outside oddly hushed.

I took a seat at the writing desk and waited. Hoping what I suspected, and wouldn't dare say aloud, was true. . . If magic existed at all, it would happen in the witching hour, well after midnight – at three o' clock, to be precise.

At first, when I saw the flicker of moonlight, I thought that perhaps I'd been wrong. For at first no new apparition, no new dream-spun gift unfolded. Then, before my eyes, a silvery golden thread appeared and began to spin itself into a minute old-fashioned birdcage. Its little moon-spun door opened and a tiny red and gold stardust thrush appeared, fluttering its wings, taking small little hops across the desk. I held out my hand, heart in my throat, as it hopped onto my outstretched palm, softer than the softest kiss.

'How are you doing this?' I breathed, eyes shimmering with unshed tears, as the little bird sprang from my hand and fluttered across the studio, out the open window.

As I stared at the desk, the birdcage disappeared, and another glimmer caught my eye. I inhaled sharply.

The creamy postcard, addressed to me, began to shimmer with an otherworldly light, words etched in silvered moonshine appeared and I watched in awe as letter-by-letter, one by one, three perfect words emerged:

I love you

My eyes spilled over as I stared at the shimmering words dancing before me.

'Mum,' I whispered. Not a question, but a statement of impossible, inexplicable fact. I stared at the card scarcely daring to breathe, hoping against hope that, somehow, she could hear. Then, slowly, the words disappeared and new ones took their place, each letter followed by an answering hammer from my heart.

Hello Darling

I gasped, tears flowing freely. Then I closed my eyes for a second, barely able to contain what I felt. My shoulders shook with happy sobs, hands clenched in excitement. I stuttered, 'How. . . how are you doing this? Where are you?'

I swallowed, waiting for her to answer, in fearful desperation that she wouldn't. But she did.

There is no language for it

I sucked in air in surprise; waiting, wondering. . . then more words appeared, more obtuse than the first.

As far as a whisper, as close as space

'Are you in heaven?' I whispered to the moonlit room.

Nothing happened and I began to fear, heart thrashing in my chest, nothing ever would.

Then slowly. . . *so* slowly, she answered. As before, the silvered words disappeared and new ones formed.

We do not use words for it, but if words were used, heaven may be one, if what one could say about the sun was that it was round

The fear that I'd had for years. . . that there was nothing after we left, was finally taken away.

'But if you're there. . . then how, how are we doing this?'

I was given time

'Time?'

To be. . . with you

I inhaled, closing my eyes. 'How much time?'

Enough

'Enough?' I asked. But she didn't answer. . . I suppose that enough was plenty.

'Oh Mum, I miss you so much.'

I'm always with you. I know it's not the same but we have this

The tears slid down my cheeks. 'This is more than I could have ever dreamt of. I love you, Mum.'

Love you more

I grinned, with aching familiarity; it *was* Mum, despite the mysterious words, and the moonlight magic, it was what she had always said to me – even when I argued that that was impossible, she'd insisted no one could love more than she.

Her last message for the night, though, was enigmatic.

Upstairs wardrobe

The words appeared then slowly faded away. I stared, waiting, yet knowing as the air changed, and the sounds came back to life and the light. . . the moonlight that had bathed the desk disappeared, that the postcard would not fill again that night.

I bit my lip, hand clutched to my heart, afraid it would burst, and went to bed. Hours later, I fell asleep, a small smile on my face.

CHAPTER SEVEN

The Hope Box

When morning came, despite broken sleep and vivid dreams, I was eager to start the day.

The postcard was like a secret held close to my chest, colouring the day with rose-tinged promise, and at around mid-morning I decided to take her message of the night before literally.

Because, despite the enigma and the mystery and how strange it sounded, Mum had always been practical, and her last message of the night had been no exception.

I stood before the upstairs wardrobe.

The one in the passageway between our room and the studio, where I'd put just one box, the only one I hadn't unpacked. The one filled with all our lost hope, broken dreams, and unfulfilled wishes.

Before the first failed IVF, the first miscarriage. . . before we knew not to dare hope at all, I'd planned, and dreamed, and bought. Babygros and teddy bears and palm-sized shoes. I sat back on my heels on the wooden floor, tenderly unfolding each little outfit, feeling the soft fabric between my fingers.

I didn't see him come, just felt his fingers brush my hair, the wooden floor creak as he settled himself next to me. I looked up into his brown eyes, gentle, soft.

'I'd forgotten about these,' he said, touching the silken leg of a Babygro.

'Me too.'

Fingers playing with my hair, Stuart asked, 'It's time? To unpack the *Everton Ten: Burnt alive?*'

I bit my lower lip and nodded. It was time, time to dream, time to hope.

I took a shaky breath. 'Stuart, we're having a baby,' I said, with a big wobbling smile, finally daring to say it aloud, to believe, to trust that if I did then it would all be all right.

He hugged me close, dark eyes shining with moisture. 'We're having a baby,' he said in wonder.

We had dinner that night at Dad's, finally breaking the news. He was overjoyed; his wild, grey hair seemed to crackle afterwards, as if whatever emotion he was feeling radiated from its tips.

I realised – as we sat in the sitting room now empty of Mum's desk, mugs of hot chocolate steaming while he made plans with Stuart to help set up the nursery and he told us that my old cot was somewhere in the attic and it could be sanded and varnished, that there was the rocker too, which could be reupholstered – that he needed this. Something besides his work as a workshop manager at a freighting company, and his long-held passion for philosophy. I suspected he'd lost the will to feel philosophical about very much since Mum fell ill.

I grinned at his enthusiasm. The next few months would be filled with decorating and restoring. The sanding, and the massive mural I was planning – well, that was all up to me.

For the first time, sitting in this room since she was gone, I felt like everything was going to be all right.

At 3 a.m. I was finally in the studio, where I'd spent all day longing to be. Each hour leading past midnight carried a double jolt of excitement through my veins. I didn't have to wait long.

The air was alive with the hush that I'd come to recognise just before the magic hour.

Tonight, the words, made in pen and ink, rather than moonlight and stardust like her messages from the night before, seemed to glow.

Darling Ivy

'Mum,' I breathed in excitement, feeling my love rush out as I told her, 'I unpacked the box, finally told Dad. . .'

The words appeared finer than thread but shimmering bright.

It was time

I nodded, past caring that each time I sat here the tears couldn't help but fall. I didn't ask how she knew that it would all be all right, just trusted that it would.

If I closed my eyes, I could see hers, soft and blue, her blonde hair fixed in its loose chignon, pearls glowing in the firelight and her gentle, ever-ready smile.

Dad is happy

I smiled. 'He is. . . happier than I've seen him in years.'

Tell him: under the stairs

'What's under the stairs?'

What he's been looking for

I frowned. 'What has he been looking for?' But she didn't answer. 'Can't – can't you speak to him too? I know it would mean everything to him. Can I bring him here one night to speak with you as well?' I asked, daring to hope.

For a long while she didn't answer and then she said:

We only get one

'One? One what?' I asked, not sure what she meant.

One life. . . one to guide

I frowned, not sure that I fully understood what she meant, except for what I feared. 'I can't tell him?' I asked, my heart breaking for her, for them both.

You could, but it would be best not as I couldn't reach him

Not like this, not like with you

I swallowed and with sudden, awful clarity, I understood. 'It was a choice. . . and you. . .'

I chose

'Oh Mum!' I cried, knowing how impossible that must have been.

He would understand if he knew

I stared at her words, watching them disappear, hoping that was true when a new one took its place.

Holly

'Holly?' I asked.

Her name

And there, once again, appeared the perfect baby bootie made from moonlight and magic. I touched it gently with a fingertip, while my other hand clasped my mouth.

I gasped. 'But – but does that mean? It's a. . . it's a girl!' I exclaimed. Did she know? Could she know that?

A Christmas name seems right

Now sleep

Don't upset the snow globe

I breathed out, blinking in the moonlight. A girl. . . was it possible?

Snow globe? What did she mean by snow globe? But before I could ask, she had gone. The night returned to dark and I slipped back into bed, knowing, despite her instructions, that sleep would elude me that night.

'Everything seems to be fine, Ivy. . . though you are looking a little tired. Not sleeping?' asked Dr Gia Harris, my obstetrician. Sleek, black shoulder-length hair tucked behind her ears, eyes concerned as she clicked her pen to make a note on her chart during my check-up the following morning.

Stuart shook his head. 'I keep telling her to take it easy,' he said worriedly.

'I am,' I denied, knowing they were empty words. 'I'm fine, I promise.'

Dr Gia leant forward to peer closely at me, a slight frown on her face. My eye fell to her pen and I couldn't help the small chuckle that escaped my lips.

There was a small snow globe on top of it. Typical!

She smiled, looking at it. 'Ah yes. . . must get in the spirit. To tell you the truth, it's my favourite time of year: roasted chestnuts, fires, mince pies. . .'

I smiled in return. The red lab coat embellished with little white sleighs that she wore was a bit of a clue too. 'Mine too, and there's nothing like Christmas in Cornwall. . . If you're going to the village fair in Cloudsea, stop past the market. . . try one of Stuart's homemade mince pies.'

Stuart winked. 'Secret new recipe. . . my latest Sea Cottage signature.'

Dr Gia answered with a swift nod. 'I will. Peter – my husband – raves about your beetroot jam. He ordered a few from your shop.'

My eyes bulged. 'He did?'

'Oh yes. . . He wants to use it with the ham this year for Christmas.'

Stuart gave me a long-suffering look. 'See.'

I laughed. 'Okay. . . well, perhaps it's better with ham than on toast.'

Dr Gia crinkled her upper lip in mock disgust. 'I should think so,' she grinned. 'So. . .' she said, her face beaming as she passed the scanner around my belly. 'Do we want to know what we're getting?'

I sat up a little straighter, looking at Stuart, who nodded, eyes huge.

'Well. . . looks like the elves will be bringing a little girl.'

My grin was enormous, matched only by Stuart's.

'A girl,' he breathed.

'Holly,' I said simply.

Stuart looked me. 'Holly?'

I nodded.

He shook his head in wonder. 'That's. . .' He closed his eyes for a second, the last traces of fatigue and worry finally seemed to lift, so that when he opened them, his eyes were full, happy. 'That's just. . . so right.'

We held hands, beaming at each other like loons.

'I'm blubbering,' said Dr Gia, reaching across her desk for a box of tissues and handing us a few, because she wasn't the only one.

CHAPTER EIGHT

Whispers in the Dark

There was a light on in the polytunnel; it shone like a sentinel from the garden.

I'd just climbed into bed with a cup of tea, and the latest sketches of Detective Sergeant Fudge, when I saw it from out of the unshuttered blinds.

'Stuart?' I said. 'Did you leave a light on outside?'

A grunt in response.

I poked him in his side.

'Love, did you leave the light on in your polytunnel?'

A noncommittal mumbling followed. Muppet opened a bleary eye at me in reproach. I stared and took a sip of tea, deciding on whether I wanted to leave the comfort of the warm room and face the cold garden to switch it off, when I nearly jumped out of my skin. A shadow moved across the polytunnel, a human-shaped shadow.

Splashing tea on my shirt, I cried, 'Stuart, someone's in there!'

Another mumble followed. This one I could just make out.

'Smudge,' he said by way of explanation, 'needed a place to crash,' he added into his pillow.

'Why didn't you tell me? I could have got the guest room ready!'

'It's the *spare* room, it's always ready,' he muttered, turning over and after about three seconds he began to snore loudly.

I snorted in exasperation and rolled out of bed, changing into a new T-shirt and wrapping myself in an old blanket that I pulled from the little chest by our bed. Smudge had had to postpone our visit to Fowey to see where Daphne du Maurier lived. She'd texted that something had come up and her plans had to change. She's been a little enigmatic, but then that was Smudge, sometimes it was like pinning down a butterfly's wing. Still, it did make her late-night visit all the more odd.

Downstairs, I shoved my feet into my wellies, opened the kitchen door to the icy exterior and the sound of the surf crashing against the rocks amplified.

I crossed the garden path quickly, following the light from the polytunnel.

When I opened the door, I found Victoria sitting on a concrete slab, touching a green shoot, looking a little forlorn.

'Smudge?' I asked.

She looked up. ''Lo,' she mumbled. Even in the semi-darkness I could see that her eyes were red-rimmed and swollen.

'Oh my goodness, are you all right?' I asked.

She offered a watery smile. 'Fine. . . just fine. Amazing, isn't it, that even now, as we move into winter, these little shoots defy the odds, don't you think?'

It was worse than I thought. I sat down next to her.

'You know, when he said he wanted to do this,' she said, raising her arms expansively at the polytunnel, taking in the rows of vegetation, and beyond, to Stuart's now-wintry potager, 'I thought he was a little mad. I mean, what did he know about gardening? But there was this small part that was. . . I don't know, a little envious, I suppose.'

'Envious?' I said in surprise. 'Why?'

Victoria was the most free-spirited person I knew. Someone who from her dress sense down to her career truly seemed to live life by her own rules.

'It's just real, I suppose,' she said, wiping her face on her shoulder, the secretive, almost child-like move making my heart twist.

'But what you do is real. . . I mean, you write incredible biographies about people's lives, you can't get more real than that.'

She took a shuddery breath. 'My career? Oh sure, I just meant. . . this,' she said, waving an arm towards the cottage. 'Creating a real home, a base, something solid, for the three of you.'

'Victoria?' I said, touching her arm, worried. This was clearly something else. . . something to do with Mark.

She shook her head. 'It's nothing. . . I mean, no one gets everything they want, do they?'

I thought about what had been happening to me lately. . . 'Sometimes they do, maybe just not how they picture it at first. . .' I looked at her. 'Is everything okay?'

'Yeah. . . just been thinking. . .'

'Always dangerous,' I joked.

She gave a slightly cracked laugh.

I considered her words then said, 'You might not get everything you want, but you can come really close sometimes, and then very occasionally, you can get everything that you need.'

She nodded. 'Yeah, that's it though. . . trying to figure out what it is you need, that's the hard part.'

'Is it?'

She sighed, 'I guess.'

I knew better than to come right out and ask if she and Mark were having problems. They didn't have the most conventional of marriages, but then again, they weren't the most conventional of couples, yet they seemed to make it work, despite the fact that they both seemed to travel so much and were rarely in the same city at the same time.

It wouldn't have worked for Stuart and me, but every couple was different.

Over the years as Victoria's career had blossomed, Mark's seemed to have stayed the same; he was still successful, but nothing like his wife.

Victoria had a way of capturing people's lives that drew you in, her writing was rich and beautiful, and her books became must-reads, whereas Mark's biography style was more suited to a military-loving audience – there was a definite fan base for it, of course, and by all rights he should have been proud of his success, but it was obvious that he felt overshadowed by his wife. Victoria had once confided in me that sometimes she regretted her popularity because it often meant that she spent far less time doing what she loved – which was the research. I'd come to suspect that perhaps that was Mark's problem – he was more interested in having his name on the spine of the book than anyone else's.

Things grew worse when the economic downturn occurred, his projects grew fewer and fewer – there just wasn't as much of a call for his type of books, whereas it seemed every publisher wanted to sign with Victoria – knowing that with her name, they were likely to sell more copies. I think this was what really made him bitter. He'd become increasingly resentful of the time she spent away. We thought that now, with his latest biography of Marcus Aurelius in the works, things would have been better, but perhaps not. It wasn't that Victoria said as much to us – or perhaps not to me, she may have confided in Stuart – but it was Mark himself who had changed. Whenever we saw the two of them and we asked how they were doing, his expression would change, his eyes would become guarded. It was as if he took pleasure in venting his frustrations with their life to others in front of Victoria, in a passive-aggressive sort of way. Like the time we came past to admire their new home in West London, a few months ago.

Victoria had been excited about the move, which had taken them ever so slightly further away from The Terrorist – their nickname for their mother, Genevieve – making her impromptu visits more infrequent, and therefore the new home thoroughly perfect in location.

I'd admired Victoria's new study, which was an incredible bi-ographer's den, a book-lined treasury, with a long desk where some of the materials she was using and transcribing from old diaries and letters appeared on display. It felt like something out of a bygone era. She had a rather impressive collection of Brontë prints and letters that I oohed and ahhed over enthusiastically, then when I noted the gorgeous colours she'd picked out for the paintwork on the walls, Mark had scoffed and said, 'Oh yes, she started to paint it. . . but then was called off for an emergency book signing in Prague. I still don't get how or why there was a "Book Signing Emergency" but apparently there was. . .' He gave a dry sort of laugh and said, 'So off she went and I finished it, didn't I, *love?*'

Victoria had looked deeply embarrassed and said that the emergency was only because one of the writers on tour had got into an accident, and the publisher asked her to step in as so many people were already coming.

Mark had given us a fake smile and said, 'Oh well, and of course they weren't disappointed because they flew in their best author to save the day. You're like Supergirl. . .' he laughed. 'Su-per Writer,' he sniggered, though it wasn't funny.

'Mark,' Stuart had said warningly, his dark eyes losing pa-tience.

Mark held up his hands. 'Oh, don't worry, big brother, I'm all right. . . I'm happy to be the wagon-hitcher to our little star here,' he said, throwing his arm around Victoria and giving her a squeeze, while she gazed at the ground. But Mark's smile didn't meet his eyes. 'I'm sure you two are the same,' he said to us.

It had been an awkward moment. One we'd tried to gloss over as best we could. Stuart made a joke about him being happy to be my toy boy, but still, it had left a sour note behind. On the ride home I'd asked Stuart if he ever felt like Mark, now that *The Fudge Files* had gained a bit of a following, but he just laughed.

'It's not a competition, is it?' he asked. 'You've got your thing, I've got mine, we're on the same team, right? Lookit, I can't draw a stick man without it looking like a crime scene, and you can't make anything in the kitchen without it looking like one either, so we have that.'

'Haha – very funny,' I said, rolling my eyes. Crime scene, indeed!

I looked at Victoria now. I'd promised myself I wouldn't say anything. I touched the small blanket I'd draped around my shoulders; it had been made by one of the founders of Mum's quirky sewing group, May Bradley. She was Irish, a little offbeat, and fun, and could be oddly profound at times. I felt a small shiver of guilt unfurl. I hadn't thought of her, or the group, in ages – I'd been trying not to. They'd each called by to invite me over to the club when I first moved here of course, as quite a few lived within the village, but I couldn't quite face seeing my mother's old friends all together like they used to be every Thursday growing up – not like that – not when I knew Mum wouldn't be there too. I ran into a few of the members in the village every so often, and it was always a bit hard to see them after all this time. Often I found myself making a bit of an excuse to get away, then wishing I hadn't, that I'd just find a way to be normal.

No one tells you how grief can twist you inside out and make the simplest thing – like seeing a group of women who'd loved the person you lost almost as fiercely as you – an impossibly hard, heartbreaking task. Particularly when, shining in each and everyone's eyes, was a reflection of what we'd all lost.

Or how much you'd hate yourself on the way home, how much you'd wish you'd turned around, and gone back. Or how much you missed them too.

I opened the blanket and put the ends around Victoria's thin shoulders, so that she snuggled closer. 'Did I ever tell you about Colin?' I asked.

Victoria turned to look at me. 'Your ex-boyfriend, The Artiste?' she said, putting on a French accent. 'Not really, you'd just broken up when you and I met.'

I nodded. 'Well, we dated all throughout my university years. He studied fine art, pretty amazing really. Postmodern, intellectual. Many of his paintings were beautiful. . . and brutal. Children in the Sudan. Rhino poaching in Zimbabwe. Mass shootings in schools in America. No subject was left unturned. He exhibited in Paris, Berlin, New York. . . he was incredibly hard-working too. Kept impossible hours.

'In the beginning it was wonderful to be with someone who shared my passion for art – though it was always hard for me to describe my work in relation to his as "art". It's not that he was unkind, just self-involved, you know. Everything took a back seat to his work. He'd ask me to cancel meetings with potential publishers so that I could accompany him to an exhibition then sulk if I declined. Over the years he started to drink more, got jealous, possessive. Our fights turned from the usual bickering to something far uglier. He became increasingly volatile. It's funny, but because he was an artist, I made excuses for it. I'd tell myself he just felt things more deeply than anyone else. I'd tell myself things like it was actually sweet that he loves me so much that he'd show up at my parents' home when my phone died, and maybe it would have been if he hadn't also been so suspicious about why I'd "let" my phone die. Like I'd done it on purpose. I didn't see it for what it was.

'As he began to drink more and more, and his behaviour grew worse, he became increasingly mean and belittling about my work, calling it a cute hobby, or labelling it cartoonish. Over time, his attention turned quickly to suffocation. It got so that it felt like I couldn't visit a friend, or go anywhere on my own without Colin showing up, suspicious. We were always fighting. I ended it so many times but he'd make sweeping promises to change. To give up drinking. To be the man I deserved.

'He wrote letters. Drew incredible portraits of me, which he'd leave outside my house. He joined the AA. I'd take him back and for a while everything would be fine, but there was always this shadow hanging over me while I waited for him to slip back. If my phone rang, his whole body would tense. I'd see him physically resisting the impulse to check my mobile to see who it was. I'd see it and think, "Well, he's trying. . ." and then one day he proposed.'

Victoria gasped. 'What?'

I nodded. 'Yeah.'

'What happened?'

'I told him I'd think about it. I mean, in retrospect that may have been the first clue, you know, with Stuart I didn't need to think. I was like, "Hurry up and ask me."'

'Which he did after, like, five minutes,' she laughed.

'I know, he took forever,' I grinned.

Stuart and I met at Victoria's flat over dinner with friends. I suspect it was a set-up now, but back then I was completely oblivious. I sat down across from one of the most divine-looking men I'd ever seen, with gorgeous brown eyes and a megawatt, toothpaste-advert smile, who was *funny*. I mean, when are good-looking men funny too? We were talking across our neighbours at the dinner table to their annoyance, then decided to share a bottle of red wine, and carried on talking even after all Smudge's friends had gone home and she'd passed out on the couch. I'd never laughed as much. By the next morning, when he walked me home, I knew I'd found The Guy. It helped that he was bloody gorgeous, I won't lie – it also helped that he really was rather oblivious to it.

After that he took my number, and I waited like an idiot for him to call for an entire day, jumping out my skin every time my phone beeped, until finally at eight that evening, he called and said, 'Ah God, it's been like bloody forever!' As if *I* was the one who was meant to call him and not the other way around. I'd put my phone in the drawer to stop myself from ringing Smudge to demand, 'Has your brother spoken about me? Does he like me?' Ugh! Then I'd taken it out just as fast in case I missed his call. I'd thought of around thirteen different 'reasons' to call Victoria to ask for Stuart's number. He'd left his jacket? His wallet? Or the truth: he'd left a big pile of girly hormones behind, who'd forgotten to take down her hot brother's number? So when he FINALLY called, I was a bit surprised and well, wildly ecstatic really, to hear him say, 'I'm not good at this – I like you, I know I'm meant to wait, or whatever, and play this cool, but do you want to do something soon, like maybe tomorrow?' My heart was thrashing about in my chest, but I said, 'No, I don't think so. How about now? You busy?' So he came over and I pretty much never let him leave afterwards.

I waited five months for him to propose; he says it took that long only because it took that long to train Muppet (who had decided that Stuart was her favourite boy in the world too) to carry the ring cushion through to the lounge to the sound of 'Don't You Want Me Baby?' which was what he'd set his ringtone to.

She grinned back, then asked, 'So, what happened? Did you just tell him no?'

'Well, the thing is. . . I wasn't quite sure, I think I would have said no eventually but that evening I drove to my parents' place – Colin and I were renting student digs in Falmouth at that time, one of our worst decisions, which was to try living together to see if that would make him less possessive – not a great plan,' I said with a snort. 'Anyway, that's when I found May Bradley, one of my mum's best friends, sitting outside with a cup of tea, unpicking her sewing.'

Driving over, I'd forgotten it was a Thursday. Which was when my mum's group got together. To be honest, seeing May there, I was a little annoyed – I'd just wanted to see Mum on her own so that we could chat. But with the group there, I hadn't wanted to air something like that to half the schoolmatrons of the village. 'Especially Winifred Jones, the headmistress of the primary school where I went. Stern to a fault. God, she drove me mad growing up,' I laughed in memory. 'Especially as a teenager, she was always suspicious of me.'

'Ivy, weren't you sort of naughty though. . . I mean, Catherine's stories. . .'

I laughed. 'Well, yes . . . but I mean, having the headmistress over almost every Thursday didn't make things any easier. But May was different; of anyone she was my favourite.

'I said something like, "Oh, I forgot it was The Thursday Club today," and she said, "Will it be a whiskey then?" in that brogue of hers that she had never lost, the kind of voice that you knew was putting an *e* in the word *whiskey*,' I said with a chuckle that Victoria shared.

'I agreed, not wanting to go inside and have Winifred demand to know why I was there – maybe May knew this too, because she slipped inside to pour us "a wee dram – something to steady the fingers, as well as the mind", as she put it, and then she came back and gave me this look and said, "Sure you're a sorry-looking sight. . . What has he done now?"

'And I choked on the whiskey, and asked her how she knew. She just shrugged, said something like when yer in yer twenties it's always about the love life. . . or the job. . . No one comes home to their mammies about their job so I figured it was worth a shot. . .'

Victoria laughed. 'Wise words!'

I chuckled. 'She's a blast! Well, anyway, the thing with May was she wasn't the interfering one in the group – she was the fun one, the one who made the others laugh when things went wrong. The one who brought the whiskey, you know. So it was really surprising when she just patted me on my knee, and said, "Now, lookit, I'm going ta tell yer something I wish with all me heart me own mam had told me. Sure she would have saved me a whole heap of trouble if I'd have heard it but she didn't know it. . . I heard it on the *Oprah Show*, you know? *Feckin'* loved that show, not sure why she gave it in . . . Anyhoos, yer listening now?"

'I must have nodded because she looked at me, her eyes serious, "Love should feel good."

'I must have sat there for a while, thinking. Eventually I said something like, "It couldn't always be good, could it? It's also something you work at, isn't it? I mean, everyone says that, don't they?"

'Well, May, she wasn't having any of that. . . She held up her latest sewing effort. God, it always came down to sewing for them,' I laughed in memory. 'It was a jacket for her daughter Jackie. The jacket was lovely, one of those classic sort of Chanel-inspired ones, navy blue with very thin piping down the lapels, which May said would give it that extra something special. May said, "Making this jacket is like love; it isn't easy but it's mostly straightforward. And like this piping, when you have love it should only ever enhance your life, it should never detract from it because if it does then it's best left in the discard pile."

'It got me thinking, you know. How if I weighed it up, Colin's presence never really enhanced my life. If anything, most of the time I felt sort of diminished by him. After that I said goodbye to Colin for the final time. May's words really helped me. I don't think I'd realised till then that for the most part, love really *should* just feel good; sure you can have your problems and bad patches, and those should be worked on, but for the most part love should feel right. If it doesn't, there's a problem.'

I felt Victoria's hand clutch mine while she cried. I hoped that, like May, I'd done the right thing in telling her my story. Victoria would speak to me about Mark when she was ready.

After some time, I led her through to the guest room, draping May's soft blanket over her while she slept.

When I closed the door behind me, I didn't need to look at my watch to know it was 3 a.m.

I took a seat in my studio. Cold now without the soft knitted blanket May had made at least two decades before when I fell off my bicycle and was rushed to the hospital. Mum had said that May worked at it tirelessly all night. I felt a lump in my throat at the forgotten memory, at thoughts of May and the other women who had been there for me whenever I needed them, whenever Mum couldn't.

I wasn't surprised when the postcard began to write, leaving behind just three words that night.

The Thursday Club

'Mum?' I asked.

But no new words followed. It was a reproach, I knew. A gentle one, but a reproach nonetheless.

How could I have done what I had to them? It was hard to see them without Mum there, but I shouldn't have let that stop me. If I was honest with myself, they were one of the biggest reasons I'd wanted to come back to live here in the first place. It wasn't just Mum I missed. Or sweet, funny May, but all of them: my mum's dearest friends, who had always been there throughout my childhood. A group of women who taught me the value of friendship, of laughter, and yes, sometimes, whiskey after dark.

The same women who were there for us in our darkest times, when Mum grew ill, and when she was no longer there. With a sinking feeling, I realised that after Mum had left, so had I.

I had been back in Cornwall for months, yet as when Dad had offered me Mum's writing desk, I'd been avoiding them as well. Or as much as you could in a village of this size. I was polite and friendly when I saw them, but they must have known that I was avoiding them. I never realised how much that may have hurt them. They'd each tried in their own way to welcome me back, but I kept putting them off. I'd tell May I'd come around 'next week some time' when I ran into her in the shop, but 'next week' never seemed to roll around. I'd tell Flavia when I saw her at The Cloud Arms that 'we must have dinner one night', but that night never seemed to come. I made up excuses when they called. More often than not, I visited Terry's café, Salt, instead of popping into the village bakery where I'd have to see Robyn. I did it to all of them, not understanding why I was doing it really as it hurt either way. Avoiding spending time with them had been a different kind of pain.

I'd been a coward, simple as that.

The truth was I loved them, and I shouldn't have tried to cut them out of my life just because it was likely to bring back sad memories.

As I sat there staring at the words etched in gold and stardust I realised that there were six other 'mothers' I'd lost as well, but this time it was of my own doing. I wiped my eyes. My gaze fell on my little wall calendar – it was a special edition of *Detective Sergeant Fudge*, and I laughed, realising that tomorrow was Thursday.

Well, of course it was. I didn't believe in coincidences, did I?

I believed in Mum, though.

CHAPTER NINE

The Thursday Club

Every Thursday afternoon for twenty-seven years they'd met. Sometimes the location changed, depending on whose home they had been to last. Sometimes they'd go to the same person's house every week for close to a year because a new baby had been born.

Sometimes they worked on something new, or the same project lasted decades. Sometimes they all worked together, or split themselves into pairs.

Sometimes a foot would pause on the pedal of a machine, so that it could take a step towards a neighbour to offer a guiding hand, or to sigh in sympathy, or bring a cup of tea, or maybe a wee bit of something stronger, when something needed to be ripped apart and started over, from the quilt they were working on for a child's nursery, to the marriage that had fallen apart. Sometimes one of their number would be ill, or couldn't be there that night.

Sometimes when that happened, you'd find them all there at that one's bedside instead. One of them getting out the Henry and giving the house a quick once-over, wiping down counters and appliances, and applying a healthy dose of lemon-scented disinfectant and common sense (Winifred Jones, it was always Winifred Jones, and you always seemed to say her full name, no one knew why), while another heated up some shepherd's pie for the family, and yet another tended to the patient – usually that was Mum, she was always the one you wanted at your bedside. The one who knew just how to make you feel better. The one whose kind visage belied the force of will inside. Which made it all the worse when she was the one who grew ill herself. I'll never forget when they heard that she was sick. Mum kept everything to herself. Always so ready to be the rock for everyone else. Till finally she had no choice but to break the news to them. . . not only that she was sick, but that she was dying too. That night May held her hand, as she began finally to cry and tell them what she'd been keeping from them for years. . .

No Henry was switched on that night. No shepherd's pie warmed up, and no helpful scent of lemon was able to wash it away or still poor Winifred Jones's shaking fingers, except the other six pairs of hands that reached out for hers.

There had always seven of them. That's the way it had always been from the start.

Winifred Jones was the eldest, and the founder. The Cloudsea Primary School headmistress, she was the one who suggested that they form a sewing circle when Mum had joined the school as art teacher. There were many reasons they decided to start the group according to Mum, but most of these had been forgotten over the years.

May, Mum's best friend, maintained that she'd agreed because the dress shop in town made clothes that were designed with little boys' bodies in mind. Mum said they decided to start the group after a flash flood swept through a neighbouring village, when people were evacuated from their homes and the roads were blocked in and people were freezing in a caravan park that the council had helped set up, so they all made blanket squares until their fingers began to knit by themselves while they slept. Robyn Glass, who ran the bakery in town, joined at around that time too. Inviting her had been May's brilliant idea, as she brought all the treats. Then Robyn invited Abigail Charming – an eccentric American, who had bought the Senderwood Estate after it was left to wrack and ruin and opened up the tea gardens there. I always suspected that she had made up the name 'Charming' but Mum insisted it was her real name. Apparently one night May had given Abigail a bit too much whiskey and dared her to show them her passport. . . and there it was, along with the fact that she was actually a good ten years older than she claimed.

And then there was Flavia. I adored Flavia, she was wildly beautiful. Employed as the rose expert at Senderwood, and as far as many of the local men were concerned she was as much of an attraction as the rose gardens themselves.

Flavia, however, was only interested in roses, in tending them, growing them, and discovering new hybrids for the garden. There was something so enchanting about Flavia, too, something about her rose-tinted view of the world that brought the sun to our living room whenever she was there, so at odds with the perpetual storm cloud that was nosy, grouchy Winifred Jones. It was bad enough going to the same school where your mum worked, but having the headmistress over every week? There were times when it was deplorable.

'Still can't ride a bike yet I see, Ivy-girl,' she'd remark, pointing out the obvious when I came home with scratches along my knees.

'Art may be your given talent, but you've got to pull your socks up in the maths department, Ivy-girl. Mr Benners said you're barely keeping up, far too interested in making cartoons for your friends. . .'

As a result, there were many occasions I'd stay away from home on a Thursday when I was in school. But I always came back to see them. . . couldn't seem to help myself.

May had given the group the name The Thursday Club, partly because in the beginning they couldn't quite decide on the purpose of their club. Was it a knitters' group, who occasionally sewed? Or a sewing circle that sometimes knitted? Were they a supper club, who occasionally crafted? Or a book group that forgot to discuss their books? When they realised that Thursday afternoon was the day they always met, rain or shine, due to old Winifred Jones's clockwork scheduling, May Bradley hit on the name, and it stuck.

It was always a part of my life growing up, this group of women, who more often than not were found seated around my mother's living room; somehow the rotation always seemed to have more circles towards Mum's house, perhaps because, in her own quiet way, she was the centre.

I'd come in to find Mum seated next to her writing desk as always, with the gaggle of women around her. The fold-up table brought in and seven sewing machines humming along to the sound of Mum's classical music in the background. Though, occasionally, May would get her way and I'd come in to hear them laughing, and working along to the sounds of the Beatles, or the Temptations or maybe the Four Seasons. There was something about sewing, May said, that brought out the sixties girl in her.

Today, I found them at May's home, like I knew I would.

The door had been open, and I let myself in.

There were always seven. Always.

Except, now there were only six. Six slightly older women, hair somewhat changed, the odd new streak of grey and white, faces a little more lined, and one empty chair: an empty chair meant for Mum. Which made me bite my lip. It was Winifred Jones, of course, who first noticed me. Her ever-busy hands grew still and she simply gasped. For once, she had nothing to say. No 'Ivy-girl' admonishment.

Flavia turned towards me, her dark eyes widening.

I heard more than one whisper: 'She looks just like Alice at her age.'

Then, suddenly Abigail's bright, Southern drawl cut through the tense mood. 'Darling girl!' which never failed to touch my heart.

But it was May who shook her head. 'Ah, lass! The prodigal daughter returns at long, bloody last.' Her eyes were sparkling, 'Shall I pour us all a wee dram and you can tell us all about it? Sure we're all dying to know. . .'

I gave them a watery smile. 'Go on then.'

So she did.

And I took a seat, realising that maybe. . . just maybe the empty seat was actually meant for me.

Later that evening, I found the little blanket folded on the end of the spare room, along with a note, saying simply:

Ivy,
Thanks for the words. I needed them.
Smudge
P.S. Beware The Terrorist. . .

Ominous words indeed.

The studio was lit when I entered. Lit with that strange light, of stardust and moonshine. A light that would now forever be associated with Mum in my mind.

She was waiting for me.

During the day, I always tried my best not to race through it, not to wish the time away; to somehow live through each day, but it was hopeless.

All I could think about was 3 a.m: getting into the studio and speaking with Mum.

When she was there, and the postcard began to glow, and write, call it fatigue or wonder, or simply magic, with my mind in an almost dream-like state, perhaps due to the early hour, and I was able to just let it be. Let it be enchanted and strange and fantastical.

Later, of course, in the ordinariness of the day, paying bills, scooping up after the dog, and mucking out the chicken coop, it was hard to imagine this time existed at all. That I hadn't, in fact, dreamt it. But I hadn't, and somehow, in some way, it was real.

I'd like to say that every night Mum could speak to me as if we existed in some time-lapse, that the postcard served like a form of telephonic exchange between my world and hers, that we could speak about anything that I desired, but it didn't always work that way.

Sometimes she didn't or couldn't respond to my questions and I would have to manage my frustration. Frustration that I had no right to feel. Not when I had this. Because most of the time what she had to say was so much more than what I wanted, it was somehow what I needed to hear.

Though, of course, I didn't always know it.

That night, the postcard only wrote once. I hated it when that happened. To wait all day for our exchange, only to feel like our precious sand in the hourglass was metered out grain by grain. I waited, my breath tight in my throat. But it stayed the same.

I didn't know exactly why she wrote what she did.

Her words, etched in moonshine and silver, glowed bright, the words slowly, ever so slowly, filling the postcard.

Stitch by stitch

I didn't know why she said it but I knew what it meant.

It was a squaring of shoulders; a testing of mettle. Most of all, it was a warning.

CHAPTER TEN

Stitch by Stitch

There is a saying amongst the members of The Thursday Club that you don't get to the end because every stitch is perfect. You get there because of the one that came before it and how you proceed from there. You get there by going stitch by stitch.

The truth is in life, as in sewing, things fall apart; it's how you deal with it that counts.

Since I was a little girl, I'd been hearing one of my mum's old sewing club members tell me that same sage advice whenever I needed it.

When I was learning how to ride a bicycle and came inside with scraped knees, and an exhausted dad who'd been running behind me up and down the street, to launch myself in a flood of tears into my mum's arms, while I wailed that at age seven I was a hopeless failure, that I'd never get it. I'd be *twelve* and I still wouldn't get it. Being in the double digits and not knowing how to ride a bicycle seemed to me back then the worst thing that could happen in the history of the world.

Mum had looked at me with her kind eyes, lifted a sewing needle and said, 'Ivy, darling, it's *stitch by stitch*, my girl, that's how you'll get there. Now go on then, dry your eyes.'

And they'd all nodded, while Mum gave me a gentle shove to get going, followed by my reluctant father, who gave them a tired smile, his long legs no doubt aching from riding the little

pink bike I'd made him get on time and again so he could prove
to me just how 'easy' it was.

Robyn, the baker, told me the same thing, when a year later
Catherine and I had our first real fight, when she admitted that
her aversion to cats stretched even to Fat Albert. Instead of ac-
knowledging her bravery in being honest with me, I was sure
this was the end of our friendship. How could I continue to
be friends with someone who couldn't see the many delights
that was Fat Albert, chief of cats, the most lovable of creatures,
whom I was sure proved the exception to every non-cat-loving
rule? Which is what I told The Thursday Club with crossed
arms, while ignoring poor Catherine's pleading knocks on the
door outside.

Robyn, herself a cat lady, and proud of it, said, 'Ivy, everyone
is entitled to their opinions. You can't force someone to agree
with you, it's how you get around that difference that makes the
friendship richer as a result. It's like this stitch right here,' she
said, lifting up a bright orange swathe of knitted yarn, with a
vividly interesting pattern, that was no doubt intended for Hast-
ings, or Morpeth, one of her many tabby cats. 'It was meant to
be a loop stitch, like in the pattern, but I made a mistake and it
turned into a knit stitch, so I kept it going, and it's a much better piece as a result. You'll see, the same thing will happen with
your friendship. Things start to get really interesting when you
trust each other enough with the truth.'

'Even *rroses* are made more bea-uti-ful, when they turn out to
be not as they seem,' said the beautiful Flavia in her molten Italian voice, like rich chocolate gelato. 'We always think of *rroses*
as being perfect . . . but they are not always – zey only get zere
because of the care and attention we give zem,' she said, rolling
each *r*.

'Stitch by stitch,' agreed Winifred Jones, the grouchy headmistress, who clacked her needles together fiercely in response.

The circle bopped their heads in agreement. Being a wilful child, though, it had taken me a few weeks to see what they meant. That, and the fact that Catherine cornered me at school and told me that actually she was wrong, Fat Albert *was* the exception to the rule. She was lying, of course. We both knew it, but I did love her for it.

Throughout the years their motto had helped me, and when I faced a life without Mum, I would think: *Stitch by stitch*, which was sometimes translated to: *Minute by minute, hour by hour.*

When we failed to conceive. When we finally did, only to miscarry, twice. Somehow, I'd think: *Stitch by stitch*, and somehow, beyond the dark abyss that seemed ready to swallow me whole, I'd find my way to the other side.

I couldn't help but wonder just what Mum had meant by sending me this message now; what did I need to face, what more could I possibly face?

I'd just finished up the latest drawings of Mr Tibbles when the phone rang. Not realising that I would need Mum's words more than ever after the call.

Somehow, despite the fact that it was a number I didn't recognise, a part of me knew: *Genevieve.*

I didn't need Victoria's warning to know that The Terrorist wouldn't stop trying to get us to do things her way – such as visiting that specialist –even though we'd asked her to.

She'd sent the news clipping from the *Telegraph* the other day, the one that outlined the fertility specialist, Marcus Labuscagne's, technique, with a note saying that if I wanted to change my mind, she'd set up the appointment for me.

I had decided to ignore it, which perhaps wasn't the best plan.

A few days later, I'd gotten a call from the specialist, Dr Labuscagne himself, who no doubt had been paid a small fortune to give me his sales pitch, which lasted for forty-five minutes to the dot, obviously making sure he got his full money's worth despite my *many, many* protestations, which went something like this:

'Yes, er. . . thank you for your call, she did tell me but I'm afraid that at this point, we're really just not interested—'

'I understand, that's, er, really great that you've managed to squeeze us onto a two-year waiting list but—'

'Yes. . . I understand she was royalty and she was moved off the list for us—'

'But—'

'Yes, that's, er, very—'

'As I was SAYING, it is unnecessary as we won't be needing your—'

'Yes, I do understand that it's a really impressive tech—'

'Yes, a sixty-eight percent success rate is unheard of, BUT—'

'Yes, that's really—'

'Look, please, I'm not trying to be rude but I have to—'

'Oh? Well, yes, I walk every day, but what has that got to do with—'

'Yes, I understand that physical health on the outside doesn't necessarily reflect on the inside, but—'

'No, I won't tell you my age!'

'How did you get all that information? How dare she send it to you!'

'Oh. . . yes, well, I am relieved you told her that I wasn't near the end of my fertility cycle, thank you for that. . . but please—'

'No, I can't come this Tuesday, as I've already said—'

'Look, please, I have to go—'

'I'm sorry to be rude but—'

'I hardly see how that's any of your business!'

'He's very. . . er, virile, ugh, now please—'

'Excuse me, I have a job to do so if you don't mind. . .'

'I'm hanging up now.'

Which was what I should have done from the beginning.

Then a few days after that, I was sent the brochure for the Collingswood House, our dream home in Knightsbridge, which Stuart and I had always loved, and said we would love to buy if ever we won the lottery and it came on sale. Well, it turned out it was finally for sale. I suspected Genevieve had placed her rather heavy hand in this as well, however. I couldn't even imagine what she must have told the Pattersons to make them finally put their house up for sale.

And now that it was finally for sale, Genevieve wrote to us and kindly 'offered' to make us a present of it so that we could have our own London base while I did the treatments she had booked with the insufferable Dr Marcus Labuscagne, the fertility specialist, the first of which she said would occur the following Tuesday.

She was good, I'd give her that.

She'd give Genghis Khan a run for his money. The Collingswood House was a low blow.

I scribbled a note of polite thanks and apology. One that was firm and to the point, saying we were not now or ever going to be seeing that specialist and while we did once love the Collingswood House, we loved Sea Cottage much more.

Now, a few days later, I'd gotten another phone call.

This time from a number I didn't recognise. A posh-sounding male voice asked me to hold for a Genevieve Everton and, before I knew it, I was once again ambushed. I'd been so careful to ignore her subsequent calls, to let Stuart deal with her instead of me. . . Perhaps that was the problem: the more I avoided her, the worse the ensuing well of emotion that came out of her eventually was, including the sheer vitriol that spouted from her mouth when we finally spoke. After a second's rather impolite introduction, she informed me, rather insultingly, 'While the success of your "picture books",' as she referred to *The Fudge Files*, 'is, I am sure, fulfilling to some extent, spending all day imagining cute adventures about your dog is sweet in a very child-like sort of way. Thankfully, you've had some success with this, but it shouldn't get in the way of having a family, or be at the expense of Stuart's hopes and dreams of becoming a father. I'm sure your child-like pursuits can help foster your creativity, but really, Ivy, you need to put on your adult cap now, and push through. I know you've had heavy, painful setbacks, but if you're ever to succeed, you need to keep going. Trust me on this – your body won't wait for ever.'

Shock made me speechless. Had she honestly just termed my entire career a 'child-like pursuit'? And my wanting to have a break from the pain and heartache of failing to conceive was 'childish'?

While my brain whirred at the avalanche of insults, Genevieve continued, perhaps to offer some measure of an explanation for her unwarranted cruelty. 'Look, I'm a straight-shooter, Ivy, I just tell it like it is, and I'm just going to say it, I know I shouldn't, I know he won't thank me for it, but I'm his mother and if I can't stick up for him, well then. . . I'm not a very good one, am I? My fear is that my son loves you, Ivy, so much so that he'll do whatever he can to make you happy. He'll mortgage his house twice, rather than accept our help to pay for all those IVF treatments because you didn't want to be in our debt—'

'That was a joint decision!' I interjected. It was Stuart who said that if he accepted her financial aid, as she put it, we'd never be able to get rid of her. She'd see it as an investment, one that we had to pay off. Perhaps not financially, but one that may have even included visitation rights to her unborn grandchild until well into adulthood. . . or perhaps an insistence that it went to Eton if it was a boy or joined some godawful finishing school if it was a girl. I mean, who knows what she'd have asked. . . Her children didn't call her 'The Terrorist' in a hyperbolic way, they meant it. And Stuart was adamant that the one thing you didn't do was negotiate with her. Because you'd lose. Every. Single. Time. Which is why the Everton children's family motto was very similar to that of the United States: 'We do not negotiate with terrorists'.

Genevieve sighed impatiently. 'I know he *said that* but he only said it because it would upset you if you thought you owed us something. That's the trouble. He would rather put himself into serious debt and give up the career he'd been working towards just when it had finally paid off than dare to upset you. Then when your royalties paid out enough to buy a house, instead of buying his dream home in Collingswood here in Knightsbridge, which is finally for sale by the way, he agreed to move down to Cornwall with you, so that you could be closer to your dad. Meanwhile he had to give up his whole family. . . I mean, do you even know how much Victoria needs her brother right now? And your best friend, Catherine. I mean, you just left her in Chelsea.'

I spluttered in rage – how dare she bring up *my* friend in all of this? The woman was relentless. 'What real prospects are there for my son down there? It's a holiday place. Unless, like you, you're lucky enough to be independently financed, there aren't that many jobs. I mean, this little business venture of his. . . it's ludicrous. For God's sake, the man has a PhD in marketing and advertising! This isn't what he worked so hard for. To be what? A glorified farmer?'

'It's what he wanted!' I protested. 'It was his suggestion – and so what? What's wrong with being a farmer? Anyway he's a smallholder, with a small business, and he loves it! And yes, we both loved the Collingswood House, but that was only because Cornwall wasn't an option. Once we had enough money that we didn't need a mortgage any more we were able to choose what we really wanted – and we chose this!'

Genevieve harrumphed. 'I know my son. He agreed because he thought that down there away from the stress and bustle from London you'd be focused on getting pregnant. Except you're not. You'd rather just give up. He's given up everything that he ever wanted and now that you've achieved a degree of celebrity, you've decided it's too hard to try again.'

My mouth fell open and closed at her harsh, cruel words. Words that I attempted to deny.

'It's not true, Stuart wanted Cornwall, we both did. . . he wanted a change,' I said, dashing away a tear, my throat constricting. 'It might have been my suggestion but he wanted it. . . he was tired of the long nights and how awful the corporate politics were. . .'

I heard a snort of derision. 'Really, Ivy? So that's why before you and Catherine were given that big print deal, he phoned me, more excited than I'd ever heard him, to tell me that he'd just been offered the position of vice president at the Red Agency – you know, the company that he always wanted to work for, the one that does the marketing for some of the biggest brands in the world, that one?' she said sarcastically, as if I didn't know which one she meant. 'He was going to surprise you by putting in an offer on the Collingswood House to celebrate. . .'

'Vice president?' I repeated numbly. Why hadn't Stuart said anything?

Genevieve answered my unspoken question. 'He came home to find you and Catherine bouncing off the walls as you'd just signed the biggest deal of your careers to date. . . the one that would make your books not just a national, but an international success, and pay off all your debts. You were so happy. He didn't want to risk that. I never said anything, he told me not to, but now, well, someone should. Especially now that you've just given up on trying for a baby.'

The phone clicked off. She hadn't even given me the courtesy of a chance to respond.

I sat down hard on the bench in the hallway. Muppet scratched my shins, eyeing me with that soulful look of hers. I placed my hand on her silky fur. It couldn't be true, could it?

Stuart hadn't given up his dream just so that I could live mine, had he? We weren't like Smudge and Mark, with one half of a couple feeling like their lights were dimmed by the brightness of the other, were we? He'd always said that we were on the same team. When had he decided that my needs were more important than his own?

I closed my eyes. He'd loved the Red Agency. For years he'd done consultancy work for them and always said that if an opening came up anywhere in the marketing department, he'd jump at it, even if it was a demotion, as it would be incredible to work for them. But it had never happened.

What happened was the economic downturn. Several failed pregnancies. And two mortgages. So he took a marketing director position for a major pharmaceutical organisation while we tried to pay it all off.

The added insult to injury came when he began to realise how much their marketing efforts covered up the multitude of unethical practices the company turned a blind eye to. It had slowly started to eat him alive, especially when on more than one occasion he was tasked with cleaning up the bad publicity and fallout. While he went about it as ethically as possible, threatening to leave if they didn't at least try to admit some of the blame, he still felt sullied by the experience. And yet when finally his success at the pharmaceutical company meant that he was offered a job at his dream firm, working on cutting-edge campaigns, he had turned it down. Why? Why hadn't he said anything to me?

I felt a rush of nausea, and barely made it to the downstairs toilet. As I dry-heaved into the porcelain bowl, tears streamed down my face. I'd been so sure that Stuart and I were on the same page – he was the one who insisted on Cornwall, hadn't he? I thought he had, but maybe, maybe in my excitement, I'd made the suggestion and he'd been so considerate that he'd swept his own wishes aside for the sake of mine.

I'd never considered that Stuart hadn't wanted what I did. He'd been so enthusiastic about our move down here, talking about a change of pace and his idea of becoming a self-sustaining smallholder that it had never occurred to me that there was a possibility that he'd just been putting on a sporting face.

I set off for the village, trying to walk away my queasiness, while sorting out what Genevieve had told me. I should have been furious with her. And a part of me was. What she'd done was cruel. I'd been completely blindsided. But then how could he have just left me in the dark like that?

How could he just roll over and let me get what I wanted without even mentioning his own wishes?

I wasn't this person; I would have been blissfully happy to have lived in the Collingswood House and for him to take his dream job. Sure I loved it down here but not at the expense of my husband's dreams. How could he have made this call? How could he not have spoken to me about any of this?

I popped into the post office, barely listening to the octogenarian post-mistress Mrs Aheary while she told me about the plight of the Royal Mail office in the village, and how pretty soon robotic drones would be delivering the mail. 'Drones! What is this, *Star Wars*?' she said in disgust, looking at me with beetle-black eyes in a face that resembled a sunken mattress. ''Tisn't right, Ivy-Rose. . . 'tisn't right at all. Mark me words, we'll be closed down soon enough if these emmets get their way. . .'

Mrs Aheary's definition of *emmets* weren't just people across the river, the Tamar, that divided Cornwall from the rest of the world (aka foreigners), but anyone who wanted to change the way things worked, young people, the wrong sorts of old people

– 'them with modern ideas' – and pretty much anyone who disagreed with her, really.

I ignored her speech. Mrs Aheary had been telling me a similar tale since I was twelve years old, just with different bad guys threatening the Royal Mail. Faxes. . . faxes were replacing letters. Then 'The Email', then courier companies, Eastern Europeans. . . . I'm not sure what they had to do with it, but she blamed them too, despite having a young Polish girl named Paulina working for the office in earshot. (Paulina, we all knew, ended up doing most of Mrs Aheary's work while the latter worked her motor mouth.) Now it was an article about mail-delivering drones that were going to finally close down her post office, the one that had been going for more than two hundred years. Sort of around when she was born, I often imagined.

I must have grunted a response of some kind, because soon enough she brought over the package from my publisher, which was a box of marketing paraphernalia for the latest edition of *The Fudge Files – The Case of the Missing Brolly*.

Even that failed to give me the usual jolt of happiness. All I could think of were Genevieve's words and Stuart.

Mrs Aheary mentioned something about a storm warning over the next week or two, but I didn't pay it any heed. Living this close to the sea, I knew that daily weather reports weren't just the aperitif at the end of most conversation but often the main course. The subject of the weather came up all the time in Cornwall, even more so than in ordinary British conversation.

A typical exchange in the village often went something like this:

'How's your knee doing now, Mrs Blume?' April Blume ran the local pub in the village, The Cloud Arms, and complained of her knees any time you dared ask for a refill. Though, once pressed, the enquiry was likely to be followed with, 'Much better now them squalls down in Penwith have finally calmed down.'

'Your new arthritis medication starting to kick in, Mrs Glass?' someone would ask Robyn, the village baker from my mum's Thursday Club, where a lifetime of kneading dough and supplying all of Cloudsea and the neighbouring town with their daily bread had taken its toll on her elbows and wrists, and she'd say, 'Oh yes, thanks, but should take a turn now with the first frosts arriving. . . Have half a mind to take up sticks upcountry to me Aunty Sheryl, where the weather is better to ride it out, but it wouldn't be right, would it?' she'd ask with a look of worry.

The sad part was that most of the villagers were likely to shake their heads that yes, it wouldn't be right. A Cornishman or -woman, as it were, stuck it out. Even if the weather in Northamptonshire would be better right now for arthritic elbows.

So, of course, I didn't really hear the storm warming.

All I heard, on repeat, were Genevieve's words, like an overplayed Christmas song on a repetitive loop in a shopping mall.

I left the post office and took my package up under my arm, trying to keep my face as close to my jumper as possible and away from the icy chill on the long walk back home. The more I walked though, the angrier I got. When I got to Sea Cottage and saw that Stuart's car was now there, I thought, *right, that's it.*

When I got into the garden I heard the sound of the radio and followed it to the little shed, where Stuart kept his gardening equipment, along with an old, worn leather sofa and his Xbox, which since we moved down here seemed to have grown a layer of dust as, even in near winter, a smallholder's job was never done. I found him with his feet beside a heater, a scarf wrapped around his head, humming along to the sounds of the Rolling Stones.

His brown eyes were barely conspicuous above the thick wool of his brown and green tweed scarf, while he sat with a protractor and a pencil, and pored over what looked like self-made blueprints.

'Hi,' I said, rather brusquely. Generally the sight of him here would have melted my heart, but today I was immune.

'A sun dial,' he said in return. 'See here. . .' he added, pointing to a really old book from the library with ancient-looking French-styled gardens. 'This is how the old masters laid out their gardens to get in more light. . . They used nature as borders to shelter out the worst of the battling winds, including the mistral, that really vicious wind that sweeps down southern France, which is no joke apparently. I was chatting to Tomas, and it got me thinking that I could apply some of these measures here, give or take a few modifications for sea and our weather. . .'

'That's great. . .' I said with little enthusiasm.

He looked up at my short tone. 'You okay, love?' he asked.

'No. No, I. . . I don't think I am, actually.'

He looked suddenly worried. 'Is it. . . the baby?'

I shook my head. 'No, the baby is fine. Were you offered vice presidency of the Red Agency? And did you decide never to tell me?'

He turned pale.

'Ivy. . . what?'

'Is it true?'

He blinked once, twice. 'Ivy, where has this come from?'

'Just tell me,' I said, my jaw clenched.

His face grew tight. 'The Terrorist,' he said, not a question, just a statement of undeniable fact. Like the sun rising in the west, and the tides going in and out, his mother could always be relied upon to not leave anything well alone.

'My *mother*,' he spat, eyes darkening.

I closed my eyes. So he had deliberately kept it from me. Why?

'Why did you keep it a secret?' I asked, trying, yet failing to keep my voice steady. 'Why would you just decide to keep that from me?'

'I'm going to kill her,' he said through gritted teeth, digging out his phone from the pocket of his jeans.

I snatched the phone out of his hand. 'No, you're going to explain to me why you didn't tell me about it first, and why I had to hear it from your mother. Why she seemed to think that I was responsible for killing not one but two of your dreams.'

He looked shocked. 'She said *that*?'

I gave him a tight smile. 'Not exactly. She phoned to tell me that I shouldn't give up on having a baby when you'd given me everything I wanted. Which isn't exactly fair as you told me that you wanted to move down here and start a new life too. But thanks for making me look like the completely selfish one, that was great,' I said, with dripping scorn. 'Please explain. Why. Did. You. Keep. It. From. Me?' I demanded.

He looked up at the ceiling boards, leant back in his chair and sighed. Then, shoving his hands into his hair in annoyance or frustration, or both, he gazed back at me and shook his head slowly. 'It just didn't matter. You were so excited. It meant we could finally move to Cornwall. . . what we'd been talking about for years. And Dr Tam said that once we were more relaxed, we'd probably have a better chance of having a baby. . . which was true, it seemed a small sacrifice. David Mortimer – the Red Agency's CEO – understood.'

'Oh, the CEO of the Red Agency understood, did he? But obviously, not your wife? I had no say. . . It was just fine for me to be the selfish one, the one whose dreams could come true, while yours didn't?'

Stuart's eyes widened. 'It wasn't like that, Ivy. . . it wasn't selfish, it's what you'd always wanted. So I found a new dream, here with you, and now we're finally going to have a baby – even Dr Harris said that she thought the move was one of the biggest reasons it has finally happened.'

I looked at him. 'And if it hadn't have worked out. . . if I hadn't have fallen pregnant, what then? Would the sacrifice that you never needed to have taken been small then?'

He frowned. 'I didn't marry you so that we could have children, Ivy. Obviously, if it didn't happen I'd have been disappointed, but I would have got over it, and anyway it worked, didn't it?'

Not the right thing to have said.

I shook my head, furious. 'Yes, you'd be the one allowed to "get over it" while I'd be the monster who dashed all your dreams, and as far as your mother is concerned couldn't even be bothered to keep trying to have a child. You couldn't even give me the chance to have a say in what may have been best for both of us. I was absolutely fine living in London. . .'

'No, you weren't,' he said flatly. 'You wanted to come home, you always spoke about it.'

'So what! People speak about things like that all the time, it didn't mean we had to do it! Despite what your mother seems to think, I'm well accustomed to being an adult and not getting every bloody thing I desire. It's give and take, isn't it? Except, of course, not when it comes to me and my "child-like" nature, is it? Where you just get to be the one who makes all the noble sacrifices.'

It wasn't fair to throw Genevieve's words at him, I knew it. But still, perhaps there was some measure of truth in it – particularly in the way Stuart was treating me. You kept information like that from a child, not from your partner. I didn't enjoy the fact that somehow, after everything we had faced, Stuart saw me as someone who could or should be infantalised.

His face paled. 'What? Ivy? It wasn't like that! I just thought that it wasn't the right time to take up the job. . . You, we, wanted to really try for a baby, and I didn't want to be the one signing us up for potentially never having children as a result.'

I pursed my lips. 'It wasn't a binary issue, Stuart. People make these things work all the time. You might have been busy, but you would have been happy, which as Dr Harris said, if you remember, was the major reason she thought that it had finally worked. . . because we weren't stressed. She said that it wasn't because we moved to Cornwall, precisely. But no, you were so sure that I'd have chosen this path for us,' I said, my arms waving to indicate Sea Cottage. 'Did you ever consider that just maybe I never wanted to be the one who made you "just get over" your dreams? That actually I'd much rather be the sort of person who helped make yours come true as well?'

Stuart stood up, cross. 'Has it not occurred to you that's all I was trying to do, for you! After everything you'd been through, miscarriage after bloody miscarriage. Your mum dying. For God's sake, couldn't I just do this for you? The one thing I could control in this fucking world that I could give you!' he shouted.

I stared at him, wordlessly. Then I shook my head, sadly. He just didn't get it.

'But see, that's just it. When you did that, you took away mine.'

'Your what?'

'Whatever little bit of control I might have had to ensure that we both had what we wanted, what we needed – that's what a marriage is, isn't it? I'm not some child that you had to create a bloody womb for,' I said, before turning on my heel.

Before Stuart could follow, I was in my car and half way up the drive.

I took the coastal road down to Cloudsea bay, not registering the flock of gannets as they flew past or the idyllic stretch of golden sand.

Mum was the one I wanted to speak to. The one who would know what to say. How I wished it was 3 a.m. I wished that I could use the postcard now to ask her advice.

Instead I parked my car in the parking lot, along the beach road, and watched the waves crashing, unsure what I thought. My phone rang, and I put it on silent. I didn't know what to think. A part of me should have been furious with Genevieve, a part of me *was* furious with her and her eternal interfering ways, but when she'd pulled the rug out from beneath my feet, she'd also exposed something that I thought I'd never find. . . something that felt like quicksand.

When I returned home hours later, I was grateful to see that Stuart wasn't there, and that he hadn't tried to come after me. He'd left a plate of food in the fridge with a note saying that he was at Tomas's and would be home late.

I hadn't eaten all day but the thought of food turned my stomach. Stuart had made a casserole, and while ordinarily I would have devoured it, right now I knew that it wouldn't sit well. Picturing Dr Harris's disappointed face, I grabbed an apple and a handful of nuts and forced myself to eat, while I fed Muppet, Pepper and Pots.

Muppet seemed to understand my mood; when I entered my studio she climbed onto my lap and closed her eyes, something she hadn't attempted since her puppy days due to her sheer size. I was grateful for her warmth, and her indomitably kind, companionable spirit.

I got to work on Mr Tibbles, knowing that the best distraction was often getting stuck into work, finally able to write and illustrate the part where the old owl Feathershloop dies, and while sitting at his bedside in despair, the Red Fairy comes to Mr Tibbles and tells him that, despite his small size, his courage has proved that he is ready to take over for Mr Feathershloop, and become the protector of the Fairy's Forest.

It was some time later when Stuart came into the studio. I hadn't heard him come in, just felt Muppet start to wriggle in my lap. I followed her gaze but didn't say anything.

He sighed and pulled up a chair. He looked angry.

'I've been trying to call. . .'

I looked away. 'I was cross.'

'That doesn't excuse it. Anything could have happened to you.'

I sighed, 'I didn't want to speak to you. . .'

'You don't have to speak to me, but Ivy, love, c'mon, you can't take off like that. . . these roads aren't great and they say a storm is coming.'

I sighed and looked away. 'They've been saying that for days. It's just this time of year, it will probably blow over, and I would have come back long before. . .'

'You can't know that! Look, you're allowed to be cross, but I don't think it's fair that you just left. If you want me to leave you alone, fine, then just say so. . . but you can't just leave.'

'Oh, I can't "just" leave, is it? But you can keep a secret like that from me. . . for what, ever? Let me think that this whole move was our idea when actually it was you just giving in to me.'

He closed his eyes for a second. 'Ivy, stop. . . I know you think that I was treating you like a child, but I wasn't. The only time you acted like one was today when you ran off!'

My eyes snapped and I opened my mouth to retaliate.

'Just hear me out for a second, please. I know what you think, that I'm some self-sacrificing saint or something, but it's quite the opposite, really.'

'What?' I said in surprise.

He wiped his hand across his mouth in irritation. 'I should have told you, I know that. But I know you too, you would have made us stay. We would have bought the Collingswood House, three bloody roads away from my mother, and we would have lived there until I became president of the Red Agency, or had a heart attack at age forty-five because I was pulling nineteen-hour days because it was "my dream". And it *was* my dream. . . ten years ago. Sure, when you told me about Cornwall, and the life you thought we could have one day, I thought as well that it was something we might do later on. I might not have originally been the one who wanted it, but bloody hell, Ivy, I fell for it too. Every time we came down here, we came alive.'

I looked at him, not ready to trust that he wasn't still playing the 'nice guy' card. 'Your mum said you were excited about the Red Agency, Stuart.'

He nodded, then sighed, 'I was. . . I really was. For about half a day, but I was more excited for the me from ten years ago, you know? When I came home and you told me about the print deal, I just felt like, I don't know, maybe it was a sign. It was me that suggested Cornwall. I know Mum said it wasn't, and you'd suggested it in the past. But I *was* the one who said we should move. That's all I could think about when you told me your news. It meant we could live a life we had only ever dreamt about. I'd always wanted to be a VP, but did I want it more than I wanted to be a husband, or a father? More than what it felt like to sit back and have a cup of bloody coffee without gulping it down? To wake up thinking ideas, ideas, ideas? To go to bed thinking ideas, ideas, ideas. . . To always feel like part of my focus was somewhere else, and to wonder just when those ideas would finally run out?

'I loved it, Ivy, I won't deny it. . . but I love you. I love our life here more. Sometimes, on your way to one dream you find a new one, a better one. One that perhaps is a surprise to everyone, including yourself. I never for a minute might have imagined that I'd be doing this,' he laughed, jerking his head towards the window and the garden outside. 'What did I know about gardening or cooking, except for my part-time hobbies?' He glanced at his brown mud-splattered wellies, and his calloused hands. 'But it's bloody great, and I've never been happier. I didn't tell you, not because I didn't trust you, but because I believed in this one more. It's really that simple.'

I sat back in my chair and let the tears fall. 'You should have just told me that. . .'

'I should have, I know, but I didn't want you to second-guess. I knew you would, if things got tough you'd be worrying if we should have stayed. . .'

'And shouldn't I?'

'No.'

'Just promise me, Mr Everton, no more secrets. . . You need to be able to tell me these things, and if I do sometimes worry that maybe you might regret something, well, that should be my right.'

He nodded, and held me close.

'Stuart.'

'Ivy.'

'Stuart, speaking of secrets. . .'

He gave me a look of mock horror. 'Don't tell me that actually you were offered chief illustrator at Walt Disney and it's based in London?'

I punched his arm. 'Not. Funny. Yet,' I growled. 'No, worse actually. . . I think. It's time we told your mother.'

He let out a massive, groaning sigh.

'You know I'm right.'

He sighed again, then buried his head in Muppet's fur.

'I mean, do you think I want to tell her?'

He looked up and said hopefully, 'No, so why don't we leave it? I mean, do you really want to unleash another *Everton Six: Electroshock therapy?*'

'More like *Everton Nine: Severed finger.*'

He gave me a wounded look. '*Seven: Bullet wound?*'

'Nope. *Nine.*'

His eyes went huge. 'Sorry, my love. But do you honestly want to go through that again?'

I shrugged. 'Your mother is like a deadly virus, Stuart. The longer she's left unattended, the worse it gets. . .'

'True, but she can just go to hell as far as I'm concerned. I'm done, this time for good.'

CHAPTER ELEVEN

Just Bobbins

It started with the book. A practical guide on child-rearing circa 1980 that found its way silently onto the kitchen table, with useful bits highlighted in faded neon yellow, alongside fresh ink scratchings in red, written in the margins; corrections from a pen that didn't know how not to be a little interfering. For instance, next to an opening on teething the red pen said, 'Hogwash. A little bit of brandy rubbed liberally across the gums puts them to sleep and helps calm everyone's nerves. . . just don't advertise it with any "busybodies".'

This controversial advice in a tomb as large as the King James Bible, along with a set of knitted jumpers in shocking pink (how did they know it was a girl, how?), an ageing baby chest of drawers in desperate need of some paint, a fossilised perambulator, and a wooden rattle from another era, had found its way quietly and without much fanfare into our home.

The Thursday Club were making their presence known.

The somewhat controversial book advice belonged to none other than Winifred Jones, who despite her strict, headmistressy persona, could surprisingly display some old-fashioned, superstitious Cornish advice in the margins too, such as 'Whooping cough: pass the child under the belly of a piebald horse'. And, 'Never have even a picture of an owl in the nursery as this is considered a bad omen', which seemed to attest at least to some of the more mythical aspects of our Cornish heritage, as well as another age.

Odd, and outdated as some of the advice may well be, I couldn't fault the kindness that had snuck back into my life, from all of them, and Winifred Jones in particular, with her guide, which must have taken some time. I could only imagine what Catherine would say to some of it. . . then again, she may well agree. Well, not about the whooping cough or owls, at least, I hoped.

It seemed hysterical and sweet that my baby-rearing advice was coming from a group of geriatrics. If anything, it made it all the more dear. Winifred had had a good twenty years on my mum, as had most of the club – apart from May and the lovely Flavia, of course.

But once they'd found out my news, Stuart and I began to notice casserole dishes wrapped up in cellophane, featuring old-fashioned dishes made from scratch, like cottage pie and Yorkshire puddings, magically appearing on our doorstep, with instructions written in Biro to warm in the oven for twenty minutes on a low heat.

Somehow, against the odds, I had discovered not just one mother, but six.

Flavia sent roses, while Abigail sent spa vouchers and a note to say, 'Darling girl, you'll need this, trust me. . . won't get much time for any pampering later.'

Robyn sent iced buns, and *pains au chocolat*; Stuart and I agreed that having a baker for a friend was a sign that we had done some good work in a previous life.

May sent a bottle of whiskey for Stuart, and herself around as often as possible for a cuppa and a bit of a laugh, and we were grateful for both.

Winifred Jones, of course, sent The Book. When I called her to thank her, she just shrugged it off. 'It's nothing, Ivy-girl,' she said. ''Twas just something useful I had lying around, some of it was rubbish. . . you won't believe, so I made a few notes for you.'

I stifled a giggle, my eye falling on the heavy tome, and her many ink corrections. 'Ah – yes, thank you so much.'

'Don't mention it. Look – I know these modern women wouldn't agree. . . it's all about being their "friend" and asking your two-year-old blighter if things are a good idea or not, as a form of discipline.' She snorted, derisively. 'Can you imagine? That's what I heard on the telly the other day. . . they had on some twenty-year-old "Expert Mum" advising you to ask your child if what they are doing is a good idea or not, instead of having a good old-fashioned naughty corner. . . Imagine asking a two-year-old if calling someone a knob is a good idea. . . Can you imagine? He's *two*, course 'tis a good idea!'

I laughed. She had a point.

'Look,' she said sobering, her voice now uncharacteristically less grouchy. 'Everyone's going to have an opinion. . . your job is just to keep your child happy and healthy, everything else is just bobbins. It's what your mum would have done. It's what she always told me when I had an opinion about you. . . and she was right too.'

I sat with my phone in my hand for some time after that call, realising that, somehow, Winifred Jones, the woman who scared me half to death as a child, had suddenly become someone I liked. Perhaps, this was one of the reasons why Mum had made sure I reconnected with The Thursday Club in the first place. Stuart and I had been so busy trying to fall pregnant that a part of me had felt I would be tempting fate if I read any baby books, or tried to prepare myself for the possibility of actually having a child. Now, when Dr Harris told us to trust that this time everything would be all right, I found that I hadn't really prepared for what it would mean to actually have *a baby*. I mean, I didn't even really know what whooping cough was.

Catherine, of course, was just a phone call away, and would no doubt be the one I turned to for more practical, and emotional motherly advice. I wished she lived nearby, but I couldn't deny how grateful, and lucky I was to have these women on my side.

Still I put in an order soon for a few parenting books from this century online, figuring it couldn't hurt. When I came across a book entitled *Now, Stevie, is that a good idea? The New Age Mothering Guide*, I had to laugh, and agree with dear old grouchy Winifred Jones, it did sound a bit daft. Perhaps she was right, everything else was just bobbins.

CHAPTER TWELVE

The Golden Pasty

'Mr Everton,' I said in dismay, entering the kitchen only to find Stuart asleep, with his face resting on an old eighteenth-century cookbook. He was obscured by flour and pastry, surrounded by the littered bodies of discarded Cornish pasties, haphazardly piled on every available surface. I brushed the flour off his forehead, worried.

He opened his tired, red-rimmed eyes – long black eyelashes now white with dust – and sighed. 'I had to try making pasties,' he said, shaking his head morosely, deep in the mire of self-pity.

'You had to try making pasties,' I echoed, shaking my head at him.

He propped his head up on his elbow and slumped. 'But why though? Why did I have to try making pasties? And on the day before the competition?'

I shrugged, smothering my smile. 'Because, well, you're. . . you. Not enough to enter the mince pies – you had to go for gold.'

He gave a long sigh and slumped even further in his chair. 'I wrote before I could spell.'

I nodded. 'You pipped before you could pipe.'

He quirked his eyebrow. 'I sang before there was song.'

'This metaphor abuse could go on a while. . .'

He sighed again, eyes downcast as he considered the piles of discarded pasties. 'You've an excellent point.'

'These look rather nice though,' I said, glancing at four-dozen pasties that looked like they'd come through unscathed.

He gave them a long-suffering look. 'They look all right.'
'But?'

'They are not pasties.'

I raised an eyebrow, picked one up, and took a bite. 'They taste.
. . very close,' I said with a shrug. 'They're quite yummy actually.'

'No cigar. . . they're not your mum's,' he pointed out.

I shrugged. Mum's were indeed rather legendary, but these
were very good. 'You're far too hard on yourself. . . these are
almost perfect.'

'Almost is not good enough,' he replied sadly. He sighed.
'You can't be Cornish and not make a proper pasty.'

I frowned. 'But you're not Cornish.'

He looked at me with wounded eyes. 'Well, technically no,
but spiritually, I am.'

'Ah, I see,' I said with a grin. 'Well, I'm Cornish, er, spiritually and otherwise, and I can't make them.'

He grinned back. 'But that's different.'

'Why?' I asked, nonplussed.

'Because you're. . . you,' he quipped.

'Very funny.'

'And there's always one. . .' he added, eyes amused.

'One?'

'Black sheep in the family.'

'Very amusing.' I narrowed my eyes. 'Come,' I said, lifting
his arm and trying to drag him off the kitchen stool. 'Bed.'

'Bed?'

'Bed,' I agreed.

He followed behind me meekly; looking a little conquered,
and fell asleep almost immediately, bathed in flour.

When I crept into the studio that night, to my surprise there
was already a message waiting for me.

Swede, never. . . ever carrot
Waxy potatoes

Lard and margarine together
Worcester sauce
'Mum?' I asked in surprise. What was this?
Never lost the Cloudsea Christmas Fair competition in my life
Not about to start now
Hurry

I shook my head, laughing aloud, and ran out the room to wake poor Stuart. 'Get up – you've got to try making them again.'

He groaned and snuggled deeper into the pillows. I poked him in the side.

'I've consulted with my mum.'

He wiggled away closer to Muppet, whose tongue lolled onto the coverlet speckled with flour, and from under the mountain of blankets I heard, 'Mmmmh?'

'You used carrots right?'

He turned, painstakingly slowly, and opened a bleary, blood-shot eye in surprise. 'Yes.'

I shook my head. 'You are never ever to use carrots. She was rather horrified. . .'

'She *was*?' he asked, somewhat amused. 'So what did she say to use instead?'

'Swede.'

'Swede?'

'Swede.' I nodded. 'A far better use than for your turnip jam.'

He laughed. 'Swede – I have some that have just come up in the winter patch.'

'Good. You'll also need lard apparently, with margarine and waxy potatoes.'

'Lard with margarine?'

I nodded solemnly.

He stared at me. 'Did you find your mum's recipe. . . her super-secret recipe that she took with her to the grave?' he asked, hopeful.

I gave him a pointed look. 'She never wrote it down, you know that. But let's just say, as you lay there, coating our sheets and dog in flour, I got in touch with my Cornish inheritance.'

'Did you phone May?'

'May is Irish,' I reminded him.

'Winifred Jones?'

'You're joking! She's one of the judges.'

'Robyn?'

'She'd be a good one, but she's entering too. Also, I'm not going to lie, her baking is amazing; her cooking, not so much.'

'Um, pots and kettles?'

'You have a point.'

'Mmmh,' mumbled Stuart, then, 'Flavia?'

'Italian.'

'Abigail?'

'She's American.'

'God, what is The Thursday Club, the bloody United Nations?'

I shrugged. 'Mum felt sorry for all the emmets. Also, she liked to drive Winifred Jones and Mrs Aheary bonkers.'

Stuart laughed. He smiled a sleepy smile and closed his eyes. Suddenly he opened them again, thinking aloud. 'Lard, not shortening. That could work – moist, flavourful. . .' He sat up and gave a heavy sigh as he looked regretfully at our sleeping bulldog. 'Okay, let's do this.'

I opened wide eyes, wrong-footed. 'Let's? As in me and you?'

He laughed. 'You wake me up and tell me to try again. . .' he looked at the bedside clock, 'at three fifteen in the morning and what. . . you thought afterwards you'd just jump into bed and leave me to it?'

I shrugged, with a sheepish grin. The honest answer was, *Yes*. Yes, of course I did. But at his expectant look, I sighed theatrically, like he would, so that he smiled and held out his arm.

We made our way down to the kitchen, where I put on a fresh pot of coffee and Stuart went to fetch potatoes and swede from the vegetable drawer. He got started on remaking the pastry, which, once finished, would need to rest for two hours, but while he waited, he did a test run on the stove for the filling, just to see if the taste would be right.

I fell asleep standing up, my face pressed against the kitchen cupboard. I woke up with a little jolt, to see Stuart preparing the pastry cases.

'Falling asleep on the job?' he asked.

I nodded with bloodshot eyes and poured us another cup. Suddenly I remembered I had forgotten something important. 'Worcester.'

He looked at me oddly. 'Worcester?'

I nodded slowly. 'Yes, sorry, I forgot to tell you about the Worcester sauce.'

His eyes widened, a light seemed to dawn. 'That's it,' he said in wonderment.

'That's it?' I asked.

He nodded. 'I tried everything I could think of. . .'

I gave him a puzzled look, then realised, 'Her secret sauce?'

He nodded. 'How did you know?'

I shrugged. 'Told you, Mum and I had a little chat.'

'Oh really? You just went and chatted to your mum for a bit and she told you about the waxy potatoes and to use margarine with lard and not shortening. Oh, and not to forget her super-secret ingredient, which you almost did.'

'Yup,' I said truthfully.

He shook his head. 'I almost believe you, especially with this,' he said, giving the test pasty filling a taste. 'Perfect, absolutely spot on.'

Then he loaded the pasties with the raw mixture which needed to bake in their pie cases.

Four hours later, nine judges had agreed. We re-entered the competition tent at the Cloudsea Christmas Fair to find not just one, but *two* blue ribbons. One for his mince pies and the other, accompanied by the rare golden ribbon – the highest accolade at the fair – was sitting next to a scrumptious mound of perfect Cornish pasties, making Stuart the only non-Cornish winner to win in the fair's history.

Which was precisely what Juniper Barnsley had to say on the subject when she found out. Her coarse grey hair was scraped back into an all-purpose bun and her boulder-sized arms were ringed with at least a dozen blue ribbons. She looked at Stuart with black gimlet eyes, making it clear that, as far as she was concerned, a non-Cornish winner was nothing to be celebrated. She had reason to be put out though, she explained with a false trilling laugh, as she had won the golden ribbon for the last five consecutive years. 'A fluke,' she commented on Stuart's win, 'but a very lucky one,' she added, in the manner of someone trying, but failing to be a good sport. Her words edged with forewarning that next year we weren't to expect a repeat performance.

It was true that she'd won it for five years, I admitted. Though, as I pointed out rather cheekily and with a smile: much to her annoyance, Mum had won it every single year for at least twenty years before that. So really, now that we had moved back, we were just bringing it home to where it belonged. Her lips compressed into a tight smile and she stomped off without a goodbye.

Stuart laughed and whispered in my ear, 'What do you reckon that next year the competition will only be open to native Cornish citizens after this?'

I shook my head, linking my arm through his. 'I wouldn't be surprised, but I don't think it'll fly.'

'Why not?'

'Well, for one, she'd have to disqualify her own husband.'

'Really? Bill?'

'Oh yes,' I stage-whispered. 'He's foreign.'

'He *is*?' he asked, dark eyes frowning as he straightened to look over at Bill Barnsley across the rows of trestle tables that lined the tent. Bill was helping himself to some of his own prize-winning mulled wine, an air of defeat about his shoulders, while his beribboned wife stood with beefy legs akimbo, gesturing expansively in our direction.

'Oh yes,' I grinned. 'He's from *Devon*.'

Stuart gave me a lopsided smirk. 'Hilarious.'

We went home with the two ribbons, over fifty orders for mince pies, Stuart's first ever fixed culinary contract (with Terry, the owner of Salt, to supply them exclusively with Cornish pasties), and two heads held firmly high.

CHAPTER THIRTEEN

Into the Light

Winter is Cornwall's best-kept secret. The beaches are almost deserted and you can walk for miles on the golden sand with only your thoughts and the jagged coastline for company, surrounded by wild beauty from all fronts. But it's the night-time festivals that herald the light, and like them, in the magic and the moonlight during the dreamlike hour that was meant for Mum and me, I too came alive.

Every night, with bated breath, I rushed to my studio, fearful that the postcard wouldn't write, that our precious sand in the hourglass would run out. But she was always there, as the clock struck three, since that first night.

Not every message was profound, or laced with hidden meaning, yet each one lodged itself in my heart. And so, for the first time in years, Christmas re-entered our lives.

Sometimes, but not always, I got to speak to her as I did on that first night. It was like, somehow, she knew, after my fight with Stuart, how much I needed to speak with her. I told her that I wished that we hadn't have had this argument, that Stuart had simply told me about the job offer he'd gotten, so we wouldn't have had to have gone through that. Or that Genevieve could have just left it alone, and she replied:

Sometimes things have to break before they can mend

*Sometimes, tiny eruptions, from a distance, look like cracks
or breaks in the surface*

*When what has really occurred has just shaped and moulded
what was underneath into something stronger, something
near impenetrable*

*Sometimes in the darkest places the most beautiful things are
formed when pressure is applied*

Like a diamond

Or a heart, tempered by love

'Oh Mum,' I cried, dashing away my tears, 'I would give anything to just hug you right now.'

Her response was so human, so heartfelt, that I truly began to cry.

Me more

I spent all week working on my lantern. I constructed it from paper, light and cut-out stars, creating a mystical heroine for the annual Christmas Lantern Parade, which had been a part of our lives for as long as I could remember. As a school teacher, Mum had played a prominent role in the festivities each year in Cloud-sea and the children had always looked forward to her creations at the Festival of Light that launched the Christmas season.

Taking a leaf out of Mum's book, I had texted Dad Mum's message shortly after our visit with the obstetrician. Short and mysterious: *You'll find it in the cupboard under the stairs.*

What? he'd texted back.

What you're looking for, I responded.

In his typical philosophical fashion, he didn't reply. I'd hoped that he'd actually look; he was just as likely to stand and wait for an epiphany as to rumble through the contents that lurked beneath. But on the day of the parade, when we called past to fetch him, I saw what he had found. All the trees and the borders of the garden path were studded with twinkly lights. The little wreath that Dad had placed on the back door was replaced with the handmade one Mum had made years before. Here, in my childhood home, where for so many years it hadn't come to visit, Christmas had arrived.

I stood on the little cobbled path, a grin plastered across my face. Dad came and gave me a hug; we didn't need to say more as we made our way to the parade with smiles held in our hearts.

The night was filled with lanterns of every shape, colour, and size, dotting the streets with their golden light. We parked on a side street and met Catherine, Richard and the three boys, who would all be forming a convoy as a dragon lantern; they always took part of the celebrations while on holiday with Catherine's father.

'Aunty Ivy,' squealed Ben, large green eyes dancing with excitement, as he raced to me and gave me a hug, 'I'm the head. . . the dragon's head!' he exclaimed in delight, his short red hair shimmering brilliantly in the dim lantern light.

'Aren't you lucky?' I said. He nodded gleefully. I looked at Catherine and had to laugh, eyeing her outfit. 'If you can't beat 'em, join 'em?' I joked, with a raised brow.

She nodded and gave me a wink. She, Richard, and the three boys were all wearing white T-shirts that read 'The Talty Five' in luminous, sequined pink with matching pink tutus.

'I wish Claire Thomas could see you now.'

She quirked a brow, mouth suppressing a laugh. 'I made sure she did.'

I laughed. 'Really, how?'

She grinned. 'Sent a photo of us all on our rather awful "Yummy Mummies" WhatsApp group. . . She must have gone puce, specially as all the other mums had only nice things to say.'

'Good lord, a Yummy Mummies WhatsApp group?' I replied in horror, to Catherine's rather resigned, "'fraid so.'

I laughed, 'Well, good for you!' noting Ben's happy smile as he raced to be at the front in utter boyish delight.

As the Taltys got into position for the parade, Stuart helped me unfurl the lantern I'd spent days creating. Even I didn't know how it would look when we added the light. My mouth parted in surprise as it came alive. The dark tresses of the mythical woman I'd created were transformed, from darkest amber to radiant gold, animated by the gentle breeze. The folds of her dress were made of stars and tiny cut-out owls, and when the light shifted her face rippled in the moonlight and I gasped to see, not Athena, goddess of owlish wisdom, but a face as familiar as my own, and for just a second, I could have sworn she winked.

Dad stood rooted to the spot, his face pale, as if he'd seen a ghost. 'Alice,' he breathed, lifting a hand to touch the whimsical lantern that seemed alive.

'Did you. . . Did you mean to do this. . .?' he asked, Mum's face reflected in his eyes.

I swallowed and shook my head. 'No, not on purpose.'

He shook his head in wonder. 'It's so strange, but this year it's like. . .'

'What?' I asked, laying a hand on his jersey-covered arm. He was wearing his old maroon jersey that Mum had knitted for him years before. He always wore it for the festive season. 'I just feel like she's here,' he said simply, his grey eyes saying so much.

My eyes were bright, laced with tears. I nodded. 'That's because she is.'

That night, when 3 a.m. rolled around, there was a message waiting for me in the moonlight.

Darling Ivy
The sea is hungry, it has many faces
It can't always control them, though it may wish to
Have faith
Show courage
Look for what lies beneath the surface
Sometimes, when we are least expecting it, we encounter a friend

CHAPTER FOURTEEN

Tempests and Teapots

Despite my warnings about deadly viruses left unattended, we hadn't told Genevieve about the baby. Stuart was holding firm that he was done.

I tried to phone her, only to discover that she was away on an international conference in New York for women in finance and wouldn't be available for most of the week as she was overseeing several panel discussions.

I felt a sense of palpable relief even though I knew we were only delaying the inevitable.

Stuart, however, was adamant that he was through with her, perhaps even for good. 'I can't stop you from telling her, but I can't forgive what she did. What she caused, she had no right.' He flat-out refused to tell her about the baby, or to speak to her after the harm she'd caused.

When Genevieve was back, I tried to call the house and got through to Stuart's father instead. Somehow, in all of the drama that his wife had created, I'd overlooked him. I felt a guilty start at hearing his voice. 'Oh sorry, Ivy, she's just having a lie-down,' said John.

I glanced at the receiver in shock. Genevieve, having a lie-down?

'Anything I can help you with, my dear?' he asked in his kind, rather posh voice, which to me always sounded like he came from another era. I could picture him in his sporting whites, while a butler with a name like Harrison shone his golf balls, even though I knew they didn't actually have a butler.

'No, nothing. . . just wanted to have a word.'

'Is this about Stuart?' he asked, surprisingly. Generally, John stayed out of family disagreements to the point when sometimes he would be holed up in his study 'working' when really we all knew that he was simply avoiding his wife and whatever family drama she had created now. When we moved to Cornwall, he practically took up refuge in his study. Stuart said he'd even found him there taking a nap, with the latest John Grisham novel on his lap.

Poor man, it was the first time I'd developed a sort of soft spot for him, and had seen a little of where Stuart and Smudge came from.

'Look, Ivy love, I know she's bruised you both. Genny's always been overly protective of the kids. . . she's such a fighter, it's her best and worst quality. Sometimes she really doesn't know how to stop herself, she so wants the best for them that she'll fight tooth and nail, even against them if she has to. But she'll come round. . . it's best to just leave it, I think. Stuart is the same, and she knows it, even if she fights against it sometimes. And if this is what he wants. . . well, then she must just respect it.'

'What he wants?' I asked, surprised.

'The smallholding. . . look, it bothers her. It shouldn't. He's happy and that's all that matters. But you know, Genny. . . well, she just wants more for him. He finished top of his class, won that scholarship. . . She thinks he's throwing it all away, so she's trying everything she can think of, and it's not working.'

I swallowed hard. 'She even tried to turn us against each other,' I admitted. 'But he's not throwing anything away, I hope you can see that. He's loving what he's doing and he's doing well. And, more importantly, he's happy.'

'I agree,' said John to my surprise. This was the longest conversation we'd ever had, apart from a long, slightly drunken chat on my wedding night.

'I think,' he started, then cleared his throat. 'Honestly, I think he's got his head on straight. What's it all for? I worked sixty-hour weeks when my children were born. I never changed a nappy. Now,' he chuckled, 'some men would think that was heaven, but I missed out on a lot of it. Back then it was the norm, but now, maybe I'm just getting old, but I can't help but think what was it all for? Just because you're good at something doesn't mean you have to devote your life to it. He was miserable in London, now he's happy and making something to be proud of. . .'

I swallowed again; that's what Stuart had been telling me the other night.

As I listened to John I realised I wasn't the one who needed to hear him say this. While Stuart may be his own man, and I doubted anyone could ever truly change his mind once it was made up, sometimes, no matter how old you were, it was nice to hear that at least one of your parents approved of what you were doing.

'Hang on,' I said, 'I'll get Stuart.'

He started to protest; I'd obviously gotten him in a contemplative mood. 'John, I really think it might help him to hear you say it . . . I know it meant a lot to me.'

'Well, all right then, if it'll help,' came John's slightly nervous voice.

I took the phone through to the polytunnel, where I found Stuart poring over his garden plans, no doubt dreaming of summer. Muppet was on his lap. 'Someone on the phone for you.'

His face darkened momentarily. 'It's your dad, don't worry. Think he has something you'd like to hear.'

I handed the phone, which he took with a quizzical expression. 'Dad?'

I stayed just for a moment, while Stuart looked at me; it seemed John was being awkward. 'Tell him what you told me, John,' I said loudly, knowing he'd hear.

Then I watched as Stuart's expression changed. His eyes grew a bit moist. I saw him hold Muppet a little firmer so I left them to speak.

Later, as I made myself a cup of tea and got to work on *The Fudge Files*, I couldn't help my smile as I heard the familiar sound of Stuart's whistling. I peeked out the window and watched him crossing the garden path with the wheelbarrow, a familiar jaunty step in place.

I looked up at the sky, as lightning cracked, and frowned.

That evening my finger began to swell. Like it hadn't in years. Not since I'd lived in Cornwall as a child. I touched it and thought: storm's brewing.

I awoke to a violent sea. A tempest that heralded the storm that blew throughout the village, taking off roofs and upturning trees, travelling through our little town, smashing windows all along Finders Lane, taking the door off Robyn's bakery, and breaking all the windows in my favourite café, Salt, till it swept through to us high up on the hill, tumbled through Stuart's potager, blighting most of his winter crop, and seemed to come to a head with the arrival of Stuart's mother, Genevieve, who arrived shortly afterwards on our doorstep.

Stuart and I had been huddling together in the little downstairs cellar where he had managed to salvage some of his prize vegetables, along with the two cats, Muppet, and our four bantam ex-battery rescue hens, when the doorbell rang. Perhaps it would have been a better idea to remain in the warmth of the cellar with the animals, but in my innocence I followed after Stuart, curious as to who was desperate enough to be out on a night like this.

As he opened the door, it flung wide with the wind to reveal Genevieve, who despite the frenzy outside, the whirling eddies of tumbling debris and the lashings of sideways rain, stood serenely under a black umbrella with a white marble and gold handle, her salt and pepper hair as sleek and dreary as her expression. Her red lipsticked mouth folded in upon itself, just as her manicured eyebrows shot up.

She had eyes only for me. With the wind billowing into the doorway it was like standing in front of several high-speed blowers. All of which seemed to be pasting my clothes to my frame, and I watched as her eyes raked my body and fell on my now conspicuous baby bump.

She pursed her lips. And set down a suitcase which I hadn't noticed before. It was frightfully large, and ominous.

'Well, well,' she said. A mix of a thousand emotions flashed across her face: pain, anger, and something I didn't recognise. I felt a shiver of guilt watching her try to process it, while trying to pull my T-shirt away from my body in a useless attempt to cover up what she had already seen, wishing I'd just gotten through to her the previous week.

Finally she looked from me to Stuart and said coldly, 'So, were you ever actually going to tell me?'

I opened my mouth in an attempt to form some sort of explanation but no words came out. When I looked at Stuart, he was just as speechless.

At our feet, Muppet, who had followed after us, began, very uncharacteristically, to growl.

'Well, I hope that when the baby comes you'll get rid of *that*, at least,' she said with a nod to Muppet.

'Stop it,' I said to Muppet. 'No, we won't,' I told Genevieve.

'Dogs are dangerous,' said Genevieve.

'So are people,' I said.

'What?' she said, eyes narrowing. Then, not to be distracted, she hissed, 'Never mind the bloody dog, why didn't you tell me?' she continued, rounding on Stuart.

'Because you would be like. . . this,' he said truthfully. 'And honestly, Mum, Ivy just doesn't need the stress, especially after what you put us through the other day,' he added pointedly. 'Did you not get my message? I'm done with whatever silly little dramas you want to enact with my family.'

I looked at Stuart. *What* message?

Genevieve's eyes narrowed. 'Yes, your message – it's why I'm here. . . I thought I'd come to make amends. Can you imagine? I felt bad when all I was trying to do was help. But this. . .' she said, pointing to my stomach, 'is too much. "Ivy doesn't need the stress" of WHAT? Having her mother-in-law know that she is about to have a grandchild? Well, I'm sorry, my dear, if that is stressful for you, just to pick up a telephone, or get your husband here to tell his only family that you are about to have a child after years and years of trying. After me trying everything I could think—' She stopped.

Her eyes seemed to X-ray me; I could see her mentally calculating the rough number of weeks. Her face grew paler still. Then her hands shook as she realised. I closed my eyes as she hissed, 'You *knew*! All this time that I've been calling. . . when I asked you to come to London, to send my driver, no expense spared. . . you were *already* pregnant. Then when I phoned you again, you just brushed me off. You actually lied to me! I don't believe it. Why would you do it, why would you be so cruel?' she asked, looking from me to Stuart. Her eyes filled with tears and her iron helmet of hair seemed to sink somewhat. 'Why?'

I felt awful. 'Genevieve, it wasn't like that, I promise.'

'So you didn't know back then?' she asked, almost hopefully.

I bit my lip. 'I. . . that is. . . yes, we did, but you don't under-stand. . .We had to keep it a secret.'

Her face grew pinched. She stood up straight. 'The baby was at risk, so you didn't want to tell me in case our hopes were raised?'

I looked down.

Stuart took a step forward. 'Yes, and no. Mum, we didn't want this,' he said, raising his hands wide to indicate the ugly scene before us, of hurt feelings, lies, and turmoil.

'I see,' she said, taking a deep breath and looking past us. 'So it wasn't that you wanted to spare our feelings, it was just that you didn't want me here, being a nuisance.' She nodded then knelt down and picked up her bag. 'You'd rather have that dog than a granny. . .'

'Mum, God, you always do this! Stop making this so dra-matic,' said Stuart, grabbing her bag from out of her hands. 'First of all, you aren't going anywhere in this bloody storm,' he said, slamming the door and bolting it behind him while the wind howled and rattled.

'Second, we do want you as a granny. . . we just want to actually get through this bloody pregnancy without you driv-ing us all mad, okay? Deny it as much as you want, but the last time. . . well. . .'

'The last time I hired you a nurse! It should have been won-derful!'

'It would have been if you'd have done it when the baby was actually there and with our full consent, not to babysit my bloody wife!' shouted Stuart.

Genevieve blinked in shock. Her mouth shook. 'Fine, if that's how you feel, I'll just go.' It was then that I realised just how tiny she really was.

I'd spent years building her up in my mind as such a formi-dable figure, wary of the raging storm that seemed always to be just beneath the surface. It was then that I understood Mum's message.

I closed my eyes and recited it under my breath:

The sea is hungry. It has many faces
It can't always control them, though it may wish to
Have faith
Show courage
Look for what lies beneath the surface
Sometimes, when we are least expecting it, we encounter a friend

Was she trying to tell me something else? I'd thought that perhaps her message had been a warning about the storm, but it hadn't made sense. How was the storm going to be my friend? But now. . . seeing Genevieve's stricken face, I realised, she'd been talking about Stuart's mother.

When John checked out and ran away to his study, Genevieve was the one who was more often than not both mother and father. She was hard, often just plain obstinate and completely ruthless at times, but she loved her children, passionately. Of that I had no doubt.

She wasn't my mum, and I needed to stop comparing her. It wasn't fair, and it did neither of us any good. Not me, not Stuart, and not Genevieve. I knew that there were still likely to be many, many more fights after this and that she'd never be the one I turned to for a hug and cup of tea, or be someone I could go on holiday with, without wanting to shut myself into a sensory deprivation tank for a month afterwards until I regained my energy and stopped hearing the high-pitched whirring of my jangled nerves. Despite all that, despite our vast differences and personalities, she wanted what we wanted, and had been trying so very hard in her own pugnacious way to help us get it. Even when she told me about what Stuart had kept from me, in a weird, rather beastly way she *was* trying to help. Mum was right: at the heart of it all, deep, very deep down, she was a friend. She was just that one that you sometimes wanted to tip out the window.

I put a hand on Stuart's arm and shook my head. 'No,' I said. He looked at me in shock. 'What?'

I picked up Genevieve's bag and said, 'You are not going anywhere. Don't you know you've got a really important job to do?'

She frowned at me. 'What do you mean?'

I grinned. 'Well, Genevieve, it turns out that you're going to be a granny. Now, I'm sorry we didn't tell you before, but I was going to tell you this week, but you were away at that conference in New York.'

I saw her eyes smart. It looked a little like she was fighting two sides of herself. Like a sea, fighting against the tide, I could see part of her wanted to defend herself.

'So I suggest,' I added, giving Stuart a look, 'that we put all of this behind us. It was wrong of me not to have told you, because I was afraid of how you might act. . .'

She took a breath. 'Just as it was wrong of me to imply that you did something to lose it the last time. I blame myself and that's the truth, if. . .' she took a shuddering breath, 'if I hadn't have interfered, and got that horrid nurse, maybe you wouldn't have gotten yourself so stressed. . .'

I touched her arm. 'It's not your fault. Pregnant women feel stress. . . it's normal, a small bit of stress like that wouldn't have caused that. . .' To my own surprise, I found myself reassuring her, finding as I spoke the words how true they were.

'We're on the same team here, Genevieve, just, I know it's hard. . . because you're. . . well, very used to being in charge, but. . .'

'I'm more like co-captain?' she said, making a joke.

Stuart grinned, 'Sorry Mum, that's my job, you're the. . .'

'Granny,' I supplied.

She closed her eyes, and bit her lip. When she opened them she looked younger, less severe. 'That's plenty.'

I grinned. 'So tell you what, let's all get ourselves down to the cellar to wait out this storm, shall we? And I'll tell you all about your grandchild and just how big she is.'

Genevieve gasped. 'It's a girl?'

We each shared massive grins. Outside, the storm waged on, but for now, we were exactly where we wanted to be.

CHAPTER FIFTEEN

Friends, Floods, and Fare Thee Wells

Genevieve stayed for four days and three nights. In many ways she was the model guest. Despite the fact that her phone rang constantly as her company flailed hopelessly without their captain.

No one was more surprised than I when she put it on silent and said, 'They can just bloody well wait, or figure it out themselves. . .'

She listened attentively as I told her about Dr Harris and the progress of the baby. I didn't know what it must have cost her to ensure that she never uttered a word against our obstetrician's rural pedigree.

She made a half-hearted attempt to get me to see an obstetric friend, but stopped herself, shaking her head. 'Sorry, no . . . this, er, doctor has gotten further than any of the others and the fact that she actually burst into tears of happiness when it finally happened, well. . .' She twiddled her watch. 'You can't buy that, can you?'

I shook my head in wonder at her. 'No, you can't,' I agreed.

Still, she sighed every time she passed the window, her eye falling on the garden outside, while Stuart tried his best to salvage what remained of his winter crop.

There were nineteen squabbles. Five mentions of the Collingswood House. Three mentions of the job at the Red Agency.

Two occurrences of slamming doors (me). Seven apologies and two occasions in which I escaped to May Bradley's house for a much-needed breather. At these moments, each time Muppet came along too.

I believe that Genevieve's comment about the benefits of having a Labrador – a real 'walking dog' as opposed to a dog that slept more than it spent time awake – had even offended her rather indomitable canine sensibilities.

May was turning out to be a great, sympathetic friend.

Her house, like May herself, was ever so slightly wacky. Painted a deep blue, she had mosaicked it in blue, white, and yellow tiles, so that it looked like something out of a Moroccan bathhouse. The locals referred to it as 'May's Mad House' in a proud sort of way, like she might be *weird*. But she was *their* weirdo, dammit.

She was constantly working on some or other knitting project. Her hands always busy, but now even more so, as The Thursday Club made it their mission to get through as many jumpers and animal jerseys as they could possibly manage in light of the recent storm, which had resulted in the largest flood in Cloudsea history.

Luckily, May's house, like mine, was built higher up on the hill so it had survived the storm relatively unscathed. 'That battle-axe driving yer mad?' she asked, looking up from her sewing, peering over pink-rhinestoned glasses that perched at the end of her long nose, as I pounded up the stairs and came into her living-cum-sewing room that was dominated by a large, dark wood table with space for exactly seven chairs. You never needed to knock when you came over as she could see you coming from a mile away from the span of windows.

Shelves lined the walls and on every available surface bolts of fabric, yarn, needles, and spools of thread sat companionably in a helter-skelter fashion. On one small fold-up table close to the main one was a kettle, toaster, assorted cups, and biscuits. May was a great believer in biscuits. Which was perhaps why at a young age I was a great believer in May. . .

'Yeah,' I sighed, Muppet at my heels.

'You too?' she asked, giving Muppet a look.

I laughed. 'Apparently, she sleeps too much.'

May sighed. 'As if you hadn't any right,' she said in her lyrical brogue, with a shake of her head at Muppet. She patted the seat next to her, and Muppet and I both took it.

'But yer good to mend the fences and all, sure me and me own mam-in-law was at each other's throats fer half our lives. . . Then when she was gone, can yer believe I missed the old goat? Used to go and see her up at the old age home in Doolin, asked her to move in with me and everything.'

'Really?' I said in shock, as she switched on the kettle to put on a pot of tea. She laughed, as she brought down two old chipped mugs from the dresser and plopped a bag of Miles tea into each. 'She told me ter go feck it.'

'She didn't?'

'Ah, well, she was right. . . we'd have half killed each other in a matter of weeks, ta be sure. Lookit, it's never easy, is it? Sometimes ye get lucky, like me sister Susie, she liked her mam-in-law better than our own mam, though hardly surprising as ours was a right bollocks.'

She made a hand-holding-a-bottle gesture to her lips. 'Liked her cups, did me old mam, but she had seven kids. . . I mean, now that I think about it, I mean, who wouldn't? Bred like rabbits in those days, bless 'em.'

I laughed again.

'It was a different time back then . . . Times were hard, ah shame, sure she tried her best, we was loved, that's what's important I always think. . . and yer mam-in-law, she loves yer, that's why she drives yer so mad.'

I couldn't argue there.

I took a sip. 'This is us getting on,' I said with a grin. 'I've decided for the sake of our relationship that when I'm near that point of wondering if I could sell her to a wandering gypsy and I start to wish to God one would come past, that it's time to get some fresh air. . . Yesterday, that only happened three times, so you know, it's progress.'

May patted me on the hand. 'Aye, that it is,' she said with a nod. 'Why don't yer stay fer supper. . . stretch it that little bit longer? Sure yer hubby will understand. . . I mean, we can say that yer helping me with this here jumper, and yer could actually feckin' do it fer once, yer lazy arse!'

I giggled, and picked up a set of needles. 'You're a hard taskmaster, May Bradley,' I said with a fake sigh.

May shrugged and gave the dog a wink. 'But don't yer worry, we won't tell anyone about yerself. Get yer shut eye, sure, but you'll be needing it fer later.'

I could swear Muppet gave her a grateful look before she promptly fell asleep.

Seeing the destruction that the flood had wrought on the town was heartbreaking. I'd never seen anything like it before. The storm had washed away roads, swept into homes, eaten up paths, and left many stranded. Some of the worst affected were in our village, people with businesses, like our friend Terry, the owner of Salt, whose entire kitchen was sitting in three feet of water.

Water that, really, had nowhere to go. So it just sat, a living thing, twirling itself around the ankles of buildings, like a cat.

The Blumes' pub, The Cloud Arms, stood empty. They had sunk all of their savings into restoring the fine old Grade II listed building that dated back to Tudor times, only to see much of their efforts washed away. It was heartbreaking to see April looking so lost. Even her bright magenta hair seemed to have lost its customary sheen as I came past. ''Tis a fine pre-Christmas present, isn't it?' she said sadly, as I offered her a cup of tea from a flask.

'You won't leave though, will you?' I asked. It would be hard to imagine the village without the Blumes, or the cheery warmth that was The Cloud Arms.

She shrugged. 'I don't know. . . honestly. . . thanks love,' she said, handing me back the cup and following her husband Jeff back into the pub, as he and a group of men carried some of their things out into a nearby van.

Stuart and I traversed the waterlogged path together, our wellington-clad feet not able to withstand the ever ready eddies of water, which entered the gaps at the tops of our shins, turning our toes numb with cold.

Mrs Aheary passed us by. 'Told you there was ter be a storm, though none of us could have predicted this. I'm sure we'll have to close up shop for good now,' she said, jerking her head towards the post office up the lane, which alone had remained impervious to the storm's assault.

I shook my head. How she could moan when the rest of the village looked the way it did was beyond me. Still, I'd never ignore her storm warnings after this though, that was for sure.

We passed by Bess Willis, the owner of the launderette, giving her a sympathetic look as she attempted to guide Gertrude Burrows, Cloudsea's geriatric busybody, back up the hill and away from the swirling water that could knock a rhinoceros off its feet, while she moaned, 'I'm not bloody feeble, just let me go. . . Been through more floods than any of you lot. . .'

We found Terry standing outside Salt, a massive figure with his crimson beard and hair, arms crossed, his grey eyes reflecting the hungry torrent that sucked at the town.

He greeted us with a sad smile. 'We won't know how bad it is until the water recedes, and no one knows how long that will take.'

It was strange to see the café so empty. The armchair that I always sat in by the fire with Muppet while I planned out my schedule for the day over a cup of Terry's finest cappuccino and a slice of one of his mouth-watering cakes, or scones with Cornish clotted cream and strawberry jam, was shoved on top of a table at a precarious angle. Even from here I could see that the velvet was ruined. I felt a sense of indefinable loss.

'You will carry on though, Terry, won't you?' I asked, tremulously, heartbroken at the idea of so many businesses like the Blumes packing it in.

Stuart clapped Terry on the back. 'We're here to help if you need us. . . We hope you won't go.'

Terry rubbed his eyes. 'Aye, I suppose. . .' He gave us a rueful grin. 'You know us Scots don't give up. . . pretty much, ever. But I have no idea how I'm going to do it. Most of me team has had to go. I couldn't afford to keep them on without an income, and in two weeks' time there's the New Year's Harbour festival, which I'm supposed to cater.'

He pointed towards the ruined kitchens. 'Though how I'm going to do it without a kitchen and no staff is beyond me.' He ran a hand through his hair, then looked suddenly at Stuart. The two of them shared a smile. 'Unless. . .'

'Unless?' said Stuart with a wide grin.

'Well, you'd really be helping me out, mate. . . I've tried your stuff, it's amazing! I can handle the bigger things like the roasts, but how would you feel about doing the canapés? We can discuss the terms later, but let me know, think about it. . .'

Stuart shrugged. 'Nothing to think about. Count me in,' he said, and the two shook hands, Terry looking a lot happier than when we first arrived.

As we left, Stuart wrapped his arm around me, and we squelched off while he tried out various canapé suggestions on me.

'How about tripe with pak choi jelly?'

'You're joking?'

He chortled. 'No, okay, I'll leave out the jelly, tripe is a delicacy.'

'Mr Everton, let's not make Terry regret his decision.'

Stuart shot me a mock offended look. 'Terry is Scottish, they eat sheep's stomachs. . .'

'Good point, but as I'd prefer that you both to stay in business, may I make a suggestion?'

He turned to me, lending me his ear. I poked him in the ribs. 'Yes?'

'Well,' I said, scanning the horizon. 'How about crostini and goats' cheese?'

'Oooh, with spinach?'

'Definitely.'

'Also, quiche.'

'Quiche,' he said, eyes lighting up. 'Oh yes, with some of my turnip jam?'

I sighed. Sometimes there was just no use arguing.

The village rallied together to do what it could to help.

Abigail Charming, the American heiress and owner of the Senderwood Estate, who lived in my old village in Tremenara, let out all her rooms to the families, free of charge. Meanwhile Robyn Glass attempted to bring as much cheer as she could by supplying the children and adults with a steady stream of muffins, iced buns, and bread.

The rest of us did what we could, bringing along food and spare blankets, opening up our homes and inviting friends and families to ride out the flood in spare rooms and attics. Some people were living in caravan parks while they waited to see what the damage to their homes had been. When finally the waters had receded, town planners, engineers, and all manner of experts began working on the problem, trying to see what had caused the freak flood, with part of the problem apparently being the ageing sea wall.

Some people like the Greens, who were hardest hit, simply left, abandoning their cottage, and leaving word that they would be considering selling when the weather finally improved.

'It's already driven down property prices,' said Robyn when I caught up with her and May in her lime green van, which they'd dubbed the 'Cat Napper' as they trawled the streets looking for any animals that had gone into hiding or lost their way. 'People forget about the animals,' she added sadly. 'They'll come together, bring soup and bread for the families, but the animals so often get left behind. . . The same thing happens during war.'

'But surely not here in our village,' I said in shock, thinking of how animal-friendly it was. Salt, along with most of the establishments, was supremely welcoming to pets; it was one of the reasons we felt so at home.

'Yer would be surprised,' said May, giving John Usett, the hardware store owner, a sour look as we drove past. 'Himself there had a dog stuck in the garden behind the shed, still tied up. Sure that old goat had been in and out of that garden seven feckin' times. I saw him meself, while I was helping Fiona Bream – his neighbour – ta move her couches out to the dry, so it's not like he didn't see the dog, but he just left. Didn't come back the whole day. That's when Fiona broke in and rescued him – shivering wreck he was. The vet said that if it had gone any longer the dog would have died of cold. As it is they don't know if he'll keep the limb. He tried so hard to free himself, tore the ligaments right out.'

I gasped. John Usett had always been a bit of a crabby man, but I never imagined that it ran to cruelty. I certainly would think twice about getting anything else from him at the hardware store from now on. . .

After that, with Muppet coming along for the ride, I helped them search for any abandoned or lost animals. Luckily most people had made sure to get their animals to safety, but there were a few that had gone missing. Like Flavia's cat, Massimow.

Flavia was the Italian rose expert, and one of the members of The Thursday Club, and it hurt to see her so devastated. 'A week before the flood, the handle broke on the cat carrier. So I throw it away, thinking I would get a new one soon. Then zis happen. We couldn't keep Massimow in the car, and we were in and out getting all our things when he disappear. We've looked everywhere,' she said with tired eyes, exhaustion etched on her pretty face.

I shrugged off my jacket and put it over her. 'You're freezing, Flavia,' I said. 'Don't worry, get in the van.' I poured her a cup of cocoa from the flask we'd prepared. 'We'll find Massimow.'

She seemed reluctant to take my jacket. May winked at her. 'Sure, Massimow would have found himself a nice warm spot by now, my love. Cats are clever creatures who don't like to suffer, don't be getting yerself a chill now.'

Flavia gave May a grateful smile, and shrugged into the jacket, new hope in her eyes. 'Do you really think 'e is somewhere safe?' she asked.

'I do,' I said. I thought of Pepper and Pots, who had been hiding beneath our home when we moved in, then frowned, remembering something. 'Flavia, you didn't always live here, did you? When I was young I seem to remember a house, closer to Mum's, about ten minutes away?'

She nodded. 'Oh yes, many years ago, we had a cute leetle cottage, covered with *rroses*. . . I used to walk to your mother's house from zere, it was that close.'

I nodded and gave May a look. 'Did you have the cat when you lived there?'

'Yes, we'd just gotten 'im. . . such a sweet leetle kitten, was 'is first home.'

'Really?' I asked. 'It's not too far away. . . I wonder,' I added.

Flavia looked at me, her face suddenly changing. 'You think 'e'd go zere?' she said in surprise.

I shrugged. 'It's possible, cats are quite territorial and there's a good chance that he sought out the last place that he felt safe. . .'

Fifteen minutes later when we rounded on the house and knocked on the door, an older woman with a blue rinse, plump arms, and a kind smile opened the door. 'Flavia?' she said in surprise, then she started to laugh. 'Ah, perhaps then that explains this,' she said, welcoming us into the warm interior, where a roaring fire was going in the cottage's open hearth, in front of which dozed a very sleepy-looking cat, who opened one eye curiously at the sound of intruders, then quite suddenly bolted straight into Flavia's arms.

'He showed up here last week. We've asked all the neighbours but no one knew who he was. . . I never imagined for a second he'd be yours. I mean, what's it been. . .' she said in surprise, 'ten years?'

Flavia nodded, tears in her eyes.

Robyn winked. 'Like we said, cats are clever.'

Having Genevieve to stay that week was good for other reasons, though she wasn't all that into animal rescuing. But, once she'd seen and heard all the orders coming through for Stuart, who had been called in to help relieve the chef at the pub in the neighbouring village, and was receiving orders from as far as the Latria Hotel in St Ives, she was beginning to see at last that he was doing well.

She even said, 'You're not as full as you used to be.'

'Are you saying I've lost weight, Mum?' asked Stuart, his brown eyes amused.

'Must be all these vegetables. . . I mean, honestly, beetroot jam? Have you not heard of strawberry?' she said with a wry twist to her mouth.

I bit my lip, and tried not to laugh. Stuart looked at me, suspiciously. 'Did you put her up to this?'

I shook my head. 'Nope, but you can't deny, your mother has a point.'

Stuart rolled his eyes. 'No taste, the lot of you!' he laughed, throwing on his jacket and heading out the door to see Tomas about flood-proofing his potager. It seemed the old Frenchie had a plan for preventing such occurrences.

In the afternoon, Genevieve and I went shopping. Having someone on hand who had given birth in relatively modern times was hugely helpful. I found to my surprise that she was quite practical. I had her figured for the type who would spend hundreds of pounds because the sales clerk let us know it was the best pram on the market, but instead she simply compared features with features and showed me (and yes, the sales clerk too), several models that had the exact same offerings. 'The only advantage on this one, Ivy dear,' she said, pointing at a rather lovely red one, 'is the commission that it would no doubt line this person's pockets with. On the other hand. . .' she whispered, 'it *is* the prettiest.'

Which was when I discovered that she could also be a little bit fun. So we got it anyway.

No one was more surprised than Smudge when I phoned to tell her that me and The Terrorist were getting along. 'You're kidding?' she said. 'It would be like having peace in the Middle East.'

'I'm not sure we were ever that bad. . . and it could happen.'

'What, peace in the Middle East?'

'Well, both.' I laughed. 'How're you doing? How's the research? I meant to come see you but with the flood, things have been mad here.'

'I know, I'm so sorry, it's so sad. I've been in Falmouth this past week, luckily it wasn't hit as badly. . .'

I snorted. 'So you've been sort of in the area and you didn't come to visit your mum?'

She laughed. 'Ah, I know! I just can't. She'll pry and ask about Mark and me, and I don't have an answer right now.'

'Oh Smudge, you don't have to have everything figured out right away.'

'But I do. . . in a way. God, I didn't want to tell you over the phone but well, I think he's having an affair. Or he's about to maybe, I don't know.'

'What?!' I gasped in shock.

Mark wasn't my favourite person, but I never thought he'd *cheat* on Victoria.

'Are you sure?'

'Not really, I saw a few texts. . . I know I shouldn't have looked but he was being weird. There's some trainer from the gym he's mentioned a few times, she's been putting him through his paces – I mean, Mark, the gym?' She laughed but there was no humour in it. 'The messages weren't explicit but there's something going on. . . flirty, you know. . .' she added, her voice catching. 'I mean, what did I expect? I'm never home.'

'That's not an excuse!'

'Yeah, but it's reality, something I've got to face. We haven't spoken about it though, not yet.'

'Why not?'

'I'm just tired. God, that sounds pathetic, but it's the truth. I don't know how to explain. When I saw it, I just wasn't up for another epic fight, had to catch a flight here for work, so I just left. It seems all we do when we see each other is fight, even without bloody, pretty personal trainers involved. I mean, he's finished up in Rome now, and he wouldn't come down here, doesn't want to be "my little tag-along" as he put it the other day. He never used to be like that, I thought it was that he. .

. you know, gets a bit funny about my work, but now, well, maybe it's because he wanted to be with her.'

I swallowed. This was bad. 'You can't know that though. . .'

'I know – I go back in a few days, will deal with it then. Though, I may just go to that gym and see Miss Thing for myself.'

'Do *not* do that,' I warned. 'That could be a recipe for a disaster. . .'

She sighed. 'See, this is why you are my sister, if only to help me avoid prison. When is The Terrorist leaving?'

'Tomorrow morning.'

'Ah okay, so I'll come for dinner then, all right?'

I laughed. 'All right – I'll help you come up with a plan of attack.'

'Oh, on the gym bunny?' she said.

I giggled. 'Er, no. . . for Mark. I'm thinking drawn and quartered. . .'

She snorted. 'I like what you're thinking. See you tomorrow – oh, but Ivy, don't tell Stu till I'm there, 'kay? He'll go crazy. . .'

'Please, I'm not stupid. He threatened to put Mark in hospital the last time he forgot to fetch you from the train station. . . can you imagine what he'd do now? On second thoughts, maybe that bastard deserves it. . .'

'Maybe, but still. . . See you tomorrow.'

I hung up, cradling the phone to my chest. Poor Smudge. Forget Stuart, I was ready to go there and wring Mark's bloody neck myself. I knew he was a whiny arse, but I hadn't thought he was a right cheating bollocks to boot.

That night, as I entered the studio, a sound made me jump. 'Ivy? Is that you?' came Genevieve's voice from behind.

I startled.

That strange light that always accompanied the postcard lit the studio. I looked at it in fear, then back at Genevieve, wondering if she saw it.

'Why are you up so late?' she said. 'Please don't tell me that you're working? I heard you walk past my room as I was sending off a report.' She gave me a pointed look that seemed to imply that if that was my plan it was a bad one.

I sighed. If I said yes, she'd lecture. I was in no mood for it. And the postcard wouldn't wait forever, either. I swallowed my impatience, and just said, 'No, I, er. . . heard my mobile ringing and thought maybe I left it in the studio. . .'

'Oh,' she said, turning to enter the studio, to my horror. 'I'll help you look.'

'No, no, that's fine. Go back to sleep, you've got a long drive tomorrow.'

'That's okay, James is fetching me, I'll be able to get some sleep then.'

I sighed. James, her poor abused assistant, seemed to think nothing of driving five and half hours straight to come and fetch her.

I closed my eyes in annoyance as she entered the room. The light from the postcard was still shining bright. I held my breath, but she didn't mention it. Next thing, she switched on the lamp, and the light from the postcard faded completely.

'That's better,' she said, her eyes scanning the studio. I felt a lump form in my throat, while I resisted the urge to scream. To demand that she get out. But she simply started rummaging through my things, lifting up drawings and sketches. She looked up, saw my face and faltered. 'Don't worry, Ivy, we'll find it. I'm sure it's nothing.'

My voice shook as I asked, 'What's nothing?'

'The phone call. If it was serious, I'm sure they'd try Stuart too. Tell you what, let me get my phone and ring yours. . . then we'll hear it,' she said, then rummaged in her bathrobe, pulled out her phone, and started to ring mine.

I tried to smile. She was being kind but all I wanted to do was tell her to get the hell out.

'It's okay, Genevieve,' I managed. 'Let's just go to sleep.'

We heard the phone ringing from the bedroom. On the night-stand, where I left it, and Stuart's voice from the receiver, sounding tired but worried. 'Mum? Where are you, what's wrong?'

'Oh nothing, love, sorry,' she answered. 'Ivy thought she heard her phone ringing in the studio, we were looking for it, must have been in the room then.'

My eye crept towards the postcard. No light shone from it now, just the cold light from the bright fluorescent lamp.

'You okay?' asked Genevieve, a worried look creasing her forehead.

I nodded, fixing a smile in place with what felt like screws. But I wasn't okay. Mum had come every night since that first night, but how long would it last? All I wanted to do was wait. Wait to see if she'd come back, but Genevieve led me slowly and carefully out.

'I'll make us some chamomile, shall I? It always helps me sleep,' she said. Her offer of a cup of tea to help me fall back asleep right then seemed more insult than comfort. I tried with every step that she led me down the stairs to stop thinking like that, to stop wishing she'd just get out of my house. Stuart's living, interfering mother, who right then was preventing me from spending the precious, magical time that my own had somehow managed to find for us. I was grateful in the dark kitchen that she couldn't see the tears that had begun to form and burn their way down my throat.

In the morning, I awoke feeling better than I had the night before, but grateful nonetheless that Genevieve would be leaving that day. I knew that last night all she had been trying to do, really, was help. She'd been kind, even. But it was the first time her presence had truly stung, though for once through no fault of her own.

Later, Genevieve and I took the rest of the things we'd bought and put them in the cupboard in the nursery. Now without the company of ghosts I could value the time she'd spent with us. Just having her here to help us get started on the baby's room had helped.

When I rolled out the cans of paint I'd ordered though, I saw her frown.

Of course she had ideas about the colours we should paint it. Seeing the tins of black paint I'd bought, however, it looked as if she might faint. 'Don't worry, this is just the base coat,' I said.

'O-kay.'

I waited. Counted to one, two, three – impressive. Then: 'Base for what exactly? I mean. . . I'm sorry but you're a children's book illustrator, why on earth would you want to paint your child's room black?' she finally exploded.

I stifled a laugh. 'Ah you know, just to be a bit different. . . I'm sort of tired of how light and fluffy my day job is. . . I mean, this will be soothing afterwards, I think. I mean, it is me who will have to be here most of the time so it should reflect what I like, right? I mean, it's just so old-fashioned to have the nursery be more about the baby than the mother, don't you think?'

Her mouth opened and closed in shock.

'I'm kidding!' I explained. The poor woman had turned an odd shade of purple. So I hastened over with my watercolour drawings of Mr Tibbles in the Fairy's Forest, complete with glittering fey folk, fairy lights, Feathershloop the owl, the Red Fairy, all of which were rather enchanting looking, if I did say so myself.

'I'm going to do this,' I said with a smile.

Her mouth fell open again. She clutched my arm. 'Oh my goodness, it's beautiful!' she cried. Looking up at her, I was alarmed to see a faint outline of tears. Genevieve had a whimsical side? 'It's so magical. . . Ivy, this is wonderful.'

Then she laughed. 'God, for a second I thought. . .'

'Goth baby?'

She grinned. 'Something like that. But this is lovely,' she said again, scanning the drawing. 'Is this a new project?'

'Not really,' I said, then told her about Mr Tibbles. 'He was sort of a secret project for a while. . . Something to help, you know, when things were a bit tough. . .'

She bit her lip. 'I'm sorry about what I said the other day, about your work being child-like. I didn't mean it. I was just lashing out.'

An *apology* from Genevieve?

Then she looked at me and shook her head. 'I don't think he should be kept secret,' she said, touching Mr Tibbles, who was looking rather fetching with his raincoat on, and a pair of flying goggles. 'He's just too adorable,' she added with a genuine smile making her look so much younger for it, and I found my eyes starting to well up.

'What a fun home my grandchild is going to be coming into, with parents like you two. You know, my own mother was a hard woman. I used to draw, just a hobby, you know. . . nothing like this. . . She always wanted me to be busy: "Make yourself useful, Genevieve," she'd say. She grew up after the war, they had to be very practical. Any time any of us kids were doing anything that she felt was a waste of time she'd put us to work. It's only now, as an adult, that I realise maybe I carried a bit of that with me when I became a parent too.'

When she left, I gave her a hug. It was the first time I'd ever done that.

When Smudge came over, I poured her a glass of wine while she filled us in about her and Mark, telling Stuart to keep calm as his face grew pale, and when he looked ready to kill.

'Oh sit down,' she told him with a laugh as he jumped out of his seat in rage.

'I phoned Mark. . .' she told me. 'After I spoke to you, I don't know. . . It was like a rush of fire to the brain or something, decided to just rip the bloody plaster, you know.'

We both nodded. Stuart was sitting gingerly near the open fireplace, where Muppet snored on, oblivious.

'Of course, he denied it. . .'

'That lying bastard!' exploded Stuart.

Muppet opened an eye, then turned over in a huff.

'Hey!' I said, widening my eyes at him. 'Keep your pants on. . .' Turning to Smudge I continued, 'Carry on, what exactly did that lying bastard have to say?'

Stuart and Smudge laughed. 'Well, he said they were just friends, you know. Then he told me that maybe if I were home more he wouldn't need to make friends with his bloody personal trainer, like it was my fault. Like he doesn't have any other bloody friends, the arse.' She shook her head. 'The trouble is he has a bit of a point.'

'What? No, he doesn't!' I cried. 'You said yourself he could have come here with you as he was back from Rome. It's not like you guys haven't done that for years – travelled wherever the other was working when you could. It's why your marriage worked in the first place, because you both don't have conventional jobs or kids.'

She nodded. 'Yeah, exactly. I said that too, but we just go around in circles. The thing is he wants more of a stable life now. That's what he said. Eventually, he admitted that there's a spark between him and this. . . personal trainer. *Jess*,' she said, with a twist of her lip.

'Jess?' I mouthed. 'What kind of a name is Jess for a man-stealing personal trainer?'

She nodded. 'I know, right. . . should be like Amber or something,' she added with an empty laugh.

'A spark!' shouted Stuart. 'That sleazy little arsehole, I'll show him some bloody sparks. . .'

I looked at him. 'Look, love, maybe you should, you know, go get us some crisps or something. '

'What?' he said, looking at me as if I'd gone mad. 'You want crisps now?'

'No, I want you to bloody bugger off or calm down,' I said, making a move to shove him out the living room.

He glared at me. 'This is *my sister*,' he huffed. '*You* bugger off!'

Smudge snorted as my eyes popped in rage. 'It's okay, you guys, oddly this is helping. . . Lets me know that I'm not going mad – Mark seemed to think I was overreacting.'

'What?!' exploded Stuart and I together.

She nodded. 'It's just a harmless flirtation, that's what he said. . . "If it bothers you, Victoria,"' she said, putting on a poncey-sounding voice just like Mark's, '"I'll just stop doing anything at all, while you flit around the world doing whatever you fancy, while I get fat and be your house husband ready and waiting like a big fat pussy for whenever you decide to come home. . ."'

'Seriously?' I asked, my mouth falling open in utter shock. 'He seriously said that?'

'Yep.'

'I'm going to kill him,' hissed Stuart.

'Me first,' I said.

'I love you idiots,' said Smudge.

* * *

That night as I slipped into a hot bath after we'd insisted Smudge spend the night in the spare room, I couldn't stop thinking about her and Mark. I couldn't believe he was acting this way. I knew she had a big decision to make. I hoped that they'd be able to work it out but, to be honest, I didn't see how. He seemed to resent Smudge for everything. It looked to me, at least, like he was using his personal trainer as a bit of an excuse. As I lay in the water I realised just how tired I really was. Pregnancy was no joke. I was used to feeling tired for most of the day, but it was so much worse after the events of the last few days.

It hadn't helped that I hadn't slept much last night after Genevieve had interrupted my time with Mum. When 3 a.m. rolled around, this time I was waiting, despite feeling dead on my feet.

When that magic hour rolled around, light and stardust seemed to fill the room and, in the moon-bright glow, I smiled.

'Oh Mum, I love you,' I said, holding back the fear that after last night, when Genevieve had broken the spell, she wouldn't be back. I couldn't, didn't know how I would handle that.

When the postcard began to write, I felt my shoulders sag in relief; it was just what I needed right then.

Love you more
Proud of you
Now go get some sleep

CHAPTER SIXTEEN

Birds of a Feather

The night before Christmas, I placed the last little ornament on the tree: a silver-gold box that I'd made in secret during the night. I sat back on my heels and admired the room: the crackling fire, the fairy lights twinkling around the French doors and the beautiful tree filled with homemade decorations, which Mum and I had crafted together over the years, sparkling amongst the white Christmas lights.

Dad had surprised me with a small package filled with our decorations, from paper snowmen to elves and sprites made of twigs, glitter, and glue, saying they belonged with us, as we started our new family.

I touched the little paper box I'd made, thinking of Mum. Every year, on Christmas Eve, she used to make a secret decoration just for us. From silver-winged angels to tiny, hand-sewn teddy bears with brown button eyes, our names embroidered on the chest. They were always more beautiful and intricate than any we could imagine. It was this that I looked forward to the most, perhaps even more so than the real gifts because they always seemed more magical than the others, more filled with love.

It had been that much harder to put up the tree since Mum had gone, knowing she wouldn't be there to surprise us come Christmas morning; we'd wake only to encounter yet again our loss.

This year though, because of Mum, I'd found something that I thought I'd lost: hope.

Stuart came in from the kitchen and set two mince pies and a glass of milk onto the coffee table. 'For Santa?' I asked with a raised brow.

'Or Pepper and Pots, whoever gets there first,' he said, eyeing the pair of cats curled up around Muppet, declaring a rather surprising Christmas truce.

'What are you doing?' I asked, as he inched towards the Christmas stocking hanging off the hearth.

'Nothing,' he said, acting rather too innocent.

'Stuart.'

'Ivy.'

'Stuart, back away from the Christmas stocking,' I warned.

He grinned sheepishly, looking like a young boy. 'I was just going to give it a little feel. . .'

I raised an eyebrow. 'Uh-huh. No touching the sock. Rule five.'

'See, you're just making up rules now,' he complained.

'Yes, I am,' I agreed. 'Keep going and we'll have a fifty-foot restraining order too.'

He backed away slowly. Muppet looked at him with one eye, while she lazed by the fire, her tongue out.

'She's got her eye on you for sure,' I said, laughing.

He narrowed his eyes at her. 'Cheeky madam, who feeds you?'

She waggled her bottom.

'I do,' I pointed out.

'Good point,' he laughed.

Muppet sat up to stare at him as if to say that it was fine by her if he'd like to change their arrangement. When he ignored her, she made a rather artful move where she feigned going for the kitchen and went past the coffee table from the other side instead, stealing a mince pie faster than we could blink and running out the room as quick as her short wrinkly legs would carry her.

I laughed aloud, while Stuart chased her up the stairs, declaring, 'That's it, madam. I was going to save you from your mother. You didn't know this, but there are reindeer ears in your future. . . I was going to protect your dignity, but no more. . .'

I checked my phone and saw a message from Smudge, who'd left the day before. We'd told her to stay to spend Christmas with us, but she wanted to be home, to try and sort things out with Mark, and to see The Terrorist. She'd told me that it was funny but while Genevieve could drive her so far round the bend she'd feel like throttling her, now that she was going through this, she wanted her mother. It's definitely something I could understand.

At 3 a.m. the studio was lit with a silver-tinged glow, brighter than I'd ever seen it. Standing in the doorway, I realised that I'd been holding my breath, wondering what the postcard would hold for me today. It had been five years since I'd spent a Christmas with her. Five years of wishing that somehow she would be there; yet she never was. And now, inexplicably, she had found a way.

The words were already there, waiting for me. The first line was, as ever, a message of love, bringing tears to my eyes.

Merry Christmas darling

'Merry Christmas, Mum,' I whispered, my hand on my throat, tears filling my eyes.

I want you to know how very proud I am of the woman you've become

'Oh Mum,' I breathed out, closing my eyes.

Things haven't been easy but you found courage and strength and despite how hard it must have been you haven't let it change you

I swallowed, tears sliding down my cheeks, unchecked. Mum's visits had been filled with love and light – each one precious. But until now, we hadn't spoken about her death or how hard it had been for me since she'd left. How alone I'd felt and how easy it would have been to let it harden me, especially the years of trying and failing to fall pregnant. To have her say what I needed to hear was perhaps the best gift she'd given me since she'd found me again.

'I thought it had changed me; hardened me in a way. I'd stopped hoping. . . not just for the big things, you know, but the little things too. . .' I answered truthfully.

I know
But my darling you can't let it
Life is as beautiful as it is brutal and over in the length of a sigh
Don't mute it by denying yourself the pleasures of living to protect yourself from ever aching, for it is the dark that makes us appreciate the light
You cannot know true pleasure unless you have experienced pain; both are an inevitable, exquisite torture

I took a shuddering breath and nodded. 'An exquisite torture seems about right.'

My darling it's time for you to fly

'What do you mean?' I breathed, hoping that she wouldn't choose this moment to be opaque.

For just a second, I could have sworn I heard her laugh – her sweet throaty chuckle that I loved so much. The light seemed brighter then and it moved across the studio, falling from the writing desk, past the window and onto the desk filled with my latest illustrations of Mr Tibbles and his night-time party in the Fairy's Forest. My secret project that I'd spent ten years creating, always with the distant promise that one day I would show it to the world, all the while far too comfortable being the one who stood in the shadows. With a silent flutter, the little golden-red moonlight thrush appeared again, to hop just once on top of the papers before it disappeared.

I closed my eyes and took a breath. 'It's time?' I asked.

It's time

I woke to find Muppet and Stuart staring at me. Two sets of brown eyes gazing at me expectantly.

'Merry Christmas?' I asked, amused.

Stuart's smile was wide. Muppet gave me her bulldog beam and settled her considerable weight on my lap, eyes never leaving mine.

'You hungry?' Stuart asked.

Muppet turned to look at him hopefully, bottom wiggling.

I laughed, rubbing my eyes, sitting up with no help from Muppet, who held her doggy ground. 'Er. . . maybe in a bit.'

'How about a scone. . .'

'A scone?' I said, surprised. 'For breakfast?'

He nodded, eyes serious. 'Good with jam.'

Good lord! More jam?

'Close your eyes,' he commanded. 'Hold out your hand.'

I did as instructed, feeling something small but heavy placed in my palm. Then I opened my eyes and exclaimed, 'Strawberry jam!' I looked up at his wide grin.

Turning back to the little jar, I peered at the label, which read: *Strawberries for Ivy. A Sea Cottage special edition.*

I looked at him, moved beyond words. 'Just strawberries? No added chilli. . . fennel or. . .?'

'Just strawberries and my love for you,' he said, eyes dancing.

I grinned, tears springing to my eyes. 'Have I told you lately how much I love you, Mr Everton?'

He shook his head. 'No, been meaning to take it up with you too,' he said, with mock self-pity and sad brown eyes.

'Really?' I asked.

'Yes, I mean I spent all day yesterday preparing the ham. . . stringing the lights, finishing the trifle. . .' He sighed theatrically.

'Ooh, trifle! With cherries?' I exclaimed.

He rolled his eyes. 'With cherries,' he agreed.

I smiled, beaming. He looked at Muppet sadly. 'It's all about food with this one.'

Muppet looked at him without comprehension, eyes alight at her favourite word.

'Wrong crowd, love.'

He shook his head, smirking. 'Indeed.'

'So. . .' he said, waggling his eyebrows expectantly.

'So?' I asked.

'So,' he said, shaking my arm.

I laughed. 'Presents?'

'Presents!' he agreed, dragging me out of bed and racing me down the stairs, where I handed him his Christmas stocking at last, and he exclaimed with a large huff, 'Finally! Been waiting months.'

I laughed. 'It's only been up a week.'

He looked nonplussed. 'A week? Can't be; must be at least three. At least. . .' He began squeezing his stocking all around, taking a guess. 'A new pie cutter?' he asked, eyes alight.

I shook my head.

'A lemon zester?' he persisted, his expression hopeful.

I laughed. 'No, look.'

He opened it. 'Bulbs?' he said, eyes wide with excitement. Laying four envelopes carefully on the table, each with hand-written labels and matching illustrations.

'Kohlrabi?' he read, looking at the first envelope in confusion at the image I'd drawn of a rather strange-looking green plant.

'Exotic wild cabbage,' I supplied.

'Really?' he said, intrigued. 'Sunchoke?' he asked, peering at the second envelope and the illustration of what looked like a mealy potato.

'Jerusalem artichoke – can be fermented apparently.'

His eyes widened at the possibility. 'Sea Cottage beer?' he exclaimed, excitedly.

I winked. 'Possibly. . .'

'Romanesco. . . good lord, feel like I'm on acid – is it an optical illusion?' he asked, looking down at the drawing on the third envelope with its weird lime green, spiralling wild broccoli that appeared to move while you looked at it.

'Yup, it's a natural approximation of a fractal.'

He studied it closely. 'Oooh, love it when you wax mathematical. . . So it repeats the pattern at every scale? No wonder I feel like I'm spacing out.'

'Not great for morning sickness, drawing that.'

He shook his head. 'You're wonderful, you. . . Where did you get these?'

I shook my head. 'I'd tell you, Mr Everton, but then you know I'd have to. . .'

He gave me a pointed look. '. . . Admit that you'd had a secret assignation with Tomas?' he said, dark eyes amused.

I laughed. 'Yes. . . that,' I agreed. Thinking of how the old Frenchman, with his grey beard, soil-splattered jeans and permanent green beret had looked at me like I was mad, when we met just after twilight in The Cloud Arms a few weeks before the flood. 'Eve. Seriousment? *Pah, Anglaise* . . . and what is wrong with good old-fashioned Engleesh vegetables?' he asked, bulbous blue eyes wide, touching his beret with a gnarled finger in exasperation. I'd stared at the bizarre sight before me – the only French Anglophile I'd ever heard of – and could only shrug. '*C'est Ivy*,' I pointed out yet again, and, '*C'est Stuart*,' I added.

He'd nodded. '*C'est vrai*,' he said resignedly at Stuart's odd yet persistent creative gardening urges. 'Okay. . . Eve, we'll talk,' he'd said and retreated under the cover of night, till he called by a few days ago with the goods.

Stuart looked like all his Christmases had come at once. He stared at the pile of exotic bulbs from all around the world and beamed, giving me a hug that swept me off my feet.

When he set me down, I gave him a kiss. 'You're an odd, but lovely man, Mr Everton,' I said, turning towards the kitchen to put on a pot of coffee, only to stop, heart beating wildly in my chest.

I should have seen it as soon as I came in. It should have captured my eye, and stolen my heart straight out of my chest. For there on the very top of the tree perched a single feather made of moonlight and air, shining brighter than gold, the most whimsical of stars.

Stuart looked at me strangely. 'Ivy?'

I wrenched my eyes away to look at him and smiled. 'Sorry. . . spaced out for a second. Just going to put the kettle on.'

He stood, head tilted to one side, as I left, his frown deepening as his eyes fell on the lone, shimmering feather.

'Take a bow,' said Richard, as Stuart, dressed in his red and white apron, black hair gleaming and dark eyes shining, delivered the enormous Christmas ham, on its silver platter and bed of wild rocket, to the centre of the table, amid applause from the assembled Talty family, my dad, and four of the six members of The Thursday Club, namely Abigail, Robyn, May, and Winifred Jones.

Smudge was spending Christmas with The Terrorist. We'd offered for them all to come and spend the day with us, but John and Genevieve had some or other benefit that they had to attend the following evening. Oddly, though I felt a sense of relief, there was a small part of me that was disappointed as well. Wonders never cease.

While we were eating, with appreciative moans, I turned to find Ben tugging on my sleeve.

'Aunty Ivy, watch this,' he said, green eyes mischievous, red hair vivid against his new Spider-Man outfit. I looked as he whistled and Muppet came out, wearing her dreaded reindeer ears and a length of red tinsel around her neck. I laughed. 'Well done, Ben. You're a better man than me. . . none of us could get it on her.'

He grinned, showing me the gap where his front tooth had recently fallen out. 'I have my ways,' he said.

I raised an eyebrow. 'Uncle Stuart's mince pies?'

He giggled. 'Yep!'

The honey-glazed wasabi ham turned out to be a hit, and after trifle followed by coffee, a game of Cluedo and a walk on the beach with Muppet, we said goodbye to the Taltys and the rest of The Thursday Club, who all left with tired smiles and trousers unbuttoned.

Afterwards, I turned to look for Dad, but he'd disappeared. I found him standing in the living room, staring at the tree. When I entered, he turned and gave me an odd, faraway smile. 'It's so strange: just now I could have sworn I heard your mother's voice. Then when I came in here. . .' He shook his head, sighed and touched a little reindeer made of twigs. 'I can still remember you making this.'

It was when I was about nine. I admired one in a shop on the way home from school one day, and next thing Mum dragged me off to Usett's Hardware for a glue gun, saying, 'We'll make one, shall we?' Then we were bundled off in mittens and woollen caps, combing the countryside for twigs while a light drift of snow tickled our faces, and later over several cups of cocoa before the fire, we put him together, twig by twig, till he seemed almost alive.

We did a lot of crazy-wonderful things like that. My throat constricted at the memory.

Dad looked up at the top of the tree, rocking back on his heels, turning his head with his Mad Hatter hair upwards, while he frowned at the feather. 'You know, she always called you her little bird. . . Funny that you'd put that there,' he said, with a small, sad shake of his head and shoving his hands deep into the pockets of his maroon cardigan.

He saw me staring wide-eyed and gave a little chuckle. 'Never mind me, going daft in my old age.'

I shook my head. 'I don't think so,' I said with a smile.

He shook his head again and gave me a kiss goodbye. Very softly I heard him say, 'Merry Christmas, Alice,' before he left.

I wouldn't have been a bit surprised if she'd said it back.

CHAPTER SEVENTEEN

Silence Is the Loudest Sound

I spent the next week in the nursery, painting the Fairy's Forest and Mr Tibbles's journey up the lantern-strewn path. We'd moved in the cot that Dad had brought over, which Stuart sanded and varnished, while I had unpacked every last someday vest, miniature one-day bootie, maybe-sometime outfit, and with it, all our unspoken dreams, and hopes.

After Christmas, I'd travelled up to London to have a coffee with my editor at Rain River Books, Jeff Marsons. Fear was riding high in my chest. Apart from Stuart, and Genevieve, I'd never shown Mr Tibbles to anyone before. But between my mother's words and, oddly enough, Genevieve's, I had been finally ready to take the plunge.

When I opened up my portfolio in the empty publishing house, as most people were away, and showed him Mr Tibbles's adventures in the Fairy's Forest, Jeff didn't say anything at first. Then he looked up at me with a frown, shook his balding head and said, 'How long have we been working together now? Ten years? And *now* you show me this?'

I couldn't believe how enthusiastic he was about it, and just two days later, I signed my first ever solo book contract.

Of course, I had to break the news to Catherine. Who demanded that she see my secret project straight away.

She came in while I was midway through creating the Fairy Forest scene in the nursery, staring at Mr Tibbles with her head cocked to one side, olive green eyes thoughtful. 'So how come you never told me about Mr Tibbles before?'

I shrugged as I painted in his little whiskers. 'Not sure. It was just a little project – something that kept me going. . . after everything, you know.'

She nodded, leaning against the door jamb. 'Well, I'm glad you've finally sent it to Jeff. . . Though I wish you'd told me about it.'

Jeff was talking about a release for summer. I couldn't believe it. My head was still spinning.

I smiled and stage-whispered to Muppet, who was lying on the floor next to the reupholstered rocker, with its pink and cream rose pattern, 'Detective Sergeant Fudge missed a case?'

'Very funny,' she said, rolling her eyes at us both.

I shrugged. 'I thought so,' I said, returning to Mr Tibbles's whiskers. I looked up in a minute to see her staring at me rather seriously. 'Cat. . .' I started.

She shook her head. 'Sorry. It's just we've worked on *The Fudge Files* for ten years and I love it, truly, but maybe you should have been doing this,' she said, staring at Mr Tibbles in awe.

I set my paintbrush down and went to give her a hug. 'Now listen here, Catherine Jayne Talty. While Detective Sergeant Fudge may be your invention, it was inspired by my dog – I can assure you that I have never regretted working on her stories, it has been one of the biggest joys of my life and I intend to keep working on *The Fudge Files* until we run out of crimes to solve. Which should be never. I mean, how many books did Agatha Christie write?' I said, mock sternly.

'Hundreds. Well, all right then. But we will be making time in the schedule for Mr Tibbles too from now on,' she declared, pointing a long, slim finger at me.

I shrugged. I'd been playing hooky with the deadlines that way for years already. Best not to tell her that though.

When Stuart came home, he popped his head into the nursery, blowing us all a kiss. He looked at me, eyes alight. 'Fairy lights,' he said approvingly at the little night scene I was working on.

I grinned, with a nod. 'Fairy lights. . . just for you.'

He held out a little pink bag. 'For the gem squash,' he said, eyes twinkling.

'Gem squash?' asked Catherine from the chair, topping up her wine glass as she watched me work.

'The baby. . . it's roughly the size of a gem squash now.'

She laughed. 'Stuart. . .'

He shrugged, giving us both a wink.

I took the little package and peered inside. They were a pair of bite-sized pink wellingtons with little strawberries all over. I pulled them out and placed them on the counter. Catherine and I stared at them wordlessly, hearts in our throats.

'As you were,' said Stuart, giving me a kiss and leaving.

I looked at Catherine, who shook her head. 'He's. . .'

I nodded, biting my lip to keep it in myself.

'And the little pink. . .'

I came over to pat her back.

'I mean – he's just so. . .' Struggling to find the words. 'I mean. . . Richard is a darling, but he'd never just come home with little pink wellies or get excited about fairy lights.'

I gave her an understanding look. 'Shall I keep him?'

She laughed. 'I think so.' She turned and narrowed her eyes at me. 'Especially after the other little thing I found out today, when he was asking if I'd like to stay for dinner. . . Apparently that's what he does. He cooks. Every. Bloody. Night. That's another thing you forgot to tell me about,' she added, with a pointed glare.

I hung my head. Some things I didn't tell her for her own good, but I'm not sure she saw it that way.

* * *

When I got to the studio that night, I hesitated at the door. The air felt different and the sounds from outside seemed louder, more intrusive. I went to the postcard and waited, but nothing happened. The room was strangely dark, like spilled ink over my eyes. No moonlight beam shone inside tonight. My heart started to pound.

I swallowed, fear constricting my throat. Wasn't she coming?

I wasn't prepared for this, not even close. I'd gotten so used to her being here, I'd begun to take it on faith. I wasn't at all prepared to let her go again.

I blinked back tears, feeling a silent scream lodge itself in my chest. What if she never came back? What if she never re-entered my life? What if that was all I got and I hadn't even realised that the last time was the last time. . . I wasn't ready for her to leave. Not again.

In the days since Christmas, her messages had been brief but filled with love. It hadn't occurred to me to be concerned, as I'd prattled on about my hopes for the nursery, Stuart's plantings and his plans for the installation of a 'storm-proof greenhouse', and that I'd finally sent off the first Mr Tibbles story to the publishers. She'd said nothing of leaving, left no warning that she may not return, and last night all she'd done was repeat her words from Christmas morning. Or at least, that's what I thought she'd said. That I should hold on to hope, no matter what happens.

It was only now, when the Mum-shaped-hole in my chest had just begun to mend and had exposed itself again, that it occurred to me to read deeper into her message. She'd been saying something more. Something that I'd missed. So caught up in my newfound bliss and hope for the future, I hadn't paid attention to her words as I normally would. I'd almost taken it for granted that she'd be there. I closed my eyes feeling infinitely stupid. I hadn't noticed the warning for what it was. I stood in the empty room, feeling desolate and alone, wondering what she'd meant and if I would ever hear from her again and how I could carry on without her if I didn't. It seemed impossible. Absurd even. How could I do the one thing she had asked me to do when faced with this endless silence? How could I hold on to hope when it had left with her?

CHAPTER EIGHTEEN

Broken Things

I awoke the next morning feeling strange. Not ready to face the day. The bed was warm and comfortable. I couldn't escape the feeling that it was where we should stay all day. Not the best feeling to welcome in the New Year.

The empty postcard was like a splinter – one that I couldn't remove – and as I lay in bed, Muppet in my arms, I tried my best not to think of what it meant. What she'd meant by her words.

No matter what

Stuart stared at me, his dark head on the pillow opposite mine, his expression uncomprehending. 'So you want to just stay here?' he asked, with a frown. 'All day?'

I opened my arms wide for him to snuggle in next to Muppet and me. He laughed and put his arm around us, smiling at Muppet's continuous snores, in unofficial competition with the waves crashing outside.

'Us,' I said, waggling my eyebrows. 'Not just me, but the three of us. . . We could have a little picnic. In fact, I'll make it. I'm rather good at sandwiches and fetching dog biscuits.'

He pressed his face against mine. Brown eyes to blue. 'You must really want to do that if you're prepared to do the food,' he said, eyes crinkling at the corners.

I nodded. But he just stared at me regretfully. 'Love, we have the party tonight and it's not like we can just skip it.'

'Why not?' I asked. 'We can have our own party,' I added, giving what I hoped was a lascivious wink.

He smiled, showing his perfect teeth. 'I like the sound of that, particularly if you'll be wearing those all day,' he said, tracing a finger along the sleeve of my pink flannel pyjamas – the ones with the white rabbits all over them. 'However, I'm also catering the party, if you remember,' he pointed out with a shrug.

I groaned, loudly, and threw the covers over all of us.

'No. . .'

Stuart laughed and gave me a kiss under the blanket.

'We can do this all day tomorrow if you like,' he suggested.

'It's not that. . . I just have this weird feeling, like we shouldn't get out of bed today,' I said, trying to explain.

'A feeling?' he asked in surprise.

I nodded.

He shook his head. 'Love, it's just New Year's Eve. You get like this *every* year.'

'No, I don't,' I protested, eyes wide with surprise.

'Yes, you do. Last year we had that big do in London and half way through, you said we needed to go home because you felt weird. . .'

I scoffed. 'That was because I did feel weird. . . I had food poisoning, remember? Horrid way to start the New Year, just so you know.'

He nodded. 'Yes, okay, brutal. . . But then the year before that, we cancelled with Catherine.'

I shrugged. 'Because you'd pulled an all-nighter, working with the Hong Kong office. . . You were slurring, you were so tired,' I exclaimed.

He laughed. 'Hardly. I was tired, but I could have rallied. Red Bull wings. . .' he said, eyes dancing. 'Face it, my love, you just don't like New Year's, never have and never will. Any excuse.'

I sighed. Rallied. . . really? He had fallen asleep ringing his own doorbell. But okay, if that's how he chose to remember it. 'Each case had its own merit. But today. . . today is different,' I said, knowing it was hopeless. 'Can we just drop the food off? I'll help you get it ready and everything, then we'll come home? Please?'

He laughed. 'Ivy, you know we have to go. Anyway, if we don't go then I won't see you in your new dress and you can't deny a man that. That's cruel. . . I mean, it's lace and everything.'

I laughed, rolling my eyes. 'It's sequins, not lace. Hopeless you are.'

He made his eyebrows dance. 'It's low-cut – that I do remember. . .'

I laughed. 'Of course that bit you remember. . .' I knew a lost cause when I saw one. 'Fine, I'll go shower then come help you.'

'Good girl,' he said, giving me a kiss and climbing out from under the covers, singing his made-up gardening song, while putting on his wellies to the tune of James Brown's 'I Feel Good': 'I see roots. . . nah nah nah nah nah neh eh. . . and I know that I shouldn't . . . nah nah nah nah nah neh eh there's sprouts. So nice. . . now I've got roots.'

He left, giving me a little hip pop before he swaggered out the door. I couldn't help but laugh.

I was probably just being silly. How I wished I could shake the feeling that we should just stay home today.

I had a long shower. Stuart's song lodged in my brain, making me giggle as I rinsed out the shampoo. When I got out, I felt better, more at ease. I was determined to put odd feelings, dead mothers, and empty postcards out of my head.

I had crostini to assemble, vegetables to peel, and flatbreads to brush with herbs and olive oil. Stuart was in his creative element and had given me strict instructions as our kitchen turned into a savoury production line, filled with the mouth-watering scents of cooked salmon, olive tapenade, grilled scallops and caramelised onions that were sure to wow the guests at the Cloudsea Harbour New Year's Eve Party tonight.

My job was top stacker really, as neither of us trusted me with any of the actual cooking.

When everything was ready and all the trays were stacked and covered with cling film for the ride over, we raced upstairs to our separate bathrooms to bathe and change. I touched the dark-grey sequined dress that hung on a hanger at the back of the door with a smile. It was pretty. I wasn't usually a sequins kind of girl, but this would probably be the last time I'd get to wear a really fancy dress until the baby came. Might as well make the most of it.

Stuart was waiting for me at the bottom of the stairs; dressed in a tuxedo, looking so handsome he took my breath away. His black hair and eyes were shining and he wore that irrepressible boyish smile of his.

He shook his head when he saw me, eyes widening. 'No, you're right, I don't think we should go out tonight. . . Let's just stay here and I'll take that off of you. . . very slowly, of course.' He grinned, so that I blushed. 'There's fire, food. . . the night is young,' he continued, eyes dancing.

I laughed, shaking my head. 'I'm tempted, Mr Everton. You look rather fabulous, by the way, but alas we have fifty platters to deliver, as you yourself pointed out this morning.'

He sighed. 'Okay, well, just so you know, if you'd put that on this morning when you asked, I would have cancelled,' he said.

I grinned. 'Not for the white rabbits?'

He shook his head. 'Sorry.'

I laughed and came down to give him a kiss. We put on our coats and with arms linked headed out to the car and set off towards the harbour.

The harbour's sparkling display of lights dotting both sides of the quay was one of my favourite things to see. We made our way to the boathouse, the perfect venue for a party, with its spectacular views along the harbour and its beautiful array of lights. It was breathtaking. It was hard to believe that just a few weeks ago a storm had swept through here. I just wished that I could get rid of the inexplicable anxiety that I had woken up with, so that I could enjoy it properly.

I helped Stuart carry through the trays, which the waiters would soon circulate, and went to say hello to Catherine, who was standing in the back near a white stage, where a jazz band was playing 'La Vie en Rose'.

Catherine was looking beautiful in a gorgeous, green silk dress that set off her red hair perfectly. 'Ivy Everton, that's some dress,' she said, giving me a hug hello, and handing me a glass of champagne. 'It's non-alcoholic, so no worries.'

'Same for you. Wow, you look stunning!'

She smiled. 'It's nice to feel like a girl. . . won't lie. Babysitters – aka Dad – are fabulous. Richard in a tux. . . I could get used to this,' she sighed happily, then frowned. 'But what's wrong?' she asked, peering closely at me.

I shrugged. 'It's nothing. Just had this weird feeling all day. Stupid, really.'

She smiled. 'It's New Year's Eve . . . You're always a little weird about New Year's Eve. . .'

I gave her a look. 'Not you too. That's what Stuart said. But this. . . I don't know, it feels different. . .'

She touched my arm. 'It's probably nothing. Pregnancy hormones, they do strange things, trust me.'

I nodded. Hormones. That made sense.

I stifled a laugh seeing Mrs Aheary walk past with a pitcher of ale, dressed in a fully lace pink dress with shoulder pads and about a yard of pleating going on around her hips – she looked like an extra from *The Golden Girls*. I avoided any eye contact, hoping to avoid a lecture on emmets and/or the inevitable decline of the postal service, but she saw me and made a beeline in my direction, calling, 'Ivy-girl, so glad to see you out and about, though in my day women in your condition didn't go out in the cold like this!'

Ah! Who had told Mrs Aheary I was pregnant? Who? I'd kill them. Must have been someone from The Thursday Club. . . just wait until I saw them. . .

Luckily, Mrs Aheary's lecture was interrupted by the timeous arrival of Bess Willis, who must have taken pity on me for some unknown reason, and took the pitcher of ale from out of her hands and said, 'Let me help you, Mrs Aheary. Come on then,' and Mrs Aheary had no choice but to follow after her booze.

Feeling someone touch my back, I turned in surprise to find Dr Gia Harris and her husband. 'Dr Gia,' I exclaimed.

She beamed at me and introduced her husband, Peter, a fit-looking blond with kind blue eyes. 'Just wanted to come say hello, Ivy, love,' said Dr Gia. 'It's so lovely to see you out and about. You're glowing,' she whispered. I grinned and thanked her, watching as she left arm in arm with her husband.

I waved at April Blume, the owner of The Cloud Arms, thrilled to see that she was still in town. Her bright magenta hair was striking against an electric blue jumpsuit. She gave me a wink, as her husband swept her onto the dance floor.

I started when a hand placed itself on my shoulder. 'Dad!' I uttered in surprise. He was wearing a slightly shabby-looking suit, his wild grey hair tamed on either side of his head. He gave me a nervous smile and whispered, 'I think I'm on a date.' He gestured subtly with a slight turn of his head, eyes wide with shock.

I blinked, following his gaze to a trim-looking woman with blonde-grey hair opposite the stage, swaying to the music, wearing a black dress and heels. 'Really?'

He shrugged. 'I think so. . . I said I'd give her a lift. Her name's Elizabeth Chaney. She's in my ballroom dancing class. But maybe she thought. . . well, anyway.' He shrugged. 'Not the end of the world.' He sounded quite pleased at the prospect, if rather surprised.

I smiled. She looked quite sweet really, very pretty in a Faye Dunaway sort of way. . . Wait. 'Dad, ballroom dancing, you?' Shock had rendered me almost monosyllabic.

He shook his head at himself. 'I know! Remember, before Christmas, when you told me to look under the stairs?'

I swallowed. It had been Mum who suggested that, but still. 'That's when you took out the Christmas box, with all the lights, right?'

He nodded. 'Yes, it was the push I needed to put them up. For so long I was stuck. Well, anyway, there was something else in the box: a pamphlet for dance lessons. Mum wanted us to do it but then she fell ill so we never did. But when I saw it there, in amongst all the Christmas stuff, I. . . It's daft but. . .' He shrugged, a soft smile about his lips.

'You saw it as a sign?' I asked, touched.

He gave a small shrug. 'And now. . .'

'Now you might be on a date,' I said, breathing out. 'Big day.'

'Big day.' He nodded, taking a sip of my fake champagne, supposedly to steady his nerves.

'It's non-alcoholic,' I laughed.

He gave a short nervous laugh. 'Probably better, though it makes little difference. . . look at what I get myself into sober.'

I laughed. 'Go on then, she won't bite.'

He gave me a slow, wide-eyed nod, took a steadying breath, gave me a kiss and went back to his date.

'Well done, Mum,' I whispered. Typical Dad – he would probably have never taken the step on his own.

'Would you care to dance, Mrs Everton?'

I turned to see Stuart, holding out his hand, impossibly handsome.

My breath caught in my throat. How did he do that? I nodded. 'Of course.' My smile wide.

He winked at me and then nodded at the band. The singer smiled at us and they began to play Etta James's 'At Last'.

My mouth fell open. 'I love this song,' I said, tears stinging my eyes.

He smiled. 'I know,' he said, pulling me into his embrace. Here in his arms, the world righted itself, and I felt completely safe. He cradled my hand in his while we swayed to the music, my heart feeling like it might burst.

He looked at me, eyes gentle. 'Have I told you lately that I love you, Mrs Everton?'

'That's my line,' I said in surprise.

He grinned. 'It's a good one. Mind if I borrow it?'

I shook my head, feeling ridiculously happy. 'Maybe just this once.'

He leaned over and kissed me, his lips firm, but soft, and my stomach did a little flip. The canopy of lanterns and the twinkling harbour lights faded away. Stuart's gentle expression, imprinted in my memory. I closed my eyes and lost myself in the moment, feeling the last trace of anxiety finally ebbing away.

As the song came to a close, I pulled away reluctantly. 'That was some kiss, Mr Everton,' I said, staring into his dark, serious eyes.

'That's nothing. Just wait; come midnight, I'll give you a kiss you'll never forget.'

'Is that a promise?'

He nodded, giving me a soft kiss on the forehead.

Terry clapped a large freckled hand on Stuart's shoulder. 'Sorry to break the moment, lass, but can I steal yer husband for a wee while? Got a crisis with the crostini,' he said.

I laughed, shaking my head. 'Terry, you know you get more Scottish as the night wears on?'

He grinned. 'Ah missus, that or the whisky,' he winked.

I shook my head, with a chuckle. 'Ah, that explains it. Okay, you can have him. . . just so long as you bring him back before the countdown.'

Stuart gave me a sweeping kiss, bending me backwards. 'That should hold you until then.'

I laughed. 'Not even close – hurry back,' I said, and went to join my dad and his date, who were standing rather awkwardly by the punch table, like a couple of shy teenagers.

It turned out that Dad's date was rather fabulous: she was a piano teacher who'd lived in Paris for most of her adult life. I spent the next forty-five minutes amazed as she told me about being a teacher at the Sorbonne, and what her daily life had been like. As a Francophile myself, I was a little bit in awe. Most of this was news to Dad, of course, but as the night wore on he seemed to really loosen up, so I filled up both their punch glasses and retreated to let the liquid courage do its magic.

Just then, someone called, 'One minute, everyone!' and the whole party stood to attention for the countdown. I turned, looking for Stuart, but couldn't see him anywhere. I scanned the room, and saw Terry standing with one of the waiting staff chatting, so I hurried over. 'Terry, have you seen Stuart?'

He shook his head. 'Ah no, I thought he'd be back by now. Sorry, love. Maybe try his cell?' he said, concerned, before another waiter came past to catch his attention. 'Sorry, love, got to go sort the champagne,' he added, leaving me staring at his retreating back.

'What do you mean – back from where?' I asked, confused, but it was too noisy, he couldn't hear me.

I felt a hand touch my shoulder and I turned with a relieved smile and said, 'Finally.' But it wasn't Stuart. I frowned to see

Catherine standing there, a stricken look on her face. Two tracks of black mascara trailed down her face and she was cradling a phone to her chest.

I blinked. 'What's wrong?' I cried.

'Oh Ivy, I'm so sorry. There's been an accident.'

My eyes widened in fear. All around me people began to shout '*ten, nine, eight. . .*'

'An accident?' I said in shock. 'The kids. . . has something happened to them?' I asked, touching her arm, frightened.

A tear escaped from one green eye. She shook her head, swallowed.

'It's Stuart.'

'But he's at the back in the kitchens,' I said. Though I knew, with awful, sick fear, that this was what I'd been fighting all day. This feeling that something horrible was going to happen.

I blinked and Catherine closed her eyes for a split second to shake her head.

'No, he's not.'

I blinked again.

'He's been in a car crash. It's. . . very bad.'

Her words seemed to come from a tunnel. I was staring at her blindly, losing all feeling in my limbs, as my world started to spin out of control, my knees gave way, and a wild guttural howl escaped my throat and split me in two.

CHAPTER NINETEEN

The Longest Night

Richard caught me before I fell. I hadn't noticed him standing next to Catherine, looking smaller than I'd ever seen him, his eyes full of sympathy.

'He's stable, Ivy. They've taken him straight into surgery, but he's alive, that's the main thing,' he spoke in soft tones.

I looked at him through my tears. Surgery? What was he saying? Through the fog of emotion, my brain zeroed in on the other word. *Alive*. I clung to that word, like I'd never clung to anything in my life. Even as I wondered how it could be. . . How just an hour ago we were dancing under a canopy of twinkly lights and now. . . now he'd been in an accident and he was going into surgery. My brain refused to process it.

I blinked while trying to breathe – through the tears that threatened to consume me – painful, wrenching breaths.

'W-w-what happened?' I stuttered, gasping. My lungs felt like they'd been injected with lead. Like I'd suffocate from my fear.

Catherine's lip wobbled. 'He went home to fetch something apparently. There was a. . . a truck. . . it didn't. . . didn't stop,' she said, collapsing into tears.

I started screaming. Deep feral screams, tinged with blood. Someone was holding me back.

I tried to get away, to get to Stuart. I needed to get to Stuart. I didn't notice the crowd that had gathered. Or the fact that the music had stopped. But while the world stopped turning, I saw Dad, his grey eyes wide, distraught. Together he, Richard and Catherine helped me into the car and we raced to the hospital. I sat bent over, clutching my chest, sobs painfully wracking my body. I didn't know what I'd find when I got there; I just knew that every second away was a second too long. Finally, we arrived. I flung open the car door – tearing fingernails in my haste – and raced inside, into the bitter, cold air. I wasn't the only one.

As soon as we skidded inside the hospital doors Dr Gia rushed over, her face almost translucent. I could only blink at seeing her there. I didn't have time to be polite; she was in the way and she needed not to be. Before I could rush past her, she reached for my arm and said, 'I came as soon as I heard. Peter got paged onto the scene, thank God. He's taken Stuart into surgery now.'

I turned slowly to look at her properly. To digest her words. Peter? Then I remembered. Her husband. 'Oh. . .' Then felt my legs begin to shake. 'Oh. He's a surgeon. . . that's. . .' I blinked, feeling like I might throw up. From somewhere in the recesses of my mind I recalled.

Heart surgeon.

My knees started to shake uncontrollably and I bent over, gripping them, loud, knife-edged tears ripping out of me. Dad gripped my shoulders.

Dr Gia touched my arm. 'The paramedics brought him in, he's alive. He's in surgery now. . . Peter said he thinks he'll pull through,' she said gently.

I closed my eyes, trying to breathe.

After what seemed like an eternity, I looked up at the ceiling; eyes clouded with my unstoppable tears, and asked the impossible. 'H-his heart?'

She blinked back tears and nodded. 'He went into cardiac arrest and one of his lungs collapsed.'

I sank. The world turned upside down. My legs didn't belong to me any more. Dad caught me and led me to a nearby chair as I gasped for a breath that just wouldn't come. Hot tears felt like acid on my face. It seemed fair that I couldn't breathe properly, if neither could Stuart.

Dad tried to speak to me. To reassure me. But I was in that dark place – the place where no light goes, where empty reassurances mean nothing. Catherine laid a gentle hand on his arm, a touch for restraint. I gave her a grateful look and she nodded; she always understood.

Catherine filled out the paperwork. I managed to sign, hands trembling, where she pointed and we waited. The longest, most interminable, agonised wait, unable to take my eyes off the glass doors, because it was through them that someone would come – someone with an update who could tell us something, anything.

Finally, a short, stocky man clad in surgical scrubs, with a dark beard and compassionate eyes, came out. 'Mrs Everton?'

I nodded, standing on unsteady legs. He continued, 'I'm Dr Collins. Stuart has had a fair bit of damage.' At my quick intake of air, he carried on in a rush, stepping forward, placing a hand on my shoulder. 'There's good news. Dr Harris is operating on his heart now. They've restored the lung function and he's confident that the operation will go smoothly. There are no other internal injuries detected at this stage, which is very reassuring, particularly considering the extent of his accident. However, he has a few broken bones, including his left arm and leg. Dr Vram, the orthopaedic surgeon, has set them already. We'll update you as soon as he's through surgery.'

'He's. . . he's going to be all right?' I asked, my heart beating out of control. None of what he was saying sounded like good news – quite the opposite. Dr Collins touched my arm. 'We are encouraged, but Dr Harris will update you as soon as it's over.'

I nodded. *Encouraged.* What did that mean? Wishing I could just follow him into the operating room so I could hold Stuart's hand.

Catherine looked at me as we tried to process the impossible. 'You had a feeling,' she breathed.

My face collapsed. I nodded – I'd had a feeling. Dad patted my back and Dr Gia placed her hand on my shoulder, a gesture filled with compassion. I bit my lip, grateful for their support.

Catherine clutched my hand and I drew strength. He was alive. That was all I could think, so I thought it over and over, concentrating on just breathing in and out.

A loud commotion in the corridor announced the arrival of The Thursday Club, and six pairs of clacking feet, then the kindest American accent saying loudly, 'Where is our girl? Oh lawd, look at her!' Followed by wild Italian mumblings and six pairs of very concerned eyes and a cacophony of sound as they all attempted to mould me into their embrace. I didn't know who had called them, but I was grateful for their presence. Especially May's, who pulled a shawl around my shoulders and said, 'Now back off, you lot! Give her some air, sure she can't get any with the lot of youse in the way. Go get some chairs.' Then she asked me, 'Have yer phoned his family, my love? Shall I call the battle-axe fer ya?'

I closed my eyes as a new horror washed over me. Genevieve. Smudge. I hadn't thought. I shook my head. Somehow I knew I had to be the one.

I searched for my mobile, as if I were wading through water. Catherine took my bag – I hadn't even realised that someone had brought it – and fished out my mobile and handed it to me.

My hands shook as I dialled Genevieve's number. Through choking sobs, I tried to explain. Suddenly the phone was out of my hands and Dad's voice was calmly telling her what had happened. He must have walked away to finish the call, because a little while later he came back and said, 'I spoke to Victoria as well. She and Genevieve will be here on the first flight. I'm going to keep this, okay?' he said, indicating my phone. 'And let them know as we know.'

I nodded, grateful for him, for *all* of them.

Hours later, Dr Harris – Peter – came out and made straight for me. 'Mrs Everton – Ivy – the surgery went well.'

I breathed out, feeling a heady, heart-stopping rush of relief. Though it was too soon. He took my arm and steered me away slightly from the others, so the fear returned in full awful force. 'The surgery went well, *very* well. His heart came through fine. We were able to restore function. . . However, with the stress of the damage to his body, Stuart slipped into a coma. I won't lie: it's serious. He'll be under critical observation. . . We'll just have to wait, monitor him, and hope.'

'Coma?' I said aloud, my heart plummeting to my feet as I started to shake, to sob. Catherine, May, and my dad rushed forward.

Dr Harris patted my hand. 'I know it's incredibly hard, Mrs Everton. You have our sympathy and support.'

I didn't speak, because I couldn't. I didn't trust myself.

Hard?

This wasn't hard; this was unendurable. I looked at him, intolerable pain naked in my eyes. 'C-can I see him?'

He nodded. 'He's in ICU. He's been through a lot, so you will need to prepare yourself,' he said, looking at me and everyone gathered around my side.

I blinked. How did you prepare for this? I clutched his arm, eyes wide. 'Thank you. . . for everything,' I said, meaning it, knowing that this man was the reason Stuart was alive. This man whom I'd met just hours earlier, unaware that later he'd literally have my husband's life – and heart – in his hands. 'Thank you,' I repeated, taking a shuddering breath.

He nodded, blue eyes sympathetic. 'I believe he will make it, I really think he will. He's a fighter. . . I saw that today.'

I closed my eyes, hot tears sliding down my face, and nodded, swallowing past the claw-like wedge in my throat, grateful for his faith beyond anything else.

Dr Gia touched my back. I looked up through my tears. She gave me a hug before they left. 'We'll be thinking of you, darling, and praying. Call me any time if you need me.'

I swallowed back the rush of tears, nodding. 'Thank you for staying with me. . . with us tonight. It meant so much. . .'

Her eyes were soft, understanding. 'Of course,' she said, giving me a last touch of support, then left.

On leaden legs I made my way to the ICU – the longest walk of my life. When finally we entered the ward, I looked up and saw the most painful, casual of cruelties. Like a salted wound, the clock behind the nurses' station read 3 a.m.

Somehow I managed not to scream. Instead, I dragged my eyes away and followed the others, concentrating on putting one step in front of the other.

Nothing can prepare you for seeing someone that you love in a hospital bed – every part of them battered, bruised, and broken. There were so many machines and wires. The noise that emitted from all the equipment, a cacophony of beeps and low electronic hums. Such an interminable noise. I wondered that he didn't wake, then wanted to turn them up even more, in the hope that he would. His arm and leg were in a cast. His face – his beautiful Stuart face – was swollen, criss-crossed with gashes and dried blood. I sat by his side holding his left hand – the only part of him that didn't seem broken – and sobbed till I thought I would never stop.

At some point I must have fallen asleep, because Dad woke me up and told me that he was going to take me home to change. I didn't want to leave; I shook my head. 'I'm fine here, Dad,' I whispered. He needed to understand. I couldn't leave. What if I left and Stuart woke up?

A kind-faced nurse, with soft brown eyes and a name badge that said Maggie, touched my hand. 'Mrs Everton, I'm so sorry. I have your number. I promise, if anything happens, I'll phone you. Go home, get some sleep if you can; get changed. I'll be here.'

My eyes stung. While I appreciated the kind words, there was no place I'd rather be. 'I'd rather just stay, please,' I said.

Maggie bit her lip. 'I'm afraid, Mrs Everton, unfortunately, the visiting hours are over. If it were up to me, or even Dr Harris. . .' she said, her words trailing off, eyes wide, sincere, and young – so young to have to deal with this kind of trauma every day.

Dad touched my arm. 'My darling, they made an exception for us tonight, but it isn't fair if the other families can't,' he said, handing me back my phone. I took it and swallowed, looking up at Maggie. Her eyes were full of pity. I nodded. With shaking hands I touched Stuart's face, gave him a kiss, tears running down my cheeks, and I held his hand as gently as I could.

'I'll be back. . . I love you,' I whispered, heartbroken.

Leaving him was the most impossible, unthinkable thing of all.

As I left the ward, I saw Catherine standing outside. Incredibly, she was still there. She stood there in her pretty green cocktail dress, waiting for me, while she had three sons and a husband who needed her. I swallowed, held out my hand for her. 'Thank you for staying,' I whispered.

She gave me a hug. 'Couldn't leave you. . .' she said, her green eyes tired, but full of love.

I nodded, biting my lip to stop it from trembling, and followed them out into cold daylight, blinking, my eyes stabbed by the bright light. I got into the car, more tired than I'd ever been in my life, still in my heels and cocktail dress; absurdly dressed for a party – the final, awful insult.

CHAPTER TWENTY

Day One

I asked them to just drop me off. Even though the prospect of a Stuart-less house was unbearable, I couldn't face company right now. Muppet raced to greet me as soon as I came through the kitchen door. I bent down to give her a hug, to stare into her soft bulldog eyes.

She ran from me, went outside, then back in through the flap again, looking confused, subdued. 'He's okay,' I said, taking a deep breath, my hands shaking as I touched her soft fur. 'He's okay. . . he's okay,' I cried, repeating the words over and over, hoping that they were true. My face twisted in pain, loud, excruciating sobs wracked my body, ripping it apart, and I crumpled onto the kitchen floor, finally able to release the howls that had been kept inside.

Muppet placed her heavy head on my shoulder. Her eyes seemed to understand. She sat next to me for the longest time, the most comforting of friends. When I could stand, I made my way upstairs. Slowly, I undressed, dropping my offending dress on the bathroom floor. I stepped into the shower and let the cleansing water wash over me – I needed its comfort, its warmth.

I was exhausted. My eyes were swollen and raw, yet the tears still came, hot and painful, squeezing out of my barely open lids. I put on pyjamas, pulling on Stuart's green jersey, swallowing as I realised it still smelt of him. I fell asleep with my phone clutched in my hands.

I woke a few hours later, Muppet lying next to me. I checked my phone. No one had called. Visiting hours were only later that afternoon. Four hours away. How could I exist in the hours between?

I lay with Muppet in my arms, dozing fitfully, one eye on the clock screen of my phone in case I overslept.

When my phone buzzed, I started in surprise. It was a message from Dr Gia.

No news yet. But he's looking good according to Peter. Please remember to eat, sleep, and look after yourself. It's very important. With love, Gia.

I blinked and re-read the message. I considered her words and took heart: *looking good.* She wouldn't say that if it wasn't true. I closed my eyes. I couldn't think about the other things she'd said. I had never wanted food less. Then painfully, resignedly, I opened them again. She was right: I had to eat. If not for me, then for Holly. I looked at Muppet, who'd offered her sweet, gentle support, tears forming as I wondered: when had she last eaten?

Mercifully, when I got downstairs I saw a note from Dad saying that he'd fed Muppet, Pepper, and Pots that morning. I touched the note in relief. I poured myself a glass of water and made myself eat two slices of dry toast, each painful swallow followed by a sip of water. I felt like time was standing still so I went back upstairs to dress, laid out some food for the animals and left. Early. It was very important that I was there early. I'd rather be there, waiting, than here slowly dying.

When I got to the hospital Dr Harris brought me in to see Stuart. He looked tired, dark circles beneath his eyes. 'He's still under, but his vitals are looking very good.'

I breathed out. 'That's good news.'

He looked at me, his eyes full of compassion. 'It's very encouraging.'

I nodded, understanding. That word again. He didn't want to get my hopes up. He couldn't offer me what I wanted, what I needed, which was a guarantee. 'Thank you,' I said. He smiled gently. 'All we can do now is hope.'

I nodded, fighting back the tears. Tired of that word that asked so much and gave so little in return.

I took a seat next to Stuart's bed and held his hand. Tried to swallow past the permanent tightness of my throat. Stuart's face was even more swollen than I remembered from earlier that morning, covered in livid purple bruises that were competing with the criss-crossing gashes. My heart ached as I thought of the pain he must be in.

I held his hand, lifted it to my lips, and gave it a kiss. Tears falling, I whispered, 'You are my hope.'

Genevieve and Victoria arrived a few hours later.

'Ivy,' said Smudge, enfolding me in a hug, my head resting alongside a Batman logo.

Genevieve just stood there, like a balloon with a puncture. Her usually pristine hair resembled a nest of rat-tails. There was a red stain on her silk blouse, near her heart, as if it were bleeding on the outside. I waited for her to scream. To shout. To throw every last venomous thought that she had at me. To tell me that none of this would have happened if we hadn't moved here, if we had listened to her. Because I'd agree. A thousand times over.

She opened her mouth, but no words came out. Then there in the silence, in the darkest hour of our pain, her hand found mine and Victoria's, and held on tight.

CHAPTER TWENTY-ONE

Night

'Mrs Everton . . . Hello,' said Maggie, the same pretty brown-haired nurse from earlier that morning, popping her head in as she checked up on Stuart.

I turned and smiled, glad to see a friendly face. 'You're still here – it's such a long shift?' I said, surprised.

She smiled. 'I'm meant to have gone home. . . I just wanted to stay.'

I was touched. 'Maggie, that's so kind of you. But I can't expect that. . . You must go home – get some rest.'

She shook her head. 'He came in so damaged and then when I found out he was your husband, I just felt that I had to stay,' she said.

I looked at her in surprise and she said with moisture in her eyes, 'I have a son, Adam – he's just turned six – and last year I got a divorce. It was so hard. He was angry and he wouldn't talk to anyone. Nothing we tried seemed to help. My sister bought him a copy of *The Fudge Files* – the one where Bartholomew Badger goes missing. . .'

I smiled, nodding my head. It was the first one of the series I'd come up with the idea for and Catherine had insisted that I co-write it with her. 'Of course – where he ran away because Mr and Mrs Badger had a fight and he thought that they didn't love him any more,' I said. I'd thought of the story soon after Mum passed while I attempted to work through my own feelings of abandonment.

She nodded, biting her lip. 'Well, that's what had happened to Adam; he'd thought that we didn't love him any more.' She swallowed. 'I think reading it. . . he got it, you know. He identified with Bartholomew but he also saw how much the Badgers were worried and afraid and I think he realised that it's what was happening with us.' Then she laughed a little. 'Detective Sergeant Fudge helped solve a case she never knew about. . . Afterwards I read up about you and the story, and I have always wanted to thank you.'

I wiped away tears and gave her a hug. 'And you have – this means so much to me, Maggie, truly. I'd love you to meet Catherine, my co-author, and for you and your little boy to meet Muppet, the inspiration behind Detective Sergeant Fudge. I think she'd be very pleased to know she'd helped. She always helps me – a source of unconditional, never-ending puppy love.'

Maggie smiled sincerely. 'I would love that.'

'But you must go home and get some rest. I'll cut you the same deal you gave me. As soon as I know anything, I'll let you know – you have my word.'

She gave a slow nod of relief. 'Okay, thank you,' she said, giving my arm a squeeze before she left.

Sometime later a night nurse came in to check up on Stuart. She was short with a matronly-looking, dependable kind of stoutness. 'Still the same,' she said, with a sad shake of her head. She touched my arm. 'I'm afraid visiting hours are over,' she added reluctantly.

I blinked. Being asked to leave always came as the worst surprise.

I stood up and gave him a kiss goodbye, touching his hair, always so sleek and smooth, now matted, full of debris. I swallowed, took a steadying breath and left.

* * *

I felt like a ghost roaming my empty house. Victoria and Genevieve were staying at a hotel close to the hospital. I was grateful for that. Here I didn't need to speak. To try to find hope. But here, too, I was suspended in limbo while I waited, held prisoner by the hospital's visiting hours. I forced myself to eat a proper meal, tears forming as I realised it was one of several that The Thursday Club had made and stored in our fridge, letting themselves in with the spare key, the one from under the flowerpot; somehow their 'break-in' felt about the most endearing thing in the world right then.

May had come over to check on me earlier, to give me the same warning that everyone was giving – that I needed to eat, to keep up my strength.

When she was gone, I wandered from room to room repeatedly, unsettled, lost in the emptiness and desolation without him. I prowled the kitchen, my bedroom, the conservatory, finally entering my studio, the room I had long been avoiding because, when I opened that door, I would be opening a door to the one emotion that I'd been trying all day to suppress. The one emotion buried beneath the pain and heartache.

Anger.

Because when I allowed myself to feel something besides the worry, the fear and the heartbreak, I knew that that's what would be waiting for me.

I wasn't even surprised when I looked at my phone and saw that it had just gone 3 a.m – I was past caring about life's cruel little ironies.

My eyes fell immediately on the empty postcard, waiting. Despite the slow bubble of my rage, I couldn't help but hope that she would have some reasonable explanation as to why she'd spent the last few months appearing every night without fail, only to abandon me the night before my whole life fell apart.

I sat and waited.

And waited some more.

But the studio stayed the same: black and empty. The post-card remained unchanged, no accompanying shimmer from the moon to divulge its untold secrets.

Rage.

There it was. Complete white-hot fury ebbed through me, obliterating everything else in its path. I stood up, the chair falling backward. 'HOW DARE YOU?' I screamed over and over till my throat felt raw.

'YOU COME BACK TO TELL ME WHAT? UTTER GARBAGE, THAT'S WHAT! RUBBISH ABOUT HOPE AND YOUR GODDAMN RECIPES!' I yelled in disgust, gasping for breath. The cold horror of it all washed over me. 'YOU FOUND A WAY TO TELL ME ABOUT YOUR FUCKING CORNISH PASTY RECIPE BUT YOU COULDN'T WAIT ONE DAY TO WARN ME. . . TO TELL ME TO KEEP STUART HOME TO KEEP HIM SAFE. . . YOU COULDN'T WAIT ONE DAY TO TELL ME THAT?'

I picked up the postcard and crushed it into a ball and threw it across the room. My body heaved with my sobs and I fell to the ground, gasping for air. My world spun and I reached for the waste-basket, throwing up what I'd been pushing down at the bottom of my heart, since my world broke apart, finally came loose, demanding to be felt. I'd never felt so betrayed in my life. When my body finally stopped heaving, I leant my head against my studio door.

'Hope?' I said with a small, mad laugh, as I wiped my mouth on my sleeve. 'You asked me to promise you hope, when hope is what you destroyed. The only hope I have left is that you stay gone.'

I peeled myself off the floor, taking my bucket of sick with me, and with cold finality shut the door.

CHAPTER TWENTY-TWO

Day Two

No change.

CHAPTER TWENTY-THREE

Day Three

No change.

CHAPTER TWENTY-FOUR

Guardians

'I'm sorry, Mrs Everton, but there are police officers outside who would like to speak to you.'

I looked up from Stuart's still, comatose face in surprise. 'Police officers?'

'It's nothing to worry about, they just want to talk to you – give you an update about the accident,' replied Maggie.

I felt both guilty and relieved that Victoria and Genevieve had gone to the hotel to shower and change. Though having someone there to hear it with me may have helped, there were some things you just had to face yourself.

I took a steadying breath and followed Maggie down the hall. She led me to a room with three seated men and a woman.

A heavy-set, balding officer wearing a uniform came forward to shake my hand. 'Mrs Everton?' he asked.

I nodded. He held out a thick hand, directing me to a chair opposite. 'I'm Officer Clark. This is my partner, Officer Turner,' he said, gesturing to the only woman. She was powerfully built, with short black hair and a firm jaw, but it softened when she smiled at me. I nodded hello.

'And this is Jason and Tim. They were the paramedics on the scene.'

I turned to the two young men, both dark-haired, barely in their twenties, who had helped save Stuart. 'Thank you so much,' I said, a lump forming in my throat.

They nodded. Tim, I believe, shook his head in awe.

'He was lucky.'

I was completely taken aback. '*Lucky*?' My husband was in a coma, recovering from heart surgery, with multiple broken bones and no one could tell me with any certainty that he was going to wake up. Lucky?

But they all nodded while I tried not to scream.

Officer Clark whistled. 'Extremely lucky.'

I looked at him, confused, but it was Officer Turner who reached over to touch my hand, her dark eyes full of sympathy, who explained, 'Mrs Everton, as you know, your husband's car was hit by an eighteen-wheeler truck.'

I shut my eyes, shaking my head quickly. I hadn't known that. To be honest, that was something that I didn't want to know. *Truck* had been enough. This was impossible.

She squeezed my hand. 'The truck lost a tyre and couldn't stop because of the build-up of black ice.' I looked up, taking a breath, which I held as I gazed into her deep-set eyes as she continued, 'He was lucky. The car took the impact on the driver's side, and was driven forward into the barrier. There is nothing left of the front of the car. There is no way on earth he should have been able to come through that accident alive. None. But he did. His only chance at survival would have been if he were in the back seat. There was no reason for him to be there. But that's where we found him.'

I stared at her in mute shock.

She nodded and continued. 'I mean, Mrs Everton, the truly crazy thing is that the seat he was in was the safest place he could have been, not just in the car, but on the entire road. If he'd jumped out, or if he'd been anywhere on that stretch of road he would have been dead – smashed by the resulting impact of the body of the truck as it rounded the corner.'

Officer Clark nodded his bald head. 'All I can say, Mrs Everton, is that if I believed in guardian angels, I'd want his.'

I stared at them, tears sliding down my face. 'He was lucky,' I breathed, in shock.

They nodded. 'Extremely,' said the other paramedic, Jason, shaking his dark head. 'I mean, even the fact that we got to him so quickly. . . hey, Tim?' he asked the other paramedic, who nodded his head. Big blue eyes solemn.

Jason continued, 'The highway was a disaster. . . If we'd been called from the hospital, he would have had to wait at least forty-five minutes for us. At least. The only reason we could respond so quickly was because we'd had a false alarm in the area just a few minutes before.'

'It wasn't just us,' pointed out Tim. 'I mean, the only surgeon on call in West Cornwall on New Year's Eve was just a few minutes away. . . a heart surgeon, no less.'

Jason nodded. 'It's true. It's so strange, because none of us should have been there, but somehow we were.'

I stared at them all in shock. 'I d-didn't know this. . . any of this,' I said. 'Thank you. Thank you so much for telling me and for helping to save him.'

They all smiled. Tim's eyes were kind, sympathetic. 'We're all rooting for him, Mrs Everton. I met him, you know, at the fair a few weeks back. I'm a fairly decent cook, though I didn't win nearly so many prizes, but he was really encouraging. I'll never forget that.'

I swallowed, smiling at him through my tears. 'Thank you so much – that means the world.'

I left them feeling lighter than I had since the accident. Dad, Catherine, Genevieve, and Victoria were waiting for me in the corridor. Dad's grey hair was even wilder than usual and he was wearing an old frayed jumper that I remembered from my childhood.

Catherine gave me a hug. 'The nurse said you were speaking with the police officers?'

I breathed out, nodding, and repeated everything they had told me.

Genevieve looked about to faint as I mentioned the word *truck*, but when I finished, for the first time since she'd arrived she was able to speak.

'He was lucky,' she said in awe.

I nodded.

Dad wiped his grey eyes. 'It must have been Mum, I'm sure.'

My mouth folded into itself and I gave him a small hard smile. I didn't want to think about her. . . or her help, ever again.

When I got home, I found Tomas watering Stuart's new plantings in the now restored polytunnel. When he saw me, he turned and I noticed that his green beret – the beret that I'd been sure he never took off – was in his hands. His rheumy eyes were sad.

Heavy with worry, he touched a wrinkly-looking runner bean and said, ''e will come through zis, Eve. I'm sure he will.'

I patted his brown and gold tweed-covered arm, not sure if he was talking about Stuart or the beans, but feeling comforted nonetheless, and for the first time, I didn't bother correcting him about my name.

Later that night I passed the closed studio door. I heard a sound, like the flutter of wings. My hand reached out for the doorknob, but I stopped myself. Part of me had been considering Dad's words – if Mum really had helped somehow. But another, larger, embittered part couldn't get over the fact that she hadn't warned me, not during any of our moonlight encounters. I touched my stomach, thinking of the baby. Of Holly. Of Mum, who seemed to know things before they happened: couldn't she have warned me of this?

I woke up and took Muppet for a walk along the beach – I needed the cold air to clear my head. The night had been full of fear. I couldn't face sleeping alone in our bed any more. I'd wake up in that place just before sleep, thinking he was there, and every time I'd have to go through the hell of remembering again. It was torture. I wished that I could just stay at the hospital, though I was no use to anyone there. As we made our way back up the barren beach, I saw Dad carrying two steel mugs. We walked over to join him and he handed me one.

'It's coffee – thought you could use it.' He held up a cellophane-wrapped sandwich and a muffin in one hand. 'Brought you some food as well. . . Now, no arguments; you're eating for two.'

I smiled at him. 'Don't worry, Dr Gia and The Thursday Club gave me the speech too.'

Dad looked relieved. As we walked back up towards the house, I glanced at him. 'Sorry we ruined your date.'

He laughed and rolled his eyes. 'Not that I even knew I was on one until I was. . .'

I smiled. 'I like her though. She seems really nice.'

'Me too. No one could ever take Mum's place, but it would be nice to have a friend.'

I nodded. I didn't say anything; I didn't want to think about Mum. I was still too full of hurt that she'd come back to tell me everything except the one thing that actually mattered – that I might lose the love of my life. I wasn't sure if I could ever think of her the same way again. I didn't really know what to think any more.

Back at the hospital, Maggie came in to find me. 'There's a large red-headed man outside who says he has to see you. I'm so sorry, but he's making a bit of a scene,' she said, annoyed.

I looked up at her with a puzzled frown, then suddenly realised something: 'Is he Scottish?'

She nodded. 'And very big.'

I smiled. 'That'll be Terry.'

'He said he'd been trying to visit for days but no one would call you and he doesn't have your number.'

I closed my eyes, feeling terrible. Poor Terry. I rushed out to find him just outside the ward. His huge form was crumpled around the corners, hair wild and unkempt; his ruddy face full of remorse.

'Oh Ivy, lass, I'm so sorry. It's all my fault. I feel sick, truly,' he said, his eyes red and swollen. 'No one would let me come find ya – they're all Nazis,' he added, indicating the staff who had barred his entry. 'I didn't have ya number. . . or ya address, felt so helpless.'

I patted his arm and tried to give him a hug, which was hard as he was over six foot and near as wide from his years in the Navy. 'I'm so sorry, Terry. I didn't know. . . they didn't tell me. But please, it wasn't your fault. It's a five-minute ride home; no one could have predicted this.'

He sniffed. 'I just feel so responsible. I mean, he was dancing with ya. . . ya were both so happy and if it wasn't for me. . .' he choked.

I caught my breath. 'Terry, don't do this to yourself. You didn't drive the truck and even then. . . it blew a tyre from the opposite side of the road – it was an accident,' I said, patting his arm – giving him the absolution I couldn't give myself.

Dad rounded the corner and saw me hugging Terry. He came forward and patted both our backs. 'No one is to blame,' he said, giving me a pointed look.

I pulled my face into a semblance of a smile. I'd had a feeling. An undeniable feeling that we should have stayed home, but I just hadn't fought hard enough. There was no absolution from that.

Terry wiped his eyes and gave me a bone-crushing hug. 'Can I see him?'

'Of course, come with me. . .' I said, leading them back into the ICU wing, towards Stuart's bed.

Terry's face fell when he saw him. 'Oh Ivy,' he said, touching Stuart's uninjured left arm.

'Terry, he's okay. . . he's alive. Actually he's looking a bit better. The bruises aren't so purple any more.' I took a deep breath, processing that thought, gaining strength and telling him everything that the officers and paramedics had told me.

'He was lucky,' he said, in awe.

'I think so,' said Dr Harris, who had arrived to check on Stuart, giving us all a smile. His eyes were thoughtful. 'You know, I wasn't meant to be at that party. I was supposed to fly out to New York for a conference but my flight was cancelled. It was so strange – no warning either – and the next available flight wouldn't have got me there in time. So I decided to stay and go with Gia to the party.'

I stared at him, open-mouthed. 'You weren't meant to be there?' I said, feeling my blood run cold.

He shook his head. 'No, it was lucky that I was because I was just around the corner when I got the page. Stuart needed an emergency heart procedure or else he wouldn't have made it to the hospital – it's why he had to be rushed to surgery straight away.'

I could only stare at Dr Harris. 'None of you were meant to be there,' I breathed. 'But you were.'

He frowned. 'Sorry?' he asked, puzzled.

I didn't believe in coincidences, I really didn't. Not any more.

'It wasn't just you. . .' I said, shaking my head in surprise as I explained about the paramedics who had been in the area because of a false alarm.

Dr Harris's eyes widened. 'That's amazing!' he said. 'I heard that the highway was a disaster with New Year's, though I never thought. . . hadn't considered that. He's so lucky that the paramedics were in the area. . . they were right – if they hadn't gotten there. . . I'm not sure he would have made it.' He breathed out and looked at Stuart. 'It's amazing!'

I nodded. Amazing was the word. I stood staring at Stuart, a lump forming in my throat. A sudden, undeniable question had begun to form. Had Mum had a hand in this after all? Had she helped? Maybe this was what she meant about not giving up hope. But why like this, why not use the postcard. . . the way she'd told me so many other things?

Dr Harris finished checking on Stuart, gave my arm a squeeze, and said: 'Mrs Everton – Ivy, I think he's doing very well. I think he's going to pull through, I really do.'

I touched his arm and swallowed. 'Thank you.'

He nodded and left.

Terry gave me a hug and patted Stuart's arm. 'Got to get back, lass. But I'll come by tomorrow. Ya'll let me know if there's any news?'

I nodded. 'I will. Thanks, Terry, for everything.'

It wasn't a Thursday, and I'd only ever sewn one very wonky piece of a jumper together when I'd tried to help May during the flood. But I awoke to someone gently placing a quilt over me as I lay on the sofa, and opened my eyes to see six pairs of eyes looking at me. Somehow, so very silently, they had all let themselves in.

Robyn handed me a cup of tea. Abigail switched on the light, and said softly, 'Not looking as peaky. That's good.'

Winifred Jones winked, then held up the Henry. 'Just going to give the place a quick once-over.'

May straightened the quilt, which I saw was a beautiful patchwork in blues, greys, and pinks. I touched it in awe.

'We've been making it for yer, got some of yer mum's old pieces in it,' she said, pointing to a piece that looked like an old French garden. 'Sure, but she got started on this quilt long ago. Funny, but I found it at the bottom of me sewing pile not long after yer showed up on me doorstep, was like she was waiting fer us to find it. . . So we've been finishing it for her. We thought yer should have it, 'tis only right.'

I felt a lump form, tears threatening.

'Mine is zere,' said Flavia, pointing to a patch of roses, and a sleeping cat, who looked just like Massimow. She winked at me. 'Wouldn't have found 'im if it wasn't for you.'

May's patch was a blue house and two women sitting in her sewing room. 'That be me and you having a right chinwag. . .' she said, then grinned.

Robyn's were a collection of seascapes, with the sun coming through. 'The sun always follows a storm,' she said, holding my hand.

Winifred Jones's surprisingly included a rattle and a pair of baby booties. She stopped the Henry and gave me a very un-Winifred-Jones-like smile.

I stared at the quilt through a haze of tears. 'It's so beautiful, thank you so much.'

'And look – this little bit here,' joked May, 'that's the only piece of sewing yer ever did, yer lazy lass!' she said, pointing to what was once the wonky sleeve of a jumper, and was now gloriously transformed into a duck-egg blue garden shed, with a grey watering can out of which sprouted a mix of vegetation. Next to the watering can was a small jar and in fine, silken thread it read 'Pak choi jelly'. 'We figured, we'll start by giving yer some lessons,' she said with a wink, pointing at the little patch that represented Stuart, which made the tears finally fall, splashing onto the silken can.

Her face grew serious. 'Life is like this, lass, a series of patches to be sure, some good, some bad. We're here to help yer get through this one, whichever way we can.'

Then she pulled out a bottle of some fine, aged Irish whiskey. 'Shall I pour us all a wee dram? Sure we be needing it.'

I looked up at them, these women, my unlikely friends, who had somehow, unofficially, baptised my entry into The Thursday Club, and said, 'Go on then.'

CHAPTER TWENTY-FIVE

The Last Postcard

It was just a flicker.

But I felt it. Stuart's hand against mine had moved. Heart pounding against my chest, I stared at it, willing it to do it again. I held my breath. Then so slowly, so agonisingly slowly, it moved again, till it was holding mine. I looked up and my heart stopped completely. His eyes, his beautiful coffee-coloured eyes, were looking at me.

I gasped aloud, tears gliding down my face. 'You're awake?' I took a shuddering breath, repeating it: 'You're awake!'

He smiled, the smallest briefest smile, the slightest movement but one that changed my entire world. His face shimmered before my eyes, my vision blurred and the tears fell hot and fast, shuddering through me. A wild euphoria overtook me and I kissed every part of him that I could, bathing him in my tears and loud, joyful sobs.

I couldn't recall happiness more pure and powerful than this, this perfect moment where we existed, together again. I kissed him on his lips – the softest, gentlest of kisses – holding on tightly to his hand. Finally, when I was able to form the words, I said in between shuddering gasps, 'You gave me the biggest fright, Mr Everton. I didn't know if you'd ever wake.' .

He nodded, blinked slowly, and squeezed my hand, his dark eyes saying so much. 'I promised you a kiss.'

I closed my eyes for a second, remembering that he had. 'You said you'd give me a kiss I'd never forget.'

He smiled. 'Kept my promise, did I?' he said, his eyes gentle, teasing.

I nodded fast and my voice cracked when I answered, 'Yes, you did.'

The room filled as doctors and nurses rushed in. Dr Harris raced in, his lab coat billowing behind him. 'Stuart, you're awake!' he cried, delighted. Looking younger suddenly than I'd seen him all week. Looking more like the handsome man I'd met on the night of the party than the worried doctor I'd come to know.

Stuart nodded. 'Hey, Doc,' he said. 'Sorry for falling asleep on you like that.'

Dr Harris grinned. 'Not a problem. How do you feel?'

Stuart gave a small nod. 'Ouch!'

We all laughed. Maggie let out a little sound and came and gave me a hug. I squeezed her back, eyes shining.

'Ouch indeed,' said Dr Harris, with a smile, looking at Stuart, and monitoring his vitals. 'You've been through the wringer but I think you're going to pull through this just fine.'

I closed my eyes, overcome.

Maggie touched my arm. 'Would you like me to tell your dad, get him to call everyone – his mum and sister – for you? So you can stay. . .'

'Bless you,' I whispered. Then remembered: 'Please ask Dad to call Terry and Tomas as well. He knows how to contact them.'

She nodded, brown eyes full of happiness for me. I gave her a quick hug. 'You've been lovely, Maggie, thank you. I couldn't have done this without you.'

She smiled, gave my arm a squeeze. 'It was my pleasure, Ivy, truly.'

I smiled at her retreating back, grateful beyond words.

Dr Harris and the other staff left. 'We'll leave you for a while,' he said with a wink. 'Be back a little later to see how he's doing.' I smiled at him, touched.

I sat back on the bed, holding Stuart's hand, staring into his beautiful eyes. Eyes I'd been so terrified I might never see again. Never wanting to look away.

'Everton Ten?' I asked with a grimace, looking at his broken leg and arm.

He shook his head. 'Twelve, I think. . . we'll need to add a new marker to the scale. *Hit by truck.*'

I shook my head, laughing despite myself. Only Stuart would make a joke like that.

He squeezed my hand, his expression turning serious. 'Ivy. . .'

I looked at him and he held my arm tightly. 'Ivy, she saved me.'

I blinked. Staring at him, the blood drained from my face. 'Who?' I asked, though I knew – perhaps I'd always known. 'W-who saved you?'

'Your mum.'

I closed my eyes, the earth falling around me. I asked only, 'How?'

'It was so strange. I was driving and my phone rang. I thought it was you. I looked around for it briefly, but couldn't find it and when I looked up, I saw her standing there in the road. I hit my brakes. When I came to a stop she was gone. My phone was still ringing, yet I couldn't find it. So I pulled up my handbrake and started searching for it. I found it behind the passenger seat. Ivy, it was her.'

I stared at him in shock as he continued, eyes dark, solemn. 'Her number. I mean, I never thought to erase it, but here I was getting a call from a number that had been out of service for five years, just before I got hit.'

I closed my eyes. 'You remember getting hit?' I asked, horrified.

He shook his head. 'No, thank God. But I was conscious when the paramedics got there and they told me what happened. The one paramedic – think he said his name was Tim?' he asked.

I nodded.

'Well, he said I was lucky – the only reason I was alive was because I was sitting there when the truck hit. The rest of the car was completely wrecked.'

I nodded. 'One of the officers said much the same thing. In fact, she said that even if you'd jumped out of the car, it was likely to have hit you considering how fast it was going and the angle it took – you would have had to have run pretty fast to avoid it. . . and on ice.'

Stuart's eyes widened. 'The way the road curved, that makes sense.'

I breathed out, realising what Officer Turner had tried to tell me was somehow, impossibly, true. 'The only way you could have survived was to be on the back seat.'

He nodded, squeezing my hand. 'Then later, I spoke to her, I think.'

I blinked in shock. 'You spoke to Mum?'

He nodded. 'I think so. . . though now it feels like maybe I dreamt it. It was very real though when I saw her. She looked so beautiful. Young. A lot like you, really. It was magical – like she wasn't wearing a dress, more like silver smoke,' he said with a soft smile.

I squeezed his hand, unable to speak, and he continued. 'We were standing somewhere wonderful, like a garden at night. There wasn't this bright light. . . It wasn't like what I would have thought if it was heaven. . . It was soft, muted, like moonlight on water or something. She stood there and handed me a postcard, like the one you found in her desk, except this one was addressed to me. When I looked up, she touched my arm and said: "I saved the last one for you. It was always meant for you."'

My shoulders started to heave and shake, the tears running down my cheeks. I clutched Stuart's hand to me and sobbed. I'd blamed her. I'd done the one thing she'd asked me not to do: I'd lost hope when she told me to hang on, no matter what, thinking that she'd abandoned me when I needed her, when it turned out she'd always been there. She was always there when I needed her the most – I just hoped it wasn't too late to tell her that.

CHAPTER TWENTY-SIX

Words Made of Ink

The postcard was waiting for me as I entered the room, propped up next to the Christmas card with Rudolph and his shimmering, golden-red, fairy-dust nose. There was no reason it should have been there, but it was. Somehow, after I'd crumpled it up and thrown it away, it had restored itself to its rightful place, as perfect as the day I'd found it. Except now, now it was no longer empty.

As I stood staring at it, I understood. It had never been empty, not really, because here was the last message, the one that, had she not found a way to come back, would have been the one I found. Gone were the gossamer-thin words made of moonlight and magic that filled and disappeared; in their place were other words, more precious than any made of light and stardust, for these were etched in permanent ink, made for me to keep.

Darling Ivy,

If love were enough, I'd tell St Peter to close his gates. I'd block out the stars and cover the moon with a fist. I'd find a place where time stands still, where no world would exist, except one where we could stand together arm in arm.

Except, my darling, here's the secret you should know: where you are, so am I. No there exists, or here. No place exists where I would not come when you need me, for you will always exist in a place where my love is without end.

My dream came true the day they placed you in my arms.

My hopes found flight, so that when you fall asleep at night, my arms are your arms, my side is your side.

And now the last, the big one, the one that I need you to hold close – for it's a manifesto, a recipe for life: be strong, be brave, be gentle, be kind; forgive easily – especially yourself; live each day with hope; begin and end each one with love, for it is this that turns life into living, and it is only love that makes it worth the living.

Love and always,

Mum

CHAPTER TWENTY-SEVEN

Holly Everton

'It's time.'

Stuart looked up from the vine tomatoes he'd been fondling with rather a dreamy expression, hand spade falling from his hands to the ground with a clatter, his brown eyes huge. 'It's time?'

I nodded.

'Is that because you are standing in a pool where your water just broke?' he said with a nervous laugh, while I stood in the too-warm polytunnel that basked in the June sunshine, my belly huge.

'It is indeed.'

'Oh Christ!' he said, standing up quickly. Looking like a startled woodland creature. Face white.

'Not so fast – that leg has just healed!' I warned.

He stopped, blinked. 'It's fine. All fine. Strong as an ox,' he said, eyes dancing. And he was; it had taken months of healing, but he was almost back to his old self. The gardening helped, according to Dr Harris, who approved thoroughly. Peter had become a great friend. He even had a polytunnel of his own now, to Dr Gia's despair. Apparently he too shared a fondness for exotic jam.

Stuart bent down, straightened the spade, and said, 'Okay, I'm ready.'

I shook my head, amused. 'Dad is on his way. He'll meet us there with The Thursday Club, and Catherine, your mum and Smudge are flying down.'

He nodded. 'The car is packed: clothes, pyjamas, food. . . We should have everything. . . Should I have a quick run through the house to make sure there's nothing I've missed?'

'Stuart, you started packing the car in February. You learned how to drive with one leg in March – causing me some grey hair in the process. You figured out how to feed a baby with one hand, practising on a watermelon that you dressed in a tea towel. You pureed most of your smallholding into baby food, though she won't be able to eat it for months. We have everything we need and if you run anywhere on that leg until it's properly healed I'll break it for you,' I threatened.

He grinned. 'All right, Mrs Everton.'

I grinned back. 'All right.'

'We're having a baby,' he said, in awe.

I nodded, my own eyes huge. 'Oh Christ, Stuart, we're having a baby!' I whispered.

Six hours later – one crushed hand, pain like no one ever warns you enough about, exhaustion to the point of tears, sweat, one vow never ever to do this madness again without drugs, followed by a single second of realisation when my baby was placed in my arms, and I knew I'd do it all over again in a heartbeat – we welcomed Holly Alice Everton into the world.

I held out my hand and she latched on, eyes closed, and I knew then what Mum had meant, as from then on my arm was her arm, my heart her heart.

Stuart traced her face with the tip of his finger. 'She's perfect. An Everton Ten, I'd say.'

I looked at him with a puzzled frown and he explained: 'I think we need a new scale, a better one. One for happiness.

One being something like you found a chocolate you forgot all about.'

Tears sprang to my eyes. 'Ten being your whole world just got made?' I asked.

He smiled and nodded.

I held out my hand for him, while cradling Holly in the other. An Everton Ten indeed.

LETTER FROM LILY

Thank you so much for reading *A Cornish Christmas*. If you enjoyed the book it would be so wonderful if you could leave a review. Your help in spreading the word is so appreciated.

Cornwall is such a special place, swathed in such mystery; you can't help feeling that there really is something magical about it. I just couldn't let it go, so I'm pleased to tell you that my next book will feature beautiful Cornwall again, and with one of my favourite characters from *A Cornish Christmas* too: the biographer Victoria Langley, Stuart's sister 'Smudge'. I can't wait to tell you more about it – there's an abandoned cottage, a mystery that goes back to the Great War, some magic and romance. . . You'll find out about this and much more besides by joining my mailing list here:

www.bookouture.com/lily-graham

Otherwise do come say hello on Twitter and Facebook. I love chatting about writing, abandoned houses, my search for the perfect she-shed, *The Bake Off*, and much more which I also share on my blog, which you can find here. Do come say hello!

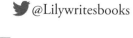 @Lilywritesbooks

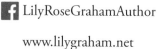 LilyRoseGrahamAuthor

www.lilygraham.net

ACKNOWLEDGEMENTS

Thank you as ever to my best friend Catherine, who read, and loved it first.

Thanks to my mom, who made childhood magical and inspired the story in the first place. My dad, for always telling me to go after my dreams, and my lovely husband, Rui, for being the visual inspiration behind Stuart, and the one who helped me the most whenever I started to lose confidence; your unshakeable faith has been such a tonic.

A huge thank you to Lydia, Natasha, Natalie, Kim and the entire incredible team at Bookouture for making dreams come true.

Thank you to my family and friends – all the Bradleys, Valentes, Da Silvas, Velozas, Wayne – for the mosh pit help! And my mad, beloved dog Fudge, my favourite writing assistant, who was the inspiration behind Detective Sergeant Fudge.

I'd like to acknowledge whimsy.org.uk for their information on Cornish superstitions.

And last, but definitely not least, a huge, massive thank you so much to all the readers who read this story first as *The Postcard*, and the amazing bloggers who took the time to read and review an untried author. Your support and kindness has meant the world – I truly hope you enjoy this longer, novel-length version.

And to all the book bloggers and readers of *The Summer Escape* – thank you so much, in particular the very lovely Kaisha

Holloway, Barbara Little, Sarah Mackins, Audrey Gibson, Rebecca Pugh, Nikki Moore, Rachel Gibson, Kath Middleton and Isabel Homfeld, amongst others, as well as everyone who took the time to leave a review or to let me know that you've enjoyed it, thank you so much!